KU-502-940

CRASHING TO A HALT

Club Twist Book Three

ALICE RAINE

ACCENT

Copyright © 2021 Alice Raine

The right of Alice Raine to be identified as the Author of
the Work has been asserted by her in accordance with the
Copyright, Designs and Patents Act 1988.

Published in 2021 by HEADLINE ACCENT
An imprint of HEADLINE PUBLISHING GROUP

Apart from any use permitted under UK copyright law, this publication may
only be reproduced, stored, or transmitted, in any form, or by any means,
with prior permission in writing of the publishers or, in the case of reprographic
production, in accordance with the terms of licences issued
by the Copyright Licensing Agency.

All characters in this publication are fictitious
and any resemblance to real persons, living or dead,
is purely coincidental.

Cataloguing in Publication Data is available from the British Library

ISBN 978 1 7861 5261 9

Typeset in 11.25/15.25 pt Bembo by Jouve (UK), Milton Keynes

Printed and bound in Great Britain by Clays Ltd, Elcograf S.p.A.

Headline's policy is to use papers that are natural, renewable and
recyclable products and made from wood grown in well-managed forests
and other controlled sources. The logging and manufacturing processes
are expected to conform to the environmental regulations
of the country of origin.

HEADLINE PUBLISHING GROUP
An Hachette UK Company
Carmelite House
50 Victoria Embankment
London EC4Y 0DZ

www.headline.co.uk
www.hachette.co.uk

This book is dedicated to Biscuit, you know who you are! The impact you've had on my life can't be put into words, but will be with me forever. Love always x

Chapter One

Sasha

I gazed at the gorgeous man sat across the table from me and I felt my heart flip with excitement. Marcus Price. My long-term crush, and miraculously, now my boyfriend. A warm flush spread over my skin as I thought about just how much I felt for him. With the way my emotions spiralled out of control every time I was near him or so much as thought about him, it seemed to indicate that it was veering dangerously towards the 'L' word.

Inwardly I smiled to myself, because in the past that would have been enough to have me running for the hills screaming like a banshee. But things with Marcus were different. *I* was different when I was with him. With his sweet ways and sexy glances, he had softened me, and I had finally managed to relax my paranoia over relationships and let him in.

Robyn said we made a perfect couple, but given both of our hang-ups with relationships we were far from perfect. The early deaths of my parents had left me with major issues about letting my emotional barriers down, and after his ex-girlfriend had attempted to stab him to death Marcus had some understandable difficulties with accepting closeness and physical contact.

Regardless of how challenging it should have been for us to be together, it wasn't; we just clicked and connected in ways that I had never imagined possible. Perhaps it was our shared issues which made things between us so good, and so easy. I had no idea, and while we might not be the perfect couple Robyn described, we were certainly living up to the nickname I had once given us: a perfectly imperfect pair.

Given Marcus's aversion to physical contact I had worried how we would manage to move our relationship forwards, especially after the tense but passionate encounters we had had before we'd got together – the quickie in the corner of the nightclub in Spain was still quite a highlight in my memories. I had wondered if we'd be able to keep our hands off each other while we eased Marcus into being able to cope with touching, but thankfully, it was going far better than I had anticipated. The magnetic chemistry between us had made it almost impossible not to launch myself at him and ravish him, and from the heated stares he sent my way I knew he was struggling with it too, but so far we'd managed to avoid the temptation and were taking things at a slower pace.

He had always been OK with hand-holding, so that was now a daily occurrence, as was kissing, and boy was he a magnificent kisser! Cuddling was becoming easier for him too, with his heart rate remaining steadier and the tension in his body less notice-able when I was in his arms. We hadn't had sex again yet, and given my usual appetite for a bit of fun between the sheets I was surprised that it hadn't been an issue at all. I knew he needed time, and because I wanted to be with him on more than just a physical level, I was more than happy to give him that.

Chapter Two

Sasha

I finished my coffee and walked through to my bedroom with an appreciative look around my little apartment. I bloody loved this place. Cosy, warm and so lovely and sunny, it really was perfect for me. Thinking about my developing relationship with Marcus I paused in the living room with a frown. This flat might not be so perfect if things with him continued to develop though, because while it was ideal for me, it would probably be a bit of a squash for two adults to share. Mind you, Chloe and I had managed for the month or so that she had been here, so it could work, I guess.

Wandering through to my bedroom I opened the skylight and rolled up onto my tiptoes so I could look down and see Robyn and Oliver's house across the street. They were arriving back from their honeymoon the next day and I couldn't wait to see them. They'd been travelling around Europe and had been gone just short of a month, but after living with Robyn for years and seeing her everyday it had felt like so much longer since I'd seen her.

Just at that moment my phone began to ring and, to my

delight, as I pulled it from my jeans pocket I saw Robyn's number. Ha! It was almost like she'd been thinking of me at exactly the same time.

'Rob! Hey! How's the honeymoon been?'

I heard a dreamy sigh down the phone and just about managed not to snort my disapproval at her soppiness. 'It's been *a—maz—ing*! Sorry I've not phoned sooner, but we've had our mobiles switched off. I have so much to update you on! And Chloe, is she there too?'

Drawing in a breath, I walked from my room and pushed open the door to my spare room. There was the faint aroma of Chloe's perfume in the air, but nothing else. The room was completely empty.

'Nope. Chloe's gone.'

There was a moment of silence down the line, and then Robyn's voice again, sounding distinctly confused. 'What do you mean *"Chloe's gone"*? I've only been away for three weeks! How can she be gone?'

I could hear the shock in Robyn's voice, and as I stared into the empty shell of a room that Chloe had left behind rather abruptly last week, I felt it resonate through me too. 'I mean she's bloody well gone!' I huffed. Closing the door, I wandered back into the lounge and dropped down onto the sofa. 'And you've been gone four weeks actually, not three.'

'Three, four, whatever,' Robyn said dismissively. 'Where is she then? Is she OK?'

'She's fine. Moved to Birmingham, apparently.' I gave a shrug, but couldn't say much else because I didn't know anything else.

'With no warning? It doesn't sound like Chloe at all, I mean

4

she was Little Miss Routine. Change was like her least favourite thing.'

'I know.' Robyn was right in her assessment of Chloe. She was so sensible it had almost been painful to witness, especially given my fly-by-the-seat-of-my-pants approach to life. 'She'd mentioned a possible new job up there a few months ago, but then she'd never talked about it again, so I'd assumed she hadn't gone for it.' I flicked at a piece of lint on my T-shirt and watched it sail through the sunbeams streaming in from my roof windows. 'I never thought she'd up and leave, but she did!'

'Wow,' Robyn murmured. Wow indeed. I might not have been as friendly with Chloe as I was with Robyn, nowhere near, but she'd been my flatmate. I'd seen her practically every day for the last year or so, so it still felt weird with her not being around anymore.

'So, are you going to apply for a new lodger?'

Looking around my lovely lounge I couldn't help but smile to myself again at how beautiful my flat was. 'Nah. I'm not adverse to someone else living here, but I don't need the extra money, so I think I'll hold off for now and just enjoy having the place to myself for a bit.'

I heard a chuckle down the line. 'What I'm reading from that comment is that you're enjoying having the apartment to yourself so you and Marcus can get down and dirty without having to be quiet!'

A filthy cackle rose in my throat, but I shook my head. For once in my life I wasn't having frantic sex with a man at every possible moment. In fact, I wasn't having *any* sex with a man. Or a woman, for that matter. I, Sasha Mortimer, was finally managing to take things slowly with someone instead of humping them silly. It was quite a novel experience. 'It's not like that, actually,' I replied tartly, trying to sound affronted at her assumption, when actually, given my track record as a serial shagger, it really was a bloody miracle that I wasn't jumping his bones at every given opportunity.

'Still taking things slow?' Robyn enquired softly, the teasing edge to her earlier voice dropping away. 'Actually, hold that answer . . . Are you free for a glass of wine in the sun and a proper catch-up?'

I frowned and immediately glanced at the date on my watch. They weren't back from honeymoon yet. Were they? 'When?'

'Now, obviously. That's why I called,' Robyn replied, a smile obvious in her tone.

Her reply had me sitting up and grinning like an excited kid. 'You're back? I though you guys landed tomorrow?'

Her soft chuckle floated down the line. 'Nope, we landed last night. Wanna meet?'

'Hell yeah!' I was standing up and walking back to my bedroom before the words were even out of my mouth.

'You might wanna bring your shades, I'm jet-lagged and I've only just woken up, so I look like arse.'

For all her modesty I could honestly say that in all my years of knowing her I'd never seen Robyn looking 'like arse'. Even back in our clubbing days when she'd had a hangover and less than an hour's sleep under her belt she'd always managed to look fresh as a flipping daisy. 'I doubt that, very much.'

She laughed again and I grinned. 'I do, I look like hell. But I think a liquid lunch might just be the perfect cure.'

'I think you might be right!' I agreed enthusiastically. 'Give me five minutes and I'll be down. I wanna hear all about your honeymoon. And when I say all about, I mean it, so get ready to share *all* the saucy deets!'

I could practically hear Robyn's eyeroll down the phone, and I hung up with a broad grin on my face.

My bestie was back, and I couldn't wait to see her.

Chapter Three

Sasha

I was so excited about seeing Robyn again that I practically flew down the three flights of stairs to my front door. Given my tendency towards clumsiness I was lucky I didn't trip, face-plant, and break my bloody neck, but miraculously I survived, and exactly four minutes and thirty-seven seconds after finishing my call with Robyn I was bursting into the sunshine and sprinting across the road to pull her into a huge hug.

'Woah! Missed me much?' She laughed into my embrace. She was joking, but still hugging me back just as tightly.

Easing off, I gave her a head-to-toe inspection and then shrugged my shoulders indifferently. 'Nah, not in the slightest,' I teased. Giving her another look over, I smiled – I'd been right, she looked pretty as a picture, showing no evidence whatsoever of being jet-lagged or sleep deprived. 'Well, the weather was obviously good. You look tanned as anything.' Raising a cheeky eyebrow, I grinned. 'Not to mention thoroughly well fucked.'

Her eyebrows flickered with amusement, but then she dismissed my comment as if I hadn't even spoken. 'Do you want to go to the wine bar, or the Club?'

I gave her a light punch on the arm and laughed. 'Don't try and give me the brush off! You've just got back from your honeymoon with Mr Fucks-A-Lot! I want to hear all about it!'

Robyn grinned at me and then linked her hand through my elbow. 'And you will. But first, we need to get our priorities right . . . I'm hung-over, I need a hair of the dog.' Wiggling her eyebrows, she smiled. 'So, Club or bar. Which is it to be?'

'Hmmm . . . I haven't been to the Club since before your wedding. Let's go there.'

'Sounds good. Let's be lazy and grab a cab.'

Living in Central London had several benefits, one of which was that a taxi was always easy to find, and luck was obviously on our side because traffic was light for a Saturday. Not wanting to be overheard, we didn't start our gossiping session in the taxi, instead sitting in eager silence exchanging grins and excited giggles. I might not be the sentimental type, but it was so good to have Robyn back.

Before long we were arriving at the Club and jumping out onto the familiar cobbled street in Soho where Club Twist was located. Robyn jerked a thumb to the side street that contained the wine bar part of the Club – simply called Twist.

'As it's lunchtime shall we go to the bar instead of the Club?'

Looking at the clear blue sky I nodded. 'Yeah, let's get some sun in the seating outside.' I gave her tanned arms an envious look and smiled wryly. 'Not that you need it, Little Miss Suntan!'

We entered the cosy little bar that was a regular haunt for us, and a quick glance around showed the bar to be quite empty. A few tables had patrons at them, and in the corner I spotted David, the owner, intently focused on something on his laptop screen. The bartender was also familiar – Natalia – a friend of both mine and Robyn's, and I greeted her with a broad smile. In the run-up to Robyn's wedding I'd become quite close friends with her and once I'd broken down her shy exterior I'd discovered a genuinely lovely girl who was now a firm member of our friendship group.

Natalia saw us and immediately came around the bar to give us both a hug. 'Hey, guys! Wow, Robyn, that's quite a tan! How was the honeymoon?'

Robyn smiled and gave her arms a self-conscious rub, as if having a tan was a bad thing. 'It was amazing, thanks, Natalia. How's things with you?'

Natalia nodded happily and then moved back behind the bar. 'Really good thanks. So, what are we having today, girls? White, rosé, or a Mojito?' She knew us so well! Robyn laughed, obviously thinking the same as me, and then pointed to the fridge behind her. 'I'll have a pink Zinfandel, please.'

'Make that two please, Natalia.' As much as I loved a refreshing Mojito, cocktails took time to prepare and I was too desperate for gossip today to wait while it was shaken and stirred to perfection.

'Come join us for a drink if you have a break soon,' Robyn offered as our drinks were poured.

Natalia smiled with obvious happiness at the invitation and nodded. 'Cool, will do,' she promised as she popped the top back on the bottle.

Now our wine was poured we made our way outside to one of the brightly coloured tables in the sunshine. There were only five tables on the roadside, but it was a quiet street with a communal park opposite containing well-developed trees, and so even though the occasional car went past it was still tranquil enough to relax and listen to the birds chirping away.

Robyn sipped her wine and let out a satisfied sigh. Noticing the leather strap around her throat, I raised an eyebrow and reached across to gently flick at the small silver disk that hung from it. Perfect. This could be an ideal starter to get the conversation moving in the direction that I wanted. 'I see you're wearing this again.'

To most it would just look like a necklace, a gorgeously soft leather band with an engraved silver pendant attached, but I knew her secret – while it *was* a necklace, it was also so much more. It was a marker of her relationship with Oliver, a collar, showing her as his submissive and marking her as his.

Truthfully, at the start of her relationship with Oliver I'd been a little concerned that Oliver's experience and dominant character would all be a bit overwhelming for Robyn – she was far more naïve and innocent when it came to relationships than me – but it had turned out that they were a perfect match. Even I, with my sceptical view on romance, couldn't deny that they were fucking brilliant together.

My observation caused Robyn's cheeks to redden slightly, and I saw an embarrassed smile curl at her lips. 'Yup.' Robyn lifted a hand and touched the pendant with a fond smile. She'd never been as open talking about sex as I was, and even though I'd softened her over the years it still sometimes felt like getting juicy details from her was like drawing blood from a sodding stone. 'I think my mum was pleased that I wore her pearl necklace for the wedding, but I really like wearing this.' Her shy smile broadened into more of a dirty grin and she wiggled her eyebrows at me. 'Oliver really likes it too.'

'I bet he does,' I remarked drily, rolling my eyes. 'So come on then, woman. Honeymoon. I need details. How was it?'

Robyn laughed and took a slow sip of her wine as her eyes wandered off to gaze at the park. 'Amazing. We drove all around France, Spain and Portugal, staying in gorgeous hotels and hidden little cabins. It was like a dream come true. I honestly couldn't have asked for anything more.'

I took a moment to imagine the magical time they must have had, while I sat waiting patiently. As glad as I was that they'd had a lovely time, Robyn knew full well that I didn't want a rundown of their journey's itinerary. I wanted sordid details, not a road map of their travels!

'I'm glad. But stop dancing around the good stuff . . . come on, how was your darling husband on the honeymoon? Back to his dominant deviousness?' Husband. Bloody hell, that sounded weird. I still couldn't quite get my head around the fact that one of us was married!

I thought she was going to do her usual and try to change the subject away from sex, but to my surprise, Robyn placed her glass down, turned her attention back to me and nodded. 'Yup. He was on top form. Dominant, devious and downright dirty.'

My eyes popped open like saucers, but I couldn't hide my glee at her apparent willingness to talk and found myself spontaneously leaning forwards in my chair and keenly grabbing her knee. 'Oooh, tell me more!'

Robyn kept me hanging for a few more seconds while she took another sip of wine, and then finally put me out of my misery. 'Well, we split our time away, there was a lot of spontaneous vanilla sex, just spending time enjoying each other and being together.'

Vanilla sex, also known as normal sex, was all well and good, but I was more interested in the less conforming activities. What can I say, I liked a bit of kink!

'I can sense a "but" coming on,' I predicted keenly. 'Tell me there's a but!'

She grinned and nodded. '*But* . . .' She emphasised the word and wiggled her eyebrows cheekily. 'But . . . there was also quite a bit of kinky stuff going on too.' Perhaps it was because we were outside and away from eavesdroppers, or maybe all my years of talking filth had finally rubbed off on her, but whatever the cause, Robyn seemed more than happy to spill the beans today. From the way she was now also leaning forwards in her chair I could only assume that she was set on continuing her sharing session.

'The night of our wedding I tried to start a little scene . . .' Her confession brought with it a reddening of her cheeks, but also a cheeky twinkle to her eye. 'He went to brush his teeth before bed and so I stripped off, put my collar on and waited for him on my knees in the middle of the floor.'

'Bloody hell!' I knew Robyn was into the whole submissive thing she had going on with Oliver, but I'd never quite imagined her to be the instigator! For some reason, her confession made me feel quite proud. I loved the fact that she'd bloomed from being a shy, relativity naïve girl into a woman in charge of her sexual experimentation.

'And do you know what?' She leant forwards and pouted. 'He turned me down!'

What? That brought my thoughts to a standstill. 'He said no?' I squawked. Surely finding a beautiful woman, naked, on her knees and presenting herself for submission was like a dream come true to a man like Oliver? 'Why the fuck would he turn you down?'

She laughed, shook her head, and then swilled her wine around her glass. 'It was quite sweet really, he said as much as he loved it when we played in those roles, he wanted us to consummate our marriage in a more traditional, intimate way.' Well I never. Oliver could be quite intense, to say the least, and when they had moved in together I had wondered if he'd have been looking for Robyn to live their lives in role as Dom and sub full time, but he hadn't, and I rather liked the dynamic they had going on.

'Plain ol' vanilla, huh?' I asked with a wiggle of my eyebrows.

Robyn laughed, her blush deepening. 'Well, I'm not sure sex with Oliver is ever entirely vanilla, but yeah, kind of. He promised we could scene on our honeymoon though, and boy did he stick to his promise!'

God, I loved talking about sex. Chuckling I re-evaluated my statement – I loved sex. Full Stop. Talking about it, doing it, imagining it, watching it . . . I'd realised recently with Marcus that it wasn't the be all and end all in a relationship, but that didn't mean I didn't still love it! A huge, huge, filthy grin spread on my face. 'Did you guys pack any toys, or did you just get imaginative with what was at hand?'

Robyn bit down on her lower lip and gave an embarrassed shrug. 'A little of both.' She took another sip of wine, as if bolstering her courage to talk naughty, and then chuckled. 'We packed a few small favourites, but let's just say that we also found several uses for the hotel dressing-gown ties.' She rubbed at her wrists and wiggled her eyebrows which caused me to cough out a laugh as I imagined Oliver binding her up tight with the plush silk. 'And Oliver managed to create a very effect-ive spreader device using a four-poster bed in one hotel . . .' She left the rest of her sentence hanging, but from her flushed cheeks I got the picture; Robyn spread wide and tied up for his pleasure, and hers . . . I bet that had been one hell of a good session.

God, it felt like years since I'd had sex! I let out a whine of frustration and scrunched my face up petulantly. 'Make me jeal-ous, Rob, were you literally shagging twenty-four seven?' I truly loved how my relationship with Marcus was developing, but for a woman who had enjoyed a *lot* of sex during my life I was certainly finding this new drier spell a little . . . different.

Read that as: *I was horny as hell, but happy to wait for him.*

Robyn opened up a packet of crisps – her breakfast replacement – and popped one in her mouth before shaking her head. 'Not twenty-four seven, no. We really did do some sightseeing too, went out for nice meals, took in a little culture, you know, the standard holiday stuff.'

Reaching over, I pinched a crisp and then raised a sceptical eyebrow which prompted Robyn to blush a deeper shade of red and then grin. 'OK, OK, we did go out, but yeah, there was a hell of a lot of sex.'

I faked a scowl and sat back in a mock huff. 'I fucking knew it! It's so unfair!'

Robyn sussed my fakery straight away and smiled before purs-ing her lips. 'So enough about me, how are things with Marcus?'

I surprised myself as an involuntary smile that felt decidedly soppy slipped to my lips as I thought about Marcus. God, what the hell was happening to me? Taking a swig of my wine I tried to neutralise my expression but found it decidedly difficult not to grin like an idiot. Marcus White was ruining my tough reputation, wasn't he?

'Quite clearly from that expression you have fallen hard for our blond wonder, hmm?'

Robyn already knew that much, but given the goofy grin still refusing to leave my lips it would be pointless to try and deny it.

I paused briefly, just to add a moment of drama, and then conceded. 'Yeah . . . I have.' I stole another crisp and allowed my mind to flood with images of the time I'd spent with Marcus since Robyn had left for her honeymoon; quiet meals together, talking late into the night about our music tastes, favourite films, intimate kisses, hand holding . . . and some tentative attempts at further contact.

I hadn't stayed over again though. With our magnetic chemistry it would have been so easy to, but the disastrous encounter we'd had in Fantasia in Barcelona was still hanging over us, and it seemed too risky to dive straight back in to anything physical, so we'd agreed to go slow. Separate apartments at night, which obviously meant separate beds, and hence there hadn't been any sex, or attempts at sex since.

I decided to start at the beginning and update her on everything. 'I think you'll be proud of me, Rob, I'm getting better at opening up to him.'

Robyn smiled, but shook her head. 'I'm already proud of you, Sasha. You're one of the strongest women I know.'

I shrugged off her compliment, uneasy with the praise, and continued. 'And he's getting better too. We've talked so much, we both understand why the other has issues now, and we're working through them. It's all really good.'

'That's amazing, Sash. I'm so pleased for you both; you seem so well matched.'

The goofy smile curled my lips again, and I rolled my eyes at myself. 'Yeah. Touching is still an issue for him, so we haven't gone back to any physical stuff,' I paused, thinking of some fairly intense kissing that had occurred, and then in the pursuit of complete honesty, corrected myself. '... well, we've kissed and held hands, but he's comfortable with both of those. We haven't done much more than that, but it's still great.' I chuckled and looked directly into Robyn's eyes. 'I'm not gonna lie though, I am horny as fuck!'

Robyn tipped back in her chair and giggled. 'Might be time to crack out a bit of porn and get busy with that vibrator drawer of yours then, eh?'

A laugh far louder than Robyn's exploded from my chest and I nodded vigorously while cackles continued to erupt from me. 'Bloody hell, how have I not thought of that sooner?' For whatever reason, sorting myself out hadn't even crossed my mind, but if things with Marcus were going to take us time to work through then maybe Robyn was onto something. A little play to ease the frustration might be just the thing. Maybe I could video it and send it to Marcus for him to enjoy as well ... now there was an idea!

Before I could lose myself to thoughts of a sexy video call with Marcus, Robyn drew my attention back to her with another question. 'So, did you get to the bottom of why he doesn't like to be touched?'

It was at that point that it dawned on me that I hadn't told Robyn about Marcus's history and his ex. Marcus's confession had come in the chaos after her wedding, and seeing as Oliver had then shipped her off on their month-long honeymoon, we hadn't had a moment together since. I had so much to update her on that I barely knew where to start!

I sat up so suddenly I nearly tipped my chair over backwards and had to grab hastily at the table to steady myself. 'Jesus fucking Christ, I haven't told you yet, have I?!' It wasn't my secret to tell, but in the past few weeks Marcus had told me he'd confided in Oliver, and was more than happy for me to do the same with Robyn, so I had no issues with spilling the beans. 'Has Oliver said anything about it to you?'

Robyn shook her head with a frown. 'No, he's very honourable like that, if something is a secret he won't tell a soul.'

She cocked her head and gave me a quizzical look. 'From your reaction I gather there is quite a story behind it all? What happened?'

I swallowed hard, trying to plan where to start. 'Have you heard of his ex? Celia?'

Robyn frowned, deep in thought and then shrugged. 'I think Oliver mentioned her in passing . . . she's American, isn't she?'

'Not quite, she's from the UK but she lives over there. They met while they were both working in the States and started dating.' My stomach gave a sudden twist and I frowned. Hum. Curious. It turned out that jealous thoughts of Marcus with another woman brought a particularly acidic taste to my mouth, but luckily, I had this rather lovely wine to wash it away. 'Did Oliver say anything else about her?'

Shrugging, Robyn finished her crisps and put the empty packet under an ashtray on the table behind us. 'No, I got the feeling he didn't like her too much though.'

I wasn't surprised. From all I'd heard, Celia sounded like a prime bitch. I felt another wave of jealousy wash over me as I thought of him with her, but supressed it as I prepared to tell the story. 'They liked to play a bit, sexually, I mean.' A gentle breeze blew my hair across my face, and I brushed it away before continuing. 'An occasional Dom/sub session. Sometimes he'd be in charge, sometimes she would be.' Another swig of wine emptied my glass, and I gave a roll of my eyes. 'Hang on, I need a top-up before I start on this story. You want another?'

Robyn nodded, and I made a quick trip to Natalia at the bar for two fresh glasses of wine, all the while mentally preparing myself for sharing the gruesome story of Marcus's past. Returning to Robyn I sat down and then saw the expectant look on her face – I'd soon change that to a look of shocked horror, that was for sure. A large gulp of wine settled my agitation and then I continued. 'So, one night they were in bed together. She'd tied his arms to the bedframe, and they were getting it on.' Jealousy swept across me again, but I shoved it into a box in my head and carried on. 'Apparently halfway through she leant across and pulled something out of his bedside drawers. He'd assumed it was a sex toy of some sort, but it wasn't ... it was one of his chef's knives.' I paused and watched as my words sunk in and Robyn's eyebrows lowered into a confused frown.

'It wasn't part of the scene,' I clarified. 'He's not into any cutting or pain play like that.'

'So why would she have a knife ...' Robyn's question faded off as a horrified expression began to dawn on her face.

'Yep. It's every bit as bad as you are imagining.' I nodded sagely. 'You were right months ago when you speculated that something bad must have happened to him in his past ... it did ... in a nutshell ... Celia tried to kill him.'

It was almost as if time suddenly shifted into slow motion, because I could have sworn I saw all the separate droplets of Robyn's wine as they exploded from her mouth in series of shocked sprays and splutters covering not only her legs, and the table, but also me, the bar window and a decent sized chunk of the pavement surrounding us.

'Fuck!' I jumped up and slapped her on the back. 'Robyn! Breathe, woman!' Robyn gasped as she tried to calm down, but I didn't like the way her cheeks were turning so red. 'Don't you dare choke!'

Finally, to my relief, Robyn swallowed, cleared her throat, plonked her wine glass on the table and then wiped a hand across her mouth to dry it. 'She tried to kill him? What the hell, Sash?'

I plopped back into my chair with a grimace. 'Sorry to shock you, but there was no way to sugar coat it. It's true. She stabbed him. Repeatedly. Luckily the wounds missed his major organs or were shallow but he still lost so much blood that apparently he was lucky not to die.'

'Jesus,' Robyn wheezed, gripping the table edge so hard that her knuckles turned white. 'Why? Why did she do that?' she asked, her voice still high-pitched with disbelief.

'Who knows? He said they had been having a bit of a rough time in their relationship because they were both working long hours, but apart from that there had been no signs of trouble.'

Robyn's eyes were bulging so wide that it looked painful. 'And in the middle of having sex? It's unbelievable!'

I nodded my agreement. 'It is. But she's been diagnosed with a psychopathic disorder. She's receiving treatment in a mental health hospital now.'

Robyn was silent for several seconds as she tried to digest the enormity of what I'd told her, and then she sat back with a shake of her head and gulped down half of her wine in one go. 'No wonder the poor guy has issues with contact!' She rubbed a hand across her face seemingly trying to wipe away the surprise, and I remember feeling just as shell shocked when I'd first found out. 'Is he OK physically? Has it affected him long term at all?'

My hand instinctively went to my stomach, gently flitting across my abdomen in the same place that Marcus had his wounds. 'He's got scars. On his torso, and they cover his stomach and up around his side too. There's a lot of them.' Thinking of the criss-cross of marks on his beautiful skin, I smiled sadly. 'Apart from that, and the obvious mental trauma, I don't think he's had any other long-term effects.'

Robyn shook her head sombrely. 'I guess it explains his fear of contact then. It must trigger memories of the attack?'

'Yeah, and rightly so. Trust is a really big issue for him.' My sweet broken boy, god, weren't we a right pair? 'Remember that first night when I nearly stayed over with him and he wanted to cuff me to the bed? This is the reason why. He said that knowing I couldn't leave the bed while he was sleeping was the only way he could feel safe.'

Robyn seemed momentarily lost for words, her expression was well and truly shell shocked. 'Jesus. Poor guy. It certainly answers a lot of questions about his behaviour back then.'

I nodded and looked at my dwindling wine. Seemed it might be a blessing that I had nothing in the diary for tomorrow, because at the rate we were going through these drinks I was going to be bedbound with a hangover. 'It does.' I drew in a deep breath and allowed my eyes to wander across to the park for a moment. Everything was calm; the sun blazed down from above, birds flitted between branches, and a gentle breeze swayed the leaves. Life was good. In a moment as peaceful as this it was hard to believe that such awful things could happen in this big wide world of ours.

'It messed with his head big time, but we're getting there though. We're developing on the hand-holding and he's getting better at letting me touch him. It's going slowly, but we're building trust.' I laughed at the complexity of it all. 'To be fair, I need the trust building just as much as he does, so going slowly is working out pretty well for both of us.'

'I'm really pleased for you both.' Robyn smiled and then leant over and gave my hand a squeeze. 'So, you two still haven't spent a full night together?'

'Nope.' Shaking my head, I thought about the progress we'd been making recently and gave a shrug. 'I think we're getting closer to trying again though, but I'm just sort of taking each day as it comes. At the moment we just talk late into the night and kiss a little bit and then one of us goes home.' A wry smile curved my lips. 'I feel a bit like a teenager again, making out on the sofa but not taking it any further!'

Robyn raised her eyebrows and laughed. 'Come on now, Sash, we both know full well that as a teenager you'd have been taking it way further than just a kiss!'

Rolling my eyes, I tried to look offended, but couldn't muster much more than a mild frown because let's face it, Robyn was spot on. 'Yeah, yeah, I was a slapper, I know!' I reverted to the old joke we use to share, and it caused us both to laugh, the tension of our previous conversation lifting, and easing back into close companionship.

Leaning forwards in her seat, Robyn raised her glass towards mine. 'Here's to the future and new beginnings for all of us.'

That was certainly something I could drink to. 'New beginnings,' I agreed, and as I chinked my glass with Robyn's I felt my heart squeeze with hope as I imagined a future developing with Marcus.

Yep, life was definitely good.

Chapter Four

Natalia

Glancing out of the window, I could see Sasha and Robyn at one of the tables deep in conversation, but their glasses were still full enough from their recent top-up, so I wasn't needed again yet. Out of habit my eyes drifted over the other tables, checking if anyone needed a fresh drink, and then my gaze fell upon David, sitting in the corner working.

When I'd first met him, I'd thought he looked scary as hell with his tattoos, muscles, and big build, but he'd turned out to be really friendly and a good boss to work for. The pay was decent, hours were flexible, and once the initial training was done, he pretty much let the staff do their own thing.

I had a one issue with him though . . . and when I say issue, what I actually mean is attraction. I was attracted to my boss. It was such a cheesy cliché that I still chided myself daily for falling into a cliché. My eyes lingered on him for just a little too long, and I felt my tummy flip as I watched him continue to tap away at his laptop, oblivious to my secret observation.

I'm not sure what it was about this man, but it had become blatantly obvious to me over the past few months that my attraction to him was real enough. I never mixed work with my personal life though, so I'd made every effort to avoid thinking about it, and to avoid thinking about *him*. I'd even joined a dating app in an attempt at distracting myself from my crush, but none of it had really worked. As soon as I walked into the Club, he was all I could think about. This place was his life's work, his little London empire, and there was evidence of him everywhere I looked. The longer I spent working here, the more often I found my eyes straying in his direction, even though my brain was silently yelling at them not to.

He was currently frowning at something on the laptop screen, and even that mildly moody expression was a real turn-on for me. My heart accelerated until I could hear it throbbing in my ears, and so I dragged my eyes away with a huffed breath and forced myself to head back to the other end of the bar, chastising myself for seemingly having no self-control when I was near him.

It was an understandable crush, because he was a gorgeous specimen of a man, and it wasn't just me wearing rose-tinted glasses that thought so. He got plenty of attention from the customers. I'd watched time after time in silent jealousy as various women tried it on with him, which definitely hadn't made my crush any easier to live with.

My traitorous eyes dragged back across the room until they settled on him again, and I glumly assessed the man currently dominating my thoughts. Tall, broad, and just a little bit rough around the edges with his stubbly jaw, biker boots and leather jackets . . . he was so different from me that I really needed to try and ignore the way my body reacted to him.

When I'd first started work here David had been chatty,

almost to the point of flirting, or so it had felt to me, anyway; but as I'd found myself stupidly attracted to him I hadn't known how to deal with it, and so had withdrawn into myself. He had persevered with being sociable for a few weeks, but with me just seizing up with embarrassment every day he'd eventually given up, and all we did nowadays was basic polite interaction. He probably thought I was some introverted loser, which probably wasn't far from the truth. I was certainly painfully shy.

Taking a frustrated breath, I turned my attention to finishing the dishwasher. Loading the final glasses, I stood up and immediately let out a yelp of shock as I found David leaning on the bar and staring at me. 'Hey, Natalia.'

Talk about timing! It was if he'd read my previous thoughts, knew I'd been thinking about him and was determined to prove me wrong and pull me out of myself.

'Why don't you knock off for the day and go sit with the girls.' He jerked his head in the direction of Sasha and Robyn outside. 'We're hardly busy, and I know you'll want to catch up on Robyn's honeymoon gossip. Go on, go and enjoy yourself.'

My eyebrows rose in surprise. What a lovely offer. 'Oh. OK, that would be great, thank you.'

'You're working tomorrow, right?' he asked as I gathered up my phone and bag.

I nodded and forced myself to look him in the eye instead of avoiding eye contact as I usually did. 'Yes. I'm on the evening shift.'

'Cool.' David sorted through some papers and frowned. 'Would you be interested in a shift on Monday? Dan's on leave so I'm short staffed.'

'No can do, I'll be at my day job. Sorry.'

Placing the papers down, David cocked his head and gave me a curious look. His blue eyes were so penetrating I felt my stomach flip and had to deliberately tear my gaze away and pretend to look at my phone. Ha! So much for my earlier attempt at bravery! God, I was such a coward.

'So you work two jobs?'

'Yeah.' I nodded with a shrug. 'I don't need the extra money from the bar work here, but I'm ... well, you must have noticed, but I'm not very confident, and at my day job I only work in a small team.' I'm not sure why I felt the need to elaborate, but I did anyway. 'I hoped working somewhere social like this would help push me a little.'

David nodded, as if impressed, but then chuckled. 'It's good to push yourself if you're shy, but choosing a sex club to work in? Surely that goes above and beyond a dedication to self-improvement?' He laughed again and I felt the lovely sound vibrate into my chest causing a smile to pull at my own lips.

I kept my eyes averted, but for some crazy reason my brain decided to confide in him further. God knows why, but who cared if he knew? He was the owner of this place, he'd hardly judge me for my sexual choices, would he? 'Plus ... I'm quite ... well, I'm a submissive, so a sex club seemed a good choice of secondary job.'

I snuck a glance at him and could see by the way his eyebrows had just jumped in his brow that my words had shocked the hell out of him. A deep-down part of me was thrilled that little ol' me could shock a man as confident and self-assured as David Halton, and I felt my shoulders straighten out a little.

'Submissive, eh?' He rubbed a hand across his stubbly jaw and smiled. 'Well, this conversation has just got a whole lot more interesting!' he commented with another deep laugh. 'Submissive, or do you just mean shy?' he enquired curiously, seeming to lean even closer across the bar.

I shrugged again and kept my eyes locked on the phone now gripped like a vice in my hands. 'No, I'm submissive.' My reply was confident, because although I was frequently withdrawn around this stunning specimen, I knew exactly what I liked sexually.

'Have you had much experience of it?' His voice sounded hoarse, as if my declaration had excited him, and a sliver of hope spiked in my veins before I pushed it away again. I knew of his reputation; he didn't date, he fucked, and that wasn't what I was looking for.

'A little,' I admitted. Risking another glance up I found his eyes still firmly fixed on me, and I decided that as I'd started talking, I may as well trust him with a bit more of my history. 'Back when I lived in Russia . . . I was a sub to a couple there for a few years.'

'Woah! Natalia!' David ran a hand through his already messy hair and let out a bark of laughter. 'Fuck, girl, I was not expecting you to say that!'

David's grin was infectious, and my face immediately lit with a matching smile. It felt good to be the one causing him to laugh. 'I'm just full of surprises,' I mumbled in an attempt at changing the subject.

'I bet you are,' David murmured, his tone dropping lower and sending a delicious shiver dancing across my skin. Reaching over, he took me by surprise and pulled my phone from my hand before placing it on the counter to the side of him. Panic burst in my system at the loss of my distraction tool . . . that had been my excuse not to look at him! Now I no longer had it to stare down at, I wasn't sure what to do with my gaze, or my hands, and I started to fidget restlessly on the spot.

'Natalia. Look at me.' There was a long pause as my body fought desperately against the compelling urge to obey him, but my will just wasn't as strong as my curiosity, and finally I found my eyes dragging up his body to meet his stare. He smiled at my compliance, and then raised an eyebrow. 'I'm probably pushing my luck here, but I can't pass up the opportunity to ask ... you wanna scene with me one day in the Club?'

Shock hit me first, followed immediately by a raging temptation to say yes. Scene with David? Feel his hands upon me ... his lips touching me ... his stubble causing goose pimples to scatter across my skin ... our bodies moving together, slick with sweat from our mutual passion?

The very thought turned me on so much that I suddenly felt far too warm and found myself squirming on the spot to try and quell the sudden throbbing between my legs. It was such a tempting thought. My god, it would be like all the fantasies I had coming true in one go ... but no. *No.* It was the worst possible thing I could agree to. I liked him too much. I'd fall for him even more if I did a scene with him, and that was not a good path to go down.

Swallowing suddenly seemed like the most difficult task in the world and when I finally succeeded my throat made a noise loud enough that surely everyone in the bar must have heard. I gave an embarrassed laugh, but shook my head, even though it felt decidedly reluctant. 'I don't think so. I've heard about your reputation, David, and no offence, but it's not the type of thing I'm after. I don't want to just play with someone at the Club.

That's not really my thing. I'm looking for a little more than that.' In short, I was looking for a relationship, not just a one-night stand.

'I . . .' But whatever David had been about to say to me was lost as Sasha came bouncing up to the bar with two empty glasses in her hand. 'It seems we're in for the long haul, so can we just get a bottle this time, please?'

I wanted to look at Sasha as she spoke to us, I really did, but David's stare held mine with such force that I honestly couldn't tear my eyes away and break the connection. I watched his brow twitch with frustration at the interruption, before he gave a reluctant smile and finally freed me from the captivity of his gaze by turning to Sasha.

My shoulders sagged as the connection was lost and I had to draw in a huge breath to settle myself. As much as I'd been perversely enjoying this time with David, I was quite glad of her distraction to give me the space I clearly needed, and I smiled across at her in relief. 'Of course.'

I started to open the fridge to retrieve a bottle, but David came around the bar and placed a warm hand on my shoulder which brought me up short. All the relief I'd felt a few seconds ago melted away as the connection between us fizzed straight back to life. Tingles were erupting across my skin and I glanced up at him with wide eyes. He had an inscrutable look on his face as if he were about to say something, perhaps continue with what he'd been saying before Sasha interrupted us, but then he shook his head and jerked a thumb at the window. 'You head out and join them, I'll bring the wine out. Go enjoy yourself.'

I almost didn't want to break the contact with his hand, but for my sanity it was advisable, so I nodded, and then stood up. His hand briefly gripped me and then fell away, and we shared a moment where we both stared at each other before the connection swamped me, overwhelming my coping mechanism and again I did my usual: I dropped my eyes and quickly fled.

My feet felt like lead as I walked away from him, each step seeming to reverberate with a parting finality on the moment we had just shared. It was a warm day outside, but the breeze felt amazing on my flushed cheeks as I practically ran the final few steps from the bar and out onto the street.

Wow, that had been intense! I tried to steady my skittering pulse before I approached the girls and I must have looked like a complete wreck.

A few deep breaths reset me, and I smiled as I approached Sasha and Robyn and saw them both grinning and bringing a chair across for me. I was really glad I'd met these two, they were so friendly, helping me develop my confidence with their laid-back ways and easy friendship.

Sasha grabbed my hand and almost dragged me down onto the chair. 'Nat! Come, sit. Robyn has just been telling me all about her honeymoon!'

'Oh! Honeymoon gossip, excellent!' I'd known Oliver since starting work at the Club, because he'd frequently been in to assist with the running and finances. Through him I'd developed a friendship with Robyn when she'd become a member, but I'd still been incredibly touched when they had invited me to their wedding – it had been such a beautiful celebration. 'I need to hear everything!'

Before Robyn could regale me with the juicy details my phone started to ring in my bag. 'Sorry.' Letting out an apologetic groan at the untimely interruption, I dug in my bag to retrieve it and then felt my heart sink when I saw the name on the screen. Brett. Pressing the red cancel button I dumped the phone down on the table with a huff.

'Everything OK?' Sasha was frowning with obvious concern, but I nodded and rolled my eyes. 'Yeah, it's just some guy I met on a dating app and went out with a few times. I told him I'm not interested in seeing him again, but he keeps calling. He'll get the message eventually.'

Sasha's top lip curled in distaste and she nodded. 'Guys can be such dicks.' Brett had certainly been that, we'd only been on a couple of dates but on our second day out he'd been so rude to the waiter that it had almost verged on aggression. He'd claimed to be a Dominant on his dating profile, but after spending just a few hours with him I'd got the feeling that he was actually just a bully, and I'd decided that that was the end of things with him.

'So, were you just not into him, or is there someone else on your radar?' Her words immediately made me paranoid – did she know about my crush on David? My eyes sprung to Sasha's to see if she was giving anything away, but she just looked genuinely curious. I wasn't going to pursue anything with David, so it seemed pointless telling them I was being distracted by my attraction to him. I decided to satisfy her curiosity a little, but not give away my crush.

'Nah, not interested in him, he was weird. A bit of a bully, I think.' I hung my bag on the back of the chair and made myself more comfortable before giving a wry chuckle. 'I always seem to attract the weird ones.'

Sasha gave an agreeing hum. 'Dating sites are such a gamble.

You just never know if it's going to turn out to be a genuine guy or a complete freak.'

She was right there; I had read some really strange profiles and had more than a few bizarre first dates. 'To be honest I only joined the site to distract myself from someone else that I liked, but I think I'm going to cancel my subscription, dating seems like too much hard work.'

'Oooooh. Who is it you like?' Sasha looked interested now, *really interested*, and I immediately regretted my words.

The deep timbre of David's voice suddenly sounded over my shoulder and I practically jumped from my seat in shock at his close proximity. 'Hmmm, sounds like juicy gossip. I timed my arrival perfectly.' His comment was casual, but his blue eyes found mine as he placed a bottle of wine on the table and I blinked rapidly to try and break the spell he was casting on me. The corner of his mouth turned up slightly as if he were amused by my gawking, and then he looked away and began to fill the glasses.

'Do tell . . .' Sasha added, leaning forwards with interest.

'I . . . um . . . err . . .' It was official. Talking was impossible. David finished pouring the drinks and was once again staring at me. His gaze was hypnotising, and far too intense for me to string together a sentence.

I could feel my cheeks overheating by the second, but just when I was losing all hope of getting myself out of this sticky situation, Robyn gave a loud click of her tongue and shoved David playfully in the shoulder. 'Would you two give the poor girl a break?' Picking up a glass of wine, she handed it to me, and I immediately took a much-needed swig. 'Ignore them, Nat. Let me tell you about Europe – it was amazing!'

Sasha pouted her disapproval, and David let out a deep, wicked laugh that vibrated right though me to my already overheated core. He flashed me a wink and headed back to the bar with the empty tray. I had no idea if that wink was just good-humoured, or hinting that he'd noticed my reaction to him, but either way, he was gone, and I was out of the spot-light . . . for now.

Thank god for Robyn coming to my rescue!

Chapter Five

David

'Is Natalia here?' The demanding tone broke my concentration, and I put my pen down on the bar with deliberate slowness before looking up with a frown. A skinny guy with a quiff was walking towards me with a scowl on his face, and then as he glanced around the Club his top lip curled with apparent distaste.

Narrowing my eyes, I sat back and let him walk all the way to me before cocking my head and examining him further. Ratty attempt at a moustache, terrible taste in shirts and what appeared to be a ketchup stain on his tie. Classy. 'No, she's not. Who wants to know?'

He gave another scowl and then looked me up and down before smirking, 'No offence, *mate*, but seeing as you just work behind the bar of this disgusting pit, I don't think it's really any of your business. When's she due in?'

What the actual fuck? I most certainly was not his 'mate' and my eyebrows leapt to my hairline at his complete lack of both tact and manners. Surely Natalia wasn't friends with this douche? She might be shy, but I'd certainly expected her to have higher standards.

35

Sizing him up again, I relaxed. I could squash him with my pinky finger if I needed to. For some inexplicable reason I could feel myself getting protective of Natalia though, and as such I wanted to know why this guy was seeking her out. I never usually get involved in my staff members' personal lives, but I ignored that thought and gave him my best steely stare. 'I'm not sure.' It was Sunday and she was working tonight so due in half an hour, but I wasn't going to tell this guy that.

At my words he threw his head back and let out a gruff noise of frustration before swiping a hand through the air and only just missing the glasses I had lined up on the bar. 'She finished with and told me it was because her job was more important.' Glancing around the Club again, my pride and joy, he sneered. 'I mean seriously? This dump?'

Dump? Disgusting pit? I was about a hair's breadth away from giving this guy a serious beating and ramming his ketchup-stained tie down his throat. I probably would have done, if I hadn't been so shocked by his words – she'd dumped him? Natalia had been dating this jerk?

What on earth had she been thinking? I couldn't imagine Natalia picking someone like this. He was an arrogant short-arsed shit, with a haircut straight from the eighties and arms like elastic bands. Natalia might be shy and seemingly terrified of talking to me, but yesterday's brief chat with her had given me a glimpse at the part of herself she kept hidden. She was beautiful and so sweet beneath her low self-confidence. She deserved so much more than this. I couldn't believe it, and then to add to my confusion an unmistakable tide of jealousy flooded my system and mixed with my irritation.

Bringing myself up short, I frowned and rubbed at the back

of my neck in discomfort. Why the hell was I feeling jealous? She was a just a colleague. Someone I worked with. Wasn't she? My brain chose that moment to remind me that I also now knew that she was a submissive that I found rather attractive. Pushing my confusion aside to consider later, I quelled my swirling mood as best I could and then resolutely set my mind on putting this guy in his place.

Pushing off from my stool I stood to my full height and then stepped out from behind the bar before crossing my arms over my chest. His ratty little eyes bulged as they followed me to my upright position, and from the way he was now rapidly blinking and looking up at me it seemed that he hadn't realised I'd been sitting down before.

He could look all he wanted. I was six foot six and I'd done an intense upper body session at the gym this morning so my arms felt pumped and taut and in perfect condition to punch some sense into his arrogant arse.

I watched with genuine pleasure as the little prick eyed me up, swallowed with difficulty and then took a nervous step back, immediately followed by another. He should fucking step away. Coming into my club and slagging it off? I don't bloody well think so.

'I said, she's not here. And seeing as you clearly have such an issue with *my* club maybe you should leave.' I emphasised the 'my' to let him know that not only was I the big guy that was behind the bar, but I was also the owner. It worked a treat as I saw the final remnants of colour drain from his face. 'That's right, arsehole, I own this "disgusting pit", and you need to leave before I stop being this polite.'

As he nodded, his head wobbled so precariously it actually

looked like it might fall off his shoulders, but as he turned to leave I reached out and grabbed hold of his wrist. 'I don't ever want to see your face in here again. Understand?' He gave another bob of his head and then made a weak attempt at pulling his arm free. I tightened my grip until I felt the bones start to grind together and he gave a pathetic whimper. 'And leave Natalia alone. She dumped you, get the fucking hint. You contact her again and you'll be dealing with me. Got it?'

His eyes popped out on stalks and then he gulped and nodded. 'Y . . . y . . . yes. I promise. She's not worth the trouble.'

My teeth clenched and it took every ounce of my self-control not to crush his wrist into tiny pieces. I'm not quite sure why I'd never realised it before, but she *was* worth it. Natalia was beautiful, and sweet and one of the most genuine people I'd met in a long time. Clearly from the raging jealousy that this encounter had ignited within me, I'd been attracted to her for quite some time, albeit unknowingly to my conscious mind.

'See yourself out,' I snarled. Throwing his arm down in disgust, I watched as he ran from the Club on wobbly legs, slamming the door behind him as he went.

Walking back to my stool I sat down and noticed just how rapidly my pulse was now beating. The encounter had had quite an effect on me, and I couldn't deny that thinking about Natalia and that guy together had sparked a seriously violent reaction in my system. I'd thought my affection for her had just been that of a co-worker who got on well with her, but clearly I had misread it.

Running a hand across my jaw I let out a breath as I tried to get a gauge on what I was feeling. I'd always found my eyes drawn to her when she was at work, and I knew that I'd found myself excited when our shifts aligned, and we were working together, but, never having gone beyond the boundary and slept with my staff, I'd left it there. Yesterday's conversation with her might have been brief, but it had left me wanting more.

Damn! My stomach swirled and flipped as I realised with a jolt that, actually, I was feeling a whole hell of a lot where Natalia Ivanov was concerned. Well, that had certainly snuck up on me! She'd said yesterday that she didn't just want to play with someone at the Club, so presumably she was looking to date someone?

If she was a sub as she claimed, then she was probably looking for a Dominant. Licking my lips, I tried to supress the wave of excitement that washed through me. I was into exploration and liked to try new things and push my boundaries, but when it really came down to it, I was happiest leading things in the bedroom.

On an impetuous moment I wondered if I should just take the plunge and ask her out for a drink sometime, but then I rolled my eyes and chuckled; it had certainly been a while since I'd asked someone out and not just invited them back to my place for a fuck.

I didn't know her that well yet, but from her words yesterday I was pretty sure Natalia wasn't the kind of girl to go for something quick and casual like that. I needed to speak to her more, get to know her better, and then see where things went from there.

Propping myself on the doorframe of my office I crossed my arms over my chest and watched unseen as Natalia unloaded the dishwasher behind the bar. She had arrived about twenty minutes ago, but I'd deliberately given her some time to settle in before telling her about the arsehole who had visited earlier. I couldn't help the smile on my lips as I watched her. She was so bloody lovely.

Thinking back, I remember liking her as soon as I met her, and I would have had to be blind not to be attracted to her, but out of professionalism I'd steered clear. I might be a reformed character now, but I'd lived a whole different life for a long time. It had opened my eyes to the excitement that could be out there, and as a result my sexual tastes were still boundary-pushing. I couldn't do vanilla, and although she might be in my sex club looking for some mild experimentation, I suspected this was just a phase and that she'd get it out of her system and leave.

My eyes soaked up her appearance and I smiled. She really was so pretty. I'm not sure she even knew it either, and her genuine innocence and modesty were incredibly attractive traits, making her even more appealing to me. I watched Natalia as she finished polishing the final glass and stretch up to place it on the shelf above the bar. Her T-shirt pulled up exposing a flat tummy and I ground my teeth together as my eyes drifted lower and settled on the curve of her arse.

Sweet natured, girl-next-door pretty, gorgeous body, submissive ... she really was stunning in all respects. I rolled my eyes at how lusty I was suddenly feeling. Hell. If my attraction to her had been happening, say, a year ago I'd have been approaching her now, intent on satisfying the lust coursing through my system. But this was different. *She* was different. I sensed that she needed treating carefully, and if I were to stand any chance with her, I'd need to take things slowly.

Natalia started a different task, and I decided that I really couldn't stand here watching her like a stalker for very much longer without getting caught. We still had a few hours before opening, and although setting up was normally quite a busy time I decided I could make the most of the quiet to update her on my unwanted visitor earlier.

I pushed off from the door and made my way across the dancefloor to the bar where she was now cleaning down the surfaces. Natalia was still unaware of my presence and was singing quietly to herself. My step faltered slightly as I paused to listen with a smile on my lips. Even her voice was sweet. I rolled my eyes at my soppy thoughts and concentrated on watching the way her hips swayed with each swipe of the cloth over the wooden bar. Hmm. What a sight.

I saw the exact moment that she spotted me, because she paused in her task, her cheeks flushed and then a small smile curled on her lips. Ha! When I'd overheard her talking with Sasha and Robyn and she'd confessed that she liked someone, was it possible that that someone was me? Could she feel something for me too? I couldn't lie, I felt smug as shit at her obvious reaction to me, but then seeing as I was now grinning like a kid and sporting a semi I could hardly talk.

Well, these last two days had certainly been a turn up for the books, hadn't they? If Natalia might possibly feel the same, then maybe I could push things and try to spend a little more time with her. I didn't really have anything to lose I guess, except maybe a barmaid, because there was quite a high possibility that she'd quit if I propositioned her again.

Nodding, I decided that my plan was set; I'd speak to her, see how things went, and maybe ask her out if it was looking hopeful. I didn't rate my chance of success though, because she always looked so terrified of me, but fuck it, maybe it was worth a try.

Chapter Six

Natalia

'Evening, Natalia.' The gravelly tone of David's voice sent chills of excitement across my skin and a spontaneous smile flickered to my lips. Instead of being brave and looking across at him though, I did my usual – dipped my head, avoided eye contact and gave a vague nod in greeting.

'Hey, David.' Yesterday's chat with him clearly hadn't helped my confidence, because I still couldn't muster up the courage to look at him. Irritated with myself, I began stacking new glasses on a shelf, when from the corner of my eye I saw his boots coming closer. My body registered his oncoming closeness with a mixture of excitement and panic, but before I could react in any way he had arrived by my side and I found myself frozen in place with my heart pounding.

'You need some help?'

Did I need help? I almost laughed out loud. With my uncontrollable reaction to this man I certainly *did* need help, but clearly that wasn't what he was referring to.

David was a hands-on manager. He wasn't the type to be found hiding away in his office, and always worked behind the bar far longer hours than any of the other staff members, but he'd never offered me help before. To be honest, until yesterday we'd never really exchanged more than a few pleasantries while at work, mostly because my attraction to him always caused a ridiculous shyness to emerge in me, which rendered me almost voiceless.

His unexpected offer today shocked me so much that I forgot myself and glanced up at him. Chatting yesterday, offering help today . . . Why was he suddenly talking to me so much?

Looking up was a big mistake, because I was instantly met by his gorgeous blue eyes twinkling down at me. They were like hypnotic whirlpools, and the second our eyes met I didn't seem to be able to look away. I felt a tingle of awareness prickle on my palms, and then spread like wildfire across my skin. It immediately reminded me of his offer yesterday to scene with him and suddenly a whole lot more than just my skin was feeling hot for him.

Now that he was gazing down at me with a cute half smile I realised I couldn't really ignore him any longer without being openly rude. Clearing my throat, I prepared myself to politely decline his offer when my eyes strayed to the five boxes by my side. If I said I didn't need the help then I would clearly be lying, because this new stock of glasses was going to take me ages to unpack, wash and stack on my own.

I really needed to get over myself and deal with this like an adult. Grabbing one of the boxes, I pushed myself to standing and placed it on the bar while I tried to suck in some self-assurance. Nodding at him, I gave a small smile. 'O . . . O . . . OK, thanks. That would be great.' It wasn't the most confident delivery, but it was a start.

David flashed me a wink that made my knees briefly go

weak, and then reached across me to take the box. As he leant past me I got a lungful of his scent. I was certainly no perfumer, but it was fresh, with a spicy undertone that I couldn't quite identify. Whatever the fragrance, it was gorgeous and suited him perfectly, and I found myself tipping my head to follow him so I could get another sniff.

I was broken from my thoughts by a shiver passing over my skin and settling deep in my core as David paused right in front of me and then leant in closer to speak to me. This was definitely inside the boundaries of personal space. His face was so close that just a small roll forwards would have brought our mouths together, and my body leapt to attention, hairs standing on end, skin tingling, and throat tightening.

'Some guy was here earlier looking for you.'

Alarmed at his words, I felt like a bucket of iced water had just been thrown over my arousal and I jerked my head up to look at him. A man had been here looking for me? It had to have been Brett, because there was no other man that would turn up here asking for me. After I had cancelled his call yesterday it seemed the likeliest option, but why on earth would he have come here?

Although I suspected I knew the answer, I asked David anyway. 'Who?'

David's huge shoulders moved lazily up and down in a shrug. 'Didn't give a name, but he said you had just finished with him.' His voice lowered as he spoke, becoming gravellier than usual, and from his almost angry tone I panicked that Brett had done something stupid or irrational while he was here.

Wincing, I took a step away from him. 'Oh god . . . what did he do?'

David was so tense that I could see a muscle flickering along his jawline, and I wondered what on earth could have happened to affect him so much. He took his time to finish drying the glass in his hand, before leaning onto the bar and raising an eyebrow.

'Not a great deal. Tried to throw his weight around a little, but he didn't get far.' He shook his head, and then frowned. 'You don't seem suited to him at all, how on earth did you meet a guy like that?'

Lowering my eyes, I gave a self-conscious shrug. 'On a dating site . . .' I admitted quietly. I ran my hands over my face in embarrassment and made a mental note to delete the apps from my phone – I certainly wouldn't be using those crappy sites again.

'Why did you finish with him?' David seemed far more interested in this topic than I would have expected, but I gave a shrug and decided just to be honest with him.

'It wasn't anything serious, we'd only been out a few times, but it was obvious to me that we had absolutely nothing in common.' I rolled my eyes as I thought about our disastrously awkward dates. We'd had *less* than nothing in common. I hadn't wanted to see him again after the first date, but I was too nice for my own good and hadn't known how to say no when he'd called me and asked me out again. 'I have no idea how they do their compatibility matching, but it hadn't worked at all for me. He was a bully.' Now I'd started talking to David I didn't seem to be able to stop, and my confessions were just falling from my tongue one after the other. 'I might be submissive, but I'm not weak. I wouldn't let someone push me around, and I'm pretty sure that's what he would have done, given half the chance.'

David crossed his arms over his chest as he gave me a curious look. 'So, he wasn't the guy you were talking about yesterday when you said you liked someone?'

I choked on a laugh. 'God, no!' The denial flew from my lips with far more vigour than I intended and I saw David's brow jump in surprise. 'He was a dick.' I winced. 'I'm really sorry that he came here causing trouble.'

David pushed my concern away with a dismissive shake of his head. 'It's fine. As I say, he tried to be the big man but didn't get far.'

I bet he didn't. I eyed David's sizable biceps and height and felt a swirl of arousal settle in my stomach. David was probably twice the weight of Brett and far taller and broader. On the rare occasions that a customer had needed ejecting from the Club for drinking too much I'd seen David's tougher side, and it was quite a sight to see. The image of Brett attempting to intimidate David and getting brought up short as he unleashed his fiercer side was making me smile, and even though it was probably wrong, I found myself chuckling. 'I would have quite liked to see him getting a taste of his own medicine as he tried and failed to push you around.'

Beside me David suddenly seemed to grow another foot in height and when I glanced up, I saw his eyes were wild and swirling with emotion. He pushed off from the bar, his hands clenched into fists by his sides, and as he drew in a ragged breath, I felt anger bristling from him in waves. 'Did that slimy shit hit you? Did he hurt you, Natalia?'

Realising how he could have mistaken my words I quickly shook my head. 'No, no, that's not what I meant. He was a bit weird, which had put me off him already, but then he was rude to a waiter when we went out once, he got aggressive, all over nothing. His temper flared from zero, to raging in a second. It gave me an insight into what he was really like, hence why I decided not to see him again.'

David's stare lingered on me for a few seconds as if he were weighing up whether I was telling the truth or not and then I saw his shoulders relax. 'OK.' He ran a hand over his jaw before pushing himself up onto one of the bar stools. 'Come and sit for a minute. We must be due a break.' David tapped the seat beside him, and even though I definitely wasn't due a break yet – I'd only been in for half an hour – I found myself obliging and walking across to join him.

'So, you mentioned your day job yesterday, but you didn't say what it was that you did,' David said, with genuine curiosity in his tone.

I'm not sure what topic I'd been expecting, but it hadn't been small talk about my job. 'I'm an accountant. A junior accountant, I guess, as I've only recently finished my studies. I've been lucky enough to bag a job at a good London firm. It's a job share so I do three or four days a week depending on our rota. That's why I can fit in some shifts here too.'

David's brow bobbed as if he were impressed and then he grinned. 'Wow. An accountant? You must be really brainy then. Well done on the job, that's brilliant.' His grin was almost enough to render me speechless again, but I managed to maintain my composure, which was a good step in the right direction.

I shrugged off his compliment and began twirling a strand of hair around a finger. 'Yeah, I know maths isn't everyone's thing, but I'm really enjoying it.'

'So, accountant by day and sex club bartender by night, huh?' he asked on a laugh. I couldn't stifle the laugh that rose in my own throat at his comical line, and a quick flick of my gaze to David showed that he was grinning that beautiful smile of his too. God, his face was so handsome when he smiled. Dimples appeared in his cheeks, and his eyes lit up. I could very easily lose myself in that expression.

'And you're sure you don't want to scene with me at some point?'

Where had that come from? One second we were talking about accountancy and then we were back to this topic again? His eyes were glinting with wickedness, and it just made the idea even more tempting, but unlike yesterday when I focused on how amazing it would be to experience that with him, today I forced myself to focus on why I *couldn't* do it.

Doing a scene with a man that I was extremely attracted to was undoubtably a very bad idea. Bad idea. *Very bad idea.* Repeating it over and over in my head seemed to help keep me grounded, and stopped me getting distracted by my attraction to him for long enough to string together an understandable reply.

'No. That would be a bit much for me. I'm ... well, I'm not very experienced, not really.'

David frowned, seemingly hanging on my every word. 'I thought you said you lived as a sub for two years with a couple? Surely you did all sorts with them?'

Why the hell had I started this line of conversation? I tried desperately to think of a way out, but after drawing a blank my shoulders bobbed up and down and I stared down at my hands. 'I did, and we did a lot of stuff, but ... well, I'm ... I'm actually still a virgin.'

My cheeks were burning from my confession, but the shocked silence beside me went on for so long that I finally dragged my gaze up to see why David wasn't speaking. His cheeks were almost as flushed as mine felt, and his eyes were blinking rapidly, almost as if he were trying – and failing – to digest my words.

As he continued to just stare at me in silence I sighed and decided to share more of my story. I'd started now, I may as well continue. 'My mother left my father and me when I was just four. She just went out one day, left a note saying she was leaving, and never came home.' Knowing that she obviously hadn't cared about me at all still hurt, even after all these years. 'I don't really have any memories of her at all. My father did his best, and things were pretty good, but then he fell ill when I was eighteen. He suddenly started getting dizzy and vomiting all the time. It was so unexpected, and I was terrified that I was going to lose him, but then after months of tests they diagnosed him with Meniere's Disease. A horrible affliction, but thankfully not life threatening for him.'

It felt strange talking about my past after so long, and even though my chest was tight from recalling the buried memories, I was oddly comfortable with David. This was a topic that should have had me paralysed with embarrassment, but with him sitting beside me, I just wasn't; in fact, it was almost the opposite, and I found myself keen to share more.

'The disease causes headaches and dizziness so once he was diagnosed, he wasn't allowed to drive anymore. He'd been working as a delivery driver so obviously he lost his job. The system over in Russia isn't like it is here, his sick pay was barely enough for a loaf of bread, so as soon as I finished college I looked for a job to help out.'

I pulled in a breath that came out sounding more like a shudder, and David immediately stood up and reached over the bar to get a bottle of water. He cracked the seal and opened it before handing it to me. I gave him a thankful look and took a swig to wet my parched throat before continuing.

'We lived in a rundown part of Moscow – there wasn't much going on except drugs and gangs really. On the next block across there was a bar. I'd walked past it every day on my way to college, but I'd never been in. It had blacked out windows and I'd gradually become convinced that it was a strip club.' I remembered back to my younger years when I'd wandered past in the snow and tried to get a peek through the covered windows. 'It had sparked my curiosity, and I'd eventually seen a few glimpses through the door and seen women in bikinis which had solidified my belief. I knew it would pay better than other jobs I'd be able to get, and even though I was shy I loved music and I was a good dancer, so I decided to give it a go and went in one day.'

Laughing, David shook his head. 'Wow, Natalia, you just keep on surprising me!'

His laugh was so lovely that I felt my body come alight in response. 'It took me two full weeks to pluck up the courage to go inside,' I admitted ruefully. 'When I finally entered, the manager turned me down for stripping work.' I chuckled as I remembered how horrifically self-conscious I'd felt that night, and how mortified I'd been when the owner Vasili had said no to me. 'At first, I'd thought he didn't think I was pretty enough, or skinny enough . . .' David interrupted my sentence with a snort and rolled his eyes.

'You have no idea how gorgeous you are, do you?'

My eyes widened at his complimentary words and I felt my cheeks flood with heat. I was aware that men found me attractive, but I didn't really see it myself. Instead of replying to his comment I cleared my throat and just continued with my story. 'Anyway ... it turned out he'd refused me work because he knew my dad so didn't feel right letting me strip. But he knew dad was sick, so he offered me a job behind the bar. I think he must have felt sorry for me because he paid me nearly the same wage as the strippers.' I shrugged, remembering him fondly as helping me out in my time of need.

'Anyway, after a year my dad was recovering and able to do some work from home, so I reduced my hours at the bar and carried on with my accountancy studies.'

'So, this isn't the first sex club you've worked at? I almost feel wounded.' David held a hand to his heart as if he'd been stabbed, but then winked at me and grinned. That wink. Cheeky, cute and sexy as hell. My heart rate went crazy and I felt a wave of heat flood my skin as I tried not to lose my train of thought and just sit here gawking at him. There was no doubt about it – this man was seriously bad for my health.

'Technically that was a strip joint, so this *is* the first sex club I've worked in.' I corrected him with a smile and then continued my tale. 'Even though it was a strip club there was still some extra stuff that went on in the private lap dance rooms. I'd made a few mentions of my curiosity about some of the things that I'd seen happening, and eventually Vasili offered to show me more. I was shy, but curious, and so I agreed.'

I took another sip of my water and thought fondly about my time with them. 'He and his wife Zoya had quite a strange relationship. They were both switches, but preferred to dominate

51

when they got the chance. Their rules were that neither could fully sleep with other people, but after a while the three of us would . . . well, we started to mess around together.' I shrugged, suddenly feeling embarrassed. 'Oral, bondage, that type of thing. They liked the excitement of having me involved and I enjoyed experimenting with submission.'

David shook his head. 'So, he was moralistic enough not to let you strip in his club, but then he takes you home and fucks you with his wife?' he asked, with a disdainful raise of his eyebrow.

The irony wasn't lost on me, and I could see exactly how badly it reflected on Vasili but I knew in my heart that he had liked the set-up because he felt protective of me and knew it kept me safe. 'Kind of. But neither of them properly slept with me. Not full sex, anyway.'

David choked out a laugh. 'I can't believe you did all that with your dad's friend!' He ran a hand across his jaw, but couldn't hide the broad grin he was displaying. 'That is some kinky shit, girl!'

My smile widened. I guess it *was* pretty kinky. I liked the fact that I was making him smile and it somehow relaxed me further. I couldn't believe I was spilling out my history to a guy I barely knew, but he was just so easy to be around that it seemed the right thing to do. 'He wasn't my dad's friend as such, more of an old colleague from one of his previous jobs. He was younger than my dad. Anyway, we kept it private, so my dad never knew about it.'

Taking another glug of water, I decided to brave it and looked him straight in the eye. 'So, there you have it, I guess I'm kinda experienced, but still sort of a virgin.'

There was a slightly awkward silence, and then David surprised me by reaching over and gently touching my hand. His finger brushed across the back of my hand, and even though it was just a brief contact, it was somehow quite reassuring, his silent way of telling me that everything I'd just told him was now our little secret. 'An experienced virgin. Don't get many of them around,' he joked quietly. I really appreciated his comment, it helped ease my self-consciousness.

Before he could strike me dumb with any more of his blistering looks, cheeky winks or offers of doing a scene with him I decided to end the conversation here while I felt like I was on top. 'I guess I better get back to work. I wouldn't want the boss to think I'm slacking.' I knew this comment would draw a chuckle, but I decided to also test out a wink, and to my satisfaction I saw that it seemed to have a similar effect on him – his eyebrows jumped up and then a soft, cute smile curled his lips as I walked away.

I made my way back around the bar, and even though I could feel his eyes continuing to track me for a few seconds I acted oblivious and unpacked the new glasses while quietly congratulating myself on how well I'd managed the conversation. I hadn't gawked, hadn't lost my words, and most importantly, hadn't lost any more of my heart to that man.

Chapter Seven

Sasha

I settled back into the sofa and glanced around Marcus's living room. It really was a lovely space. Fairly minimal, but somehow cosy too. We'd shared a delicious dinner of salmon and stir-fried vegetables and were now relaxing on the sofa with a glass of wine. There was a film on the television, but with a string of easy, free flowing conversation passing between us neither of us was really watching it.

'Have you seen Oliver yet?'

'Yeah, I saw him briefly yesterday, he suggested we all meet this weekend for catch up.'

I smiled at the thought of life returning to normal with our best mates, it really was so nice to have them both back in the country. 'Sounds good to me.'

Marcus smiled at me. 'Oliver is so tanned. That sodding Spanish blood of his!' He rubbed a hand across his arm and laughed. 'He really puts me and my pale boy skin to shame!'

Marcus continued to smile across at me, but then suddenly his expression began to shift; his eyes became more intent, he ran his tongue across his lower lip and then as he pressed his lips together I watched as a muscle began to twitch in his jaw.

My stomach clenched at the searing look he was now giving me, but I had no idea what had prompted it. 'What's that look for?' My voice came out with a slight quiver and I realised that my whole body was now tight and throbbing with anticipation from the sudden shift in mood.

'Thinking about tanned skin made me think about your skin and how gorgeous and smooth it is . . .' And just like that the atmosphere in the room changed, tension growing as the ever-present sexual pull between us grew. He swallowed, and then shifted closer on the sofa, before running a single fingertip from the tip of my shoulder across my collarbone and up my neck. His touch was so slight, but so arousing that a shudder ran through my entire body. 'And that train of thought made me think about how long it's been since I've seen you naked . . .' He leant in closer to me and a warm rush of his breath across my ear had me arching my head sideways to give him access to my neck. I desperately wanted to grab onto him to help ground myself, but I knew that might freak him out, so instead I took hold of a safe zone – one of his hands – and gripped it with all my might.

How had we gone from light-hearted and jokey to hot and heavy this quickly? I had no idea, but I wasn't complaining. I was so horny for this man that I felt dizzy as arousal shot around my body. I allowed my eyes to flutter shut as I soaked up the attention, trying not to get too carried away with where this might be leading. Our make out sessions had become hotter and hotter recently, and I was determined not to rush him, so if this were just another session of amazing kissing followed by me grabbing a cab home then that was just fine by me.

He placed a hot kiss just below my ear and then lightly nipped at my earlobe which caused me to let out a groan of pleasure. 'It also reminded me just how much I want to see you naked again.'

Hmm. Maybe he wasn't just after a quick kiss tonight then? My eyes opened and I shifted my head enough so that I could look him in the eye to try and gauge his intentions. It was almost impossible to read his thoughts because his eyes were swirling with a mixture of lust, need and something much darker. 'I want to strip you naked and explore every single inch of your body . . .' His eyes stayed latched on mine as he vocalised what he wanted, and in response my entire body was thrumming with the need to stand up and just strip off for him right here and now. 'Then I want to fuck you until you come apart in my arms over and over again.'

Ho-ly shit. I wanted that too, so much that I could hardly breathe.

'Go to my bedroom, strip and wait for me on the bed.' Marcus's voice was so rough with anticipation that he barely managed to get the words out, but I understood his need and desperation, because it was reflected in my own. We'd been so good these past weeks, but the connection and sexual potency between us was just impossible to deny. How we'd lasted this long was quite frankly a miracle.

'You're sure?' I asked softly, wanting to be certain that he was comfortable.

'I'm sure.' He nodded, his whole body now tight with need and anticipation. 'Go. Now.'

I wanted to take my time undressing him, exploring his body and reacquainting myself with each and every one of his muscles, but we both knew that amount of contact would be too much for him at this point in time, which is why I suspected he'd sent me to undress myself so we could avoid any awkward moments.

Undressing him would come with time, it was just something else I could look forward to experiencing at a later date when he was ready.

Now I had his confirmation that he definitely was OK, I moved to the bedroom with the speed of a ninja, undressing on the way and throwing my clothes aside with the impatience of a teenage virgin as I climbed onto the bed and tried to calm my hammering pulse.

I tried to present myself in an attractive way, laying on my side and propping my head on my hand, but that felt too staged. Next I lay on my front with my bum out and feet crossed at the ankles in an attempt at looking beguiling and attractive, but just ended up feeling posy and stupid. Why was it that when you were deliberately trying to look sexy it felt awkward as fuck?

With a sigh I gave up on attempting to present myself and flopped over on to my back. I wiggled up the bed, propped my head and shoulders on a pillow so I could see the door, and then as a final touch I slightly parted my legs. That would have to do.

Just seconds later Marcus arrived at the door, shirtless, barefoot and also panting, if his rapidly rising and falling chest was anything to go by. His eyes devoured me with such intensity that I felt my skin heat from his attention and I wiggled on the bed in expectation.

A low growl escaped his mouth and then, after running a hand roughly through his hair, he shook his head in apparent awe. 'Babe, you are seriously gorgeous.'

I may not be some sultry siren laid out and offered to him in perfection, but Marcus certainly seemed keen enough, so perhaps my presentation skills were better than I'd thought.

Tossing his shirt aside he then wasted no time in removing his jeans and boxers and standing before me in all his naked glory.

My eyes greedily absorbed him; trailing from the tips of his toes, up over the downy covering of blond hair on his legs until I came to his manhood and stopped. My eyelids flickered and I couldn't help but lick my lips at just how perfect it was. And erect. Let's not forget that part, because boy oh boy was my man excited!

Eventually I dragged my eyes away across his taut tummy and then faltered slightly as I saw the scars adorning his torso. They were still reddened, and in the time that had passed since I'd seen him naked I'd forgotten just how many there were. He was seriously lucky to be alive. Knowing that he wouldn't want me to focus on them, I continued my journey, letting my gaze wander up his beautiful chest until our gazes met.

His eyes were burning into mine, and then, as if he couldn't wait a second longer, he began to walk towards me. It was more of a prowl really, each step determined and purposeful until he was beside me, and then suddenly pouncing onto the bed. His hands found my wrists, pinning me down, and then his lips landed on mine, devouring me with the strength of his passion. I gave just as good as I got, straining my head up to kiss him back, and wishing that I could use my hands to dig into his hair and drag him closer.

The kiss lingered, his mouth kissing and exploring my neck, ears and lips as if he had never kissed me before, and then his hands left mine and began to join in. He cupped my breasts, his thumbs finding my nipples and rubbing the taut nubs until I arched from the bed and let out a rough moan of pleasure. Letting out a wicked chuckle, he lowered his head and explored the valley between my breasts with his tongue, tracing and licking a path to first one nipple and then the other.

One of my hands moved of its own accord, lifting and gripping at his hip but as soon as I made contact, I felt his body tense like marble. Realising my mistake, I quickly threw my arms away from him, thinking that spreading myself wide again would help relax him. One hand landed on a pillow, and the other rested on the bedside table, both well and truly away from touching him.

Marcus remained above me, but his eyes darted to first one of my hands and then the other before he let out a strange, growl of a noise and rapidly stood up. His eyes were wide and darting around frantically as he backed off towards the side of the room with his hands digging into hair in apparent panic.

He let out a growl and then spun around and slammed a palm into the wall. 'Fuck! Fuck! Fuck!'

I sat up in the bed, unsure about what was happening, but understanding enough to know that my man was having a bit of a moment. He turned again so he was facing me and as I saw the frustrated grimace on his face, I felt my heart clench for him. 'I'm so sorry, Sasha, I'm such a mess.'

'You're not at all, we just have some things to work through. Talk to me, babe. What's the matter?'

He snorted in apparent dismissal of my words and then threw

his hands up in the air again. 'I trust you completely, so I don't know why I'm feeling like this.'

My mind was whirling at a thousand miles a second but I needed to get my head straight and try to bring him back from whatever was freaking him out. 'Explain it . . . what are you feeling?' I asked, deliberately keeping my tone soft and calm.

Marcus's shoulders softened slightly and then he moved to the end of the bed and sat down. He was closer, but still not within touching distance. 'I . . . I . . . I feel like I'm about to have a panic attack,' he admitted in a rasp, quietly dropping his head as if ashamed. Raising a hand, he rubbed the centre of his chest and took several deep breaths, as if getting air into his lungs was far more difficult than usual. 'When your hand touched the bedside table . . . I . . . I freaked . . .'

Oh fuck! Of course. I closed my eyes and winced. His ex, Celia, had hidden the knife in the bedside table on the night she had stabbed him . . . I was such an idiot! In trying to do the right thing and not freak him out by touching him I had inadvertently done the worst possible thing and triggered his deepest fear of being attacked again.

'Shit. I'm so sorry, Marcus. I realised I had touched you, and to try to make it better I moved my hands away, but I didn't think about where I'd placed them.' I wasn't sure what else to say to make the situation better.

Wrapping a blanket around my nakedness, I watched as Marcus began to pace up and down the room. He wasn't kidding about the panic attack either, he looked like a terrified animal; his eyes were wide, his skin had drained of colour and there was now a sheen of perspiration forming on his brow.

Thinking logically about his past and all that he had been

through, I tried my best to softly reassure him. 'It must be association. We were about to have sex, which obviously triggered memories of when you were with ... *her* ... and then I touched the bedside table, and obviously that's a trigger too.' I couldn't bring myself to say her name out loud – Celia – but realising that that also might have triggered further reactions I was glad that I had avoided it.

'Things are getting close between us now, Marcus. *Intimate*. And it makes you remember that night, which makes you tense and probably hyper alert. It's only logical. And seeing as it was no doubt one of the worst nights of your life it's not surprising that it still affects you.'

He let out a huge sigh but nodded glumly in acceptance. Seeing my big man standing there naked and defeated was utterly heartbreaking. 'I swear on my life I would never hurt you, Marcus.' My words were quiet, but buoyed by complete sincerity, and Marcus's eyes raised and his gaze softened as they locked with mine.

'I know that, Sash. I truly do. That's why I can't understand my fucking over-reactions.'

'Me and you, yeah?' I asked softly. 'Both a bit broken, but so much better together.' I added with a supportive smile. Jesus. I was getting soppy in my old age!

'Isn't that just the truth!' Marcus agreed with a sad chuckle. Shifting towards me he sat on the edge of the bed and reached out to take hold of one of my hands. 'I want to be with you, Sasha. I just need to man up and get over my hang-ups.'

With my background and my own hang-ups, I knew exactly where he was coming from, but letting go of the past wasn't something that could be rushed, as I well understood. It had taken me a lot of little steps to get over my fear of emotional commitment and finally let Marcus in.

My final thoughts prompted me to pause ... *little steps*. Nodding to myself I smiled as an idea popped into my head and then I carefully pulled my hand from his and slowly rose from the bed. Without saying a word, I stood up and walked to the back of the door and pulled the belts free from his cotton dressing gowns. My action prompted Marcus to lift his head, and the frown on his brow morphed into an interested observation as he tracked my every movement inquisitively.

Moving back to the bed I let the blanket I had wrapped around myself drop to the floor to reveal my nakedness again and sent him a coy smile and flutter of my eyelashes as I took my time crawling up the bed to the pillows. I swayed my hips as I went, making sure he'd get a good look at my bum as I went and then settled myself comfortably by the bedhead.

Looking across at him my heart flipped as I saw that my actions had indeed caught his attention, and he was now staring at me hungrily with a devilish grin beginning to break on his face. I smiled at him and felt my heart flip as he returned my look with a wink.

With his eyes firmly fixed to me, I began to tie the sashes around each of my wrists, and then secured my left hand to the bedframe. I was now effectively shackled with one hand, so hopefully I'd relaxed him enough to partake because I was going to need his help with tying the other hand.

'I would never hurt you, Marcus, we both know that. We just need to give your subconscious some time to get used to it too.' Lifting my head to look at him, I found him still watching me intently. 'We can take small steps.' I explained softly giving the sashes a wiggle. 'Restrain me. I need your help to tie this one.' Lining my wrist up with the bedframe I then lay back and hoped that he wasn't so freaked out that he wouldn't come to me.

I clearly needn't have worried, because he was beside me on the bed within seconds, so fast in fact, that I had to stifle a giggle. Taking my wrist, he didn't tie it to the bedframe as I'd asked though, but instead lifted it to his lips and placed a lingering kiss on each and every knuckle before staring down at me with wide eyes.

'You're sure you are OK with this?'

Nodding immediately, I smiled. 'Yes. I'm sure.'

Marcus watched me intently and slid his fingers through mine so we were holding hands. His flushed cheeks told me he was excited, as did his throbbing erection, but he was still hesitating, and then he sighed heavily and dropped his head down to rest it on my shoulder. 'I hate that I'm like this, I'm so sorry, Sasha.'

My heart ached to see him feeling so despairing. 'Don't be, Marcus. This is all new for us. We've only just let each other in on our secrets.' Giving his hand a squeeze, I smiled at him. 'Technically this is our first proper night together, we need to take it slow, build up carefully and do whatever it takes to make sure we're both comfortable.' Licking my lips, I decided to add one more little secret to the mix, hoping it might be enough to persuade him. 'I . . . I know it made you feel safer to have me restrained, and . . . well, I really liked it last time when you tied me up.'

His eyes jumped to mine, and I felt his fingers tighten around my hand. 'Oh yeah?'

Lifting my head, I kissed his neck and then whispered in his ear. 'Yes. It was fucking hot.' My cheeks heated and I repeated the kiss, this time adding in a quick nip to his earlobe. I certainly wasn't lying to make him feel better; when he'd tied my hands I'd felt completely at his mercy and I'd bloody loved it, which was quite a revelation for a control freak like me.

Lowering my head back down onto the pillow I found Marcus watching me like a hawk, seemingly trying to work out if I was being genuine or not. I saw in his eyes the second that he changed his mind, because his pupils dilated, and his shoulders straightened with confidence.

'You liked it when I took control of you, hmm?' he asked, shifting on the bed and lifting my free hand up towards the bedhead, pressing it down into the pillow so I could feel just how much control he had over me right this very second. *Hmm.* That felt so good.

Wiggling my eyebrows, I gave a slow nod. 'I did.' Marcus straddled me so he could reach up and tie the second knot and then to my surprise he tugged it sharply to tighten it. '*Oh!*' My breath left my lungs in a shocked gasp, but I instantly felt a buzz of increased excitement between my legs that spread like a warm glow into my body.

Lowering his lips beside my head he nuzzled into my ear. 'Me too,' he whispered hotly, before placing a kiss on my temple and then trailing his lips across my cheek towards my mouth. My skin burnt deliciously with every touch he made, and it didn't take long before I was squirming uncontrollably beneath him and desperate for him to move things along.

Marcus chuckled at my reaction, and then with one perfectly placed hand he pressed down on my hips and stilled my desperation. Staring into my eyes he gave a shy smile. 'You should know that if you ever want this thing between us to end then you'll have to be the one to walk away, because I can tell you right now, Sasha, I'm not going anywhere. Ever.'

I felt an instant lump of emotion rise in my throat, and in response to his heartfelt words I very nearly blurted out that I'd fallen in love with him. Almost. But seeing how fragile and new this thing between us was, I held back, just in case it put too much pressure on our new relationship or freaked him out.

Truth be told it was kind of freaking me out, but for the first time in my life the nerves and excitement associated with my emotions actually felt good.

It was true though, as I gazed up at the handsome man above me there was no doubt in my mind that I had well and truly fallen in love with Mr Marcus Price and all the baggage that came with him. As visions of love filled my mind Marcus shifted on the bed and buried his face between my legs, licking and sucking on my sensitive flesh until there was no space in my mind for anything other than thoughts of him.

Chapter Eight

Marcus

I paused midway in my approach to the bed and glanced down at the leather cuffs held in my hands. They were soft and forgiving, never leaving marks on Sasha's delicate wrists, and had become our go-to restraint over the last few weeks since we'd started having sex again.

I flashed a quick glance at Sasha, who was already gloriously naked and lying with her hands raised above her head as she waited for me.

My eyes skimmed across her gorgeous curves and the pile of discarded clothes and I felt a flinch of frustration pass through my body. I so desperately wanted to undress her myself, take my time exploring every inch of her skin, discovering the spots that made her squirm, and the ones that made her body flush with heat. But no. It wouldn't be fair, because I knew how badly Sasha wanted to do the same with me, and I just wasn't sure I was ready for all over contact on my body. I just had no idea if I would freak out again.

Perhaps I was being too tough on myself. It had been weeks since my last near panic attack. Maybe I'd be able to cope now?

Weighing it up, I let out a defeated sigh. If I freaked out we'd be back to step one; holding hands and no sex, and selfishly, as much as I wanted to try letting her touch me, I just wasn't willing to give up what we'd achieved so far.

My body hummed with awareness as I skimmed my gaze over her gorgeous face and sweet, come hither smile. My eyes continued to devour her, full breasts, slim body and long, long legs. She was just stunning. The complete package.

My brain continued its internal argument – did I really need to tie her up? Things were pretty great between us, and she'd been so supportive of me and my issues, even though recently she'd admitted on several occasions that she was getting desperate to touch me. I glanced at the cuffs again as a wave of concern swept through me. I suddenly became consumed with a fear that Sasha might be getting bored of me tying her up. She was a very sexual woman, experienced and confident and seeing as I didn't have a rack, or St Andrews cross, at my place, tying her up didn't exactly lend itself to the most exciting of positions. We were basically limited to face up on the bed, or face down. It wasn't exactly thrilling stuff.

Hmm. I wasn't willing to lose her because of my own self-doubt, so maybe it was time to start working through my issues. I could start by leaving one hand free, couldn't I? As I considered placing one of the cuffs down, or perhaps not even using them tonight, my heartbeat accelerated so rapidly that I felt briefly dizzy. A vision of flashing silver filled my mind, followed by the recollection of the agonising pain I'd felt as Celia had stabbed me over and over again.

Panic engulfed me so quickly that the edges of my vision went blurry and I had to desperately try and suck in some oxygen to stop myself passing out.

Flashing a glance at the bed I saw Sasha looking at me with a frown. *Sasha.* This was Sasha, *not* Celia. Sasha wouldn't hurt me, I knew that with certainty, but no matter how much I told myself that, I couldn't seem to calm my hammering pulse.

Sasha must have read the terror and indecision on my face, because she sat up and slid slowly from the bed. 'Hey, what's that worried face for?' Keeping her hands away, she leant up and placed a lingering kiss on my lips. The warmth of her mouth, and familiar smell of her perfume helped me relax and push the past away.

Once I had grounded myself in the present, I dipped my head in an invitation for her to kiss me again. A small smile flickered at the corners of her lips, and then she obliged, her mouth exploring mine so seductively that my concerns were lost to the lust flooding my system, and predictably, my dick was solid within seconds.

Now that I had temporarily put my issues aside, I lifted my head and decided to voice my earlier concerns. 'I was just wondering if you're getting bored of being tied up? I don't want to lose you just because we aren't varying things enough in the bedroom.'

Leaning back so she could look in my eyes, Sasha shook her head. 'I love how things are going between us, Marcus,' she confessed softly, that rare, shy smile, she saved only for me, gracing her lips again and making me feel like the king of the whole world. 'And even though I'm tied up, you've made sure we've had plenty of variety in our positions so far.' Her eyebrows lifted in a seductive wiggle and then she winked. 'I have absolutely no complaints. Quite the opposite in fact . . .' Her lips found mine again, and now that I had been put at ease by her words I joined in, groaning as she parted her mouth for me and let my tongue delve inside.

Once we were both panting from our arousal, I broke the kiss, and was about to steer her towards the bed when Sasha stopped and fluttered her eyelashes at me in a way that made my dick jerk with excitement. 'Can you tie them behind my back tonight? There's something I want to try.'

From the very promising look in her eyes I was pretty certain I was going to enjoy what she had in mind, so I chucked aside one set of cuffs and shortened the link on the other pair so it would hold her arms like handcuffs at the base of her spine. I circled around behind her, admiring her gorgeous full arse and trim waist and placed a hand on the nape of her neck. Gripping lightly, I held her still while I leaned forwards to place a kiss on her shoulder. She seemed to tremble below my touch, and my ego lapped up the fact that it was me affecting her in this way. My lips trailed across her skin, loving the delicate fragrance and the softness beneath my mouth.

Once I'd had my fill of her scent, at least for now, anyway, I stood back and guided her wrists together so I could cuff her. Once she was secured, Sasha turned around and smiled at me before licking her lips. I was just about to ask what she had in mind, when she dropped to her knees before me, and then looked up at me through those long eyelashes like some siren sent straight from heaven.

Wow, what a sight.

My cock lurched in anticipation. Sasha dropped her eyes to watch it before giving a soft chuckle and then leaning forwards and licking the tip of me like her favourite lollipop. Christ. Just that initial touch felt so good that my legs weakened and it was just as well that I could reach out an arm and steady myself on the wall.

With my palm firmly planted on the wall I watched her with fascination. I'd gone down on Sasha multiple times now, her unique taste was quite literally my favourite thing in the whole world, but because of the way she'd always been tied up we hadn't experimented with her giving *me* head.

I was really fucking glad that we were starting now though, because she was giving out all the signs that she was going to be bloody good at it. She started off by exploring me; her tongue circling the head of my dick, licking down the length and back up again and then teasing the sensitive underside, but then I nearly blew my entire load when she sucked me into her mouth. Sasha hollowed her cheeks and sucked me hard, shockingly hard . . . hard enough that I swayed on my legs and placed my free hand in her hair to give me something else to grip onto.

Even with her hands tied, Sasha was managing to get enough movement in her bobbing head to have me furiously turned on and close to coming within just a few moments of her starting. I'd been planning on letting her lead the show, but I couldn't resist tightening my grip in her hair just a little, and as I felt my climax getting ever nearer I started to use my hold on her to thrust into her mouth in time with her movements.

The tip of my cock hit the back of her throat as I ground forwards and I felt her jerk against the contact. Worried that I was pushing her too far I quickly tried to pull away, but was surprised when she looked up at me and gave a small shake of her head before pressing her mouth onto me again and trying to swallow me down with a groan of apparent appreciation.

This was incredible. *She* was incredible. All the sensations started to get too much for me to hold back any longer; the sight of her on her knees taking my dick in her mouth, the feel of her warm tongue and mouth working me, the little sexy sounds she was making . . . with a groan, and one final thrust forwards I started to come across her tongue in a series of jerking, ball tingling releases until her mouth was so flooded she had to lean back and swallow it down.

'Fuck, Sasha . . .' I could barely breathe, let alone speak, but after that phenomenal start to the night I had to try and say something. 'That was unbelievable.'

As I grinned lazily to myself, I looked down at her and watched as she slowly licked her lips, cleaning up every last drop of my release. She really was quite the showgirl, it was almost as if she were savouring the taste of me, and it was such an erotic sight that my cock didn't soften at all, in fact it was more than ready for me to scoop her up, move things to the bed and start round two right now.

As I watched Sasha swallow again though, I realised there was something different about her demeanour as she looked up at me. Her expression was almost anxious, and her eyes were displaying a vulnerability I wasn't sure I'd seen in her before. She was usually so cocky and confident that this was quite a surprise.

It was also quite alarming.

Was this expression my fault? Had I pushed her too far? Perhaps when I'd gripped her hair and thrust into her mouth it hadn't been sounds of arousal she'd been making, but sounds of distress?

'Shit, Sasha? Did I push you too far?' I asked quickly,

71

dropping to my knees so our eyes were level, and then reaching up to cup her face.

A trace of confusion fluttered across her features and then she smiled and shook her head. 'No, not at all.'

She was saying the right things, but I was certain I'd seen anxiety on her features just a second ago. 'Are you OK?'

This time her shy smile returned. 'I am . . . I'm more than OK. Was that . . . was that really OK for you?' she suddenly blurted, her cheeks heating with a blush and her eyes watching me carefully for my reply.

'What?' How could she even ask that? That had been the best blow job of my entire life. 'Of course, it was amazing.' Sasha was no blushing virgin, she'd probably slept with more people than me in the past, and I'd certainly been no saint, so she must have been told before that she was bloody good at giving head. 'You have quite a magic tongue,' I added softly, hoping to convince her.

She blinked across at me, and then her cheeks reddened further. 'That . . . that was the first time I've ever done that.'

The first time?

The *first*?

'You . . . What?' My reply was nowhere near as smooth as I had intended, but I could barely believe what I was hearing.

Her gaze dropped to the carpet between us and she shrugged. 'I know I have a bad reputation, I've slept with a lot of guys, so I can see why you wouldn't believe me, but it's true, I've never done that until tonight.'

'Wow . . .' Cursing myself for my crappy replies and inability to deal with this situation, I shook myself from my stupor and then quickly set about un-cuffing her hands. Regardless of my issues with intimacy and touching, I had the sudden urge to just forget it all and be with my girl in this moment. Helping her to her feet we moved to the bed and I dragged Sasha across onto my lap before tugging a blanket up around to cover her.

I could see the surprise on her face at our close position, but as soon as I had her settled on my lap, she linked her fingers with mine, as if instinctively knowing that it would soothe my need to keep her arms captive. It also provided us both with some much-needed contact, and then I gazed down at her, hoping she might tell me more.

When I didn't speak, Sasha sighed and averted her eyes, her grip tightening around my hands. 'Sex is just sex . . . but a blow job, it's just so much more intimate, you know?'

I suppose I could see where she was coming from, but I was still slightly in shock that she'd chosen me to be her first, so I didn't manage to say anything.

'I mean I've just had your cock in my mouth, that's a pretty big deal to me.' She shrugged, still looking self-conscious. 'I've never wanted to open myself up like that before.' She dropped her gaze, before finishing on a whisper. 'It always scared me.'

The story she'd told me about the pain of losing her parents was never far from my mind, and I realised that this must just be another aspect of her fear. She was right, blow jobs *were* intimate, and Sasha didn't do intimacy. Not until me, anyway. That thought still thrilled me.

All her life Sasha had been holding herself behind a carefully constructed wall of confidence, living her life like she was carefree, when in actuality, she'd spent the entire time being afraid of getting too close to anyone.

Wow. I still couldn't quite believe it. I was her first blow job? This was a pretty major development for her, not to mention for us as a couple. I felt my chest tighten as my heart swelled with love for this amazing woman and decided there and then that I needed to reciprocate and show her just how much she meant to me too.

Chapter Nine

Sasha

I think I'd struck Marcus speechless with my 'that was my first blow job' confession, because the poor guy had been unable to speak for the last few minutes, instead just holding me tight and gripping my hands like he was scared I was going to evaporate.

Telling him had made me feel really exposed, but I was glad I had. He had very quickly become the most important thing in my life, and I was starting to see that opening up to him wasn't as scary as I'd always thought it would be. I'd always feared intimacy, been terrified that I'd get hurt, but actually, I was starting to see just how full my life could feel, and being with him was definitely worth the risk.

Giving him that blowie had been a monumental moment for me. I'd been wanting to for weeks now, but a rare cloud of self-doubt had stopped me until today. I'd been worried that I'd be unskilled and rubbish, which considering my experience in all other areas of sexual exploration was rather ironic, but from his reaction he'd seemed to enjoy what I'd done, and I had definitely liked it too. Making him come apart like that had been a massive turn-on.

Grinning, I decided that I was excited about practising it more over the coming weeks and perfecting my skills. Below my bum I could feel the solid heat of Marcus's erection as it throbbed against me, but then suddenly he shifted me from his lap, stood up and paced a few steps around the room before returning to the side of the bed with a thoughtful expression on his handsome face.

'I ... I ... don't think I want to tie you up,' Marcus stated, before staring at me intently as he hovered over me. Leaning back, he continued to stare at me, but then he lifted his hands and buried them in his hair, gazing at me with a look of complete torment on his face.

Both of us were butt naked and had been mere seconds away from getting down to some serious sexy action, but apparently my confession had triggered a change in the mood, and now the air around us had changed from one of pure lust to something much deeper and more significant.

So, he didn't want to tie me up tonight? His words were the exact ones I'd wanted to hear for weeks, but now he'd said them I felt stunned into silence. I wasn't usually someone who found themselves speechless, but right now that was exactly how I felt. Seeing as I'd just shocked him mute a few seconds ago it seemed like he'd gotten his own back on me rather swiftly.

I mulled his words over in my head and tried to work out what had prompted them and also, how to interpret them. I wanted to touch Marcus more than anything in the world, but equally I knew I couldn't push him into it. If he wanted to take things between us to that next level, then I wanted him to be the one to initiate it.

Beside me, Marcus continued to stare down at me, but I noticed that his chest was now heaving with deep breaths as if he'd realised that he'd said his words out loud and was starting to panic about it. I watched the rapid movements of his chest and noticed that his scars almost sparkled in the dim lamp light from the bedside table, each one highlighted and telling the tale of the horrific things he'd gone through and survived all those years ago.

Climbing onto the bed he sat back so that he was straddling my thighs, and so I slowly placed my hands on the bed and carefully began to push myself upright. I made my movements deliberately careful so he wouldn't think I was going to over-step his boundaries, but as I got closer to him, I noticed he didn't flinch away as I'd thought he might. I was careful to keep my hands away, but leant forward and placed my forehead into the crook of his neck. I sat silently with him for a second or two, enjoying the scent of his skin and the feel of his warmth. Our bodies were now so close that the soft hair on his chest was brushing against my nipples and causing them to harden, and as if reflecting my need, his erection was trapped between us, puls-ing against my stomach.

As much as I loved his cock and the delicious things he did with it, this moment between us was way more significant than just sex, so I focused instead on the man trembling against me, and then very slowly and carefully raised one hand and gently slid it to rest on the scars on the side of his stomach.

Marcus tensed below my fingers, but didn't move away, and so I left my hand there, and turned my head so my cheek was resting on his shoulder and I could whisper beside his ear. 'I will never, ever hurt you, Marcus.'

He pulled in a rough, wheezy groan, and then I felt him nod his head. 'I know.' He sighed, and then returned my embrace, his arms sliding around my back and pulling me more firmly against his warmth. His hands were gently rubbing up and down my back, but not wanting to ruin the moment I kept my hands still, resting on his torso and resisting the almost overwhelming temptation to explore.

We sat like that for what felt like an age, and then Marcus turned his head and placed a kiss on my neck before whispering in my ear. 'Touch me, Sasha. Please.'

His request had been a barely audible hoarse whisper, so I sat back to allow me to see his face properly and check that he definitely wanted this. There was still some tension in his frame, but his expression was open and seemed to be willing me on. Tilting my head, I stared into his eyes and saw them glowing with something so deep and powerful that I felt my chest constrict.

Suddenly I felt nervous. I'd wanted to touch him for so long, explore his body, learn what he liked, and what turned him on, but now it had come to the moment I didn't know where to start.

'Do it,' he urged. 'Touch me, Sasha.' As if sensing my hesitancy, he gave a small nod and took one of my hands, lifting it so my palm was hovering just above his shoulder.

Very carefully I put both of my hands onto his shoulders. The heat of his skin was so hot it felt like it was searing my palms and I sat for a second and just absorbed the contact between us. Staring into his eyes, I started to knead my hands, gently gripping and relaxing my fingers in a massaging motion to try and relieve some of the remaining tension from his body.

The firmness of his muscles was a real turn-on. Obviously from seeing him naked I'd known he was a seriously toned guy, but finally getting a proper feel of him was heaven. Keeping my hands in one spot seemed to be helping Marcus to loosen up, his shoulders had relaxed, and I noticed that his breathing was calmer now too. As my hands continued to rub at his shoulders, I smiled at him in happiness. 'I've wanted so badly to touch you for so long.'

His eyes were now heavily lidded, and he smiled back at me, looking relaxed and content. 'It feels good,' he admitted, before grinning. 'Really good.'

Even though he'd already touched me all over my body Marcus's hands were doing some exploring of their own too, drifting across my back until finally coming to rest on my hips and gripping lightly.

'Your face is the part I most want to explore,' I admitted quietly.

Marcus leant back looking perplexed. 'My face?' He frowned, as if he couldn't possibly understand why that would be my fascination and then wiggled his eyebrows with a grin before casting a quick glance down at his cock. 'You're sure my face is the bit you want to touch the most?'

My eyes dropped too, and as I watched his erection bobbing eagerly between us, I let out a cheeky laugh. 'Well, obviously there are lots of parts of you I want to touch.' Lifting my gaze, I let my eyes rove across his face and gave a small shrug. 'But yeah. Your face is pretty high on my list.'

Sobering his expression, he tilted his head, seemingly giving me an invitation, and then he backed it up with words. 'Go ahead.'

My heart gave a flutter of excitement, and then as I raised my hands I noticed that I was trembling. Jeez. I needed to get a grip! Trying to steady my nerves I cupped his jaw. 'I want to know how rough your stubble feels under my thumbs,' I murmured. Running my thumbs across his jaw, I smiled like a stupid kid as I felt the bristly hairs tickling me.

'I want to run my hands through your hair and see if it's as soft as it always looks,' I confessed next. Trailing my hands up the strong angle of his cheekbones I skirted past his eyes and rested my fingers on his temples. His hair was as wild tonight as it always was, a sexy mess of half floppy, half spiky locks that somehow looked as if it had been styled to look that way. I slid both hands through his hair, marvelling at the sleekness between my fingers, and then grinning when it fell messily over his brow again.

'Anything else you want to explore while you're up there?' he asked in apparent amusement, and I nodded keenly before sliding my hands through his hair again, and then down to the back of his neck. Resting my fingers on his collarbones for a moment I then traced my way to the pulse points in his neck. 'I want to see if your heartbeat accelerates when I kiss you,' I murmured teasingly.

Brushing my thumbs over his pulse points again, I leant in and placed my lips against his. Marcus hummed against my mouth, and as I kissed him again and then darted my tongue out to request entry to his mouth he moaned. I pressed my tongue onto his lips with more force, demanding entry, and felt his heartbeat give a kick of excitement under my fingertips and start to beat far faster than before.

I smiled against his mouth. It seemed that he was just as affected as me by our physical contact, and that knowledge thrilled me to my core.

We kissed lazily for several minutes, and I was enjoying this new intimacy so much that I could quite happily have just spent the entire night kissing and touching him. Sex had always been great with Marcus, but touching him like this after so long of him being wary was just so special that I wanted to cling to the moment for as long as I could. I still kept my movements slow and careful, and didn't allow my hands to wander too far, but I was loving the new ability to slip my fingers into the soft hair at the nape of his neck.

Marcus pulled back slightly, not so far that I could look into his eyes, but just enough to allow him to speak. 'Anything else on your wish list?' he asked, brushing his lips back and forth across mine.

Between us we'd taken some giant leaps tonight, and I purred my happiness at how relaxed he now seemed to be. 'I just want to touch and love every single part of you.'

As his body stilled beneath my fingertips, I replayed my words and realised exactly what I had just said. The words hung between us for a second and then I froze.

Fuck. Had I really just used the 'L' word? *Love*? Had I just said it out loud?

Shit, shit, shit! We might be taking some serious steps forward tonight, but was I ready to announce something like that? I'd never said those three words before. *Never*. I'd never ever told any man that I loved him. My heart rate was out of control, skittering wildly through my veins until I felt dizzy from it. I wasn't brave enough to look up at Marcus, but even without seeing his gorgeous face, I knew my words were true.

Me, Sasha Mortimer, the woman who had declared that she would never fall in love had gone and done just that. Pretty spectacularly too, if the rapid beating of my heart and swirling stomach were any indication.

'Seems like we both have some fast pulses going on, hmm?' Marcus murmured softly. He was right, my heart was absolutely hammering in my chest, but I still wasn't sure what to say. Did I back my words up with a proper confession, or just leave it hanging it the air between us?

We sat like that for several minutes in silence, me unsure what to do next, and him seemingly trying to dissect my words and discover the truth within them. After several painfully slow minutes I couldn't take the silence any longer and I gave a small shrug. 'I umm . . . I just meant . . . I mean . . .'

'I love you, Sasha,' Marcus murmured, cutting off my bumbled words and causing my eyes to spring back to his. He had a small, shy smile on his lips, and as my eyes met his he nodded slowly. 'It's true. I've wanted to tell you for weeks, but I know you said emotion scares you, and I didn't want to frighten you away.' Blinking several times, he gripped my hips tighter as if worried that I was about bolt. 'I hope it won't?'

It should have, given my beliefs and history, but for some reason, it didn't.

Licking my lips, I slowly shook my head. 'It won't.' My promise came out as a husky whisper, and incredibly, it was true. His declaration of love didn't scare me, quite the opposite in fact – it excited me. This amazing man – admittedly he was amazingly complicated too, but amazing nonetheless – loved me, just as I loved him.

'I . . .' my voice was a croak, and I laughed self-consciously before clearing my throat and trying again. 'I love you too, Marcus.' At my words, his eyes widened in surprise and then after blinking at me several times in apparent shock he slid his arms around me again. Leaning forwards, he buried his head into the crook of my neck, kissing the skin there with a hot, open mouthed suck. I groaned in pleasure as desire danced across my skin and leant my head sideways to give him better access.

Deciding to clarify everything now before we got carried away with other things, I spoke again. 'I'm not just saying that because you said it. I mean it, Marcus. You've made me feel things I never thought I could.'

'I'm so glad.' His lips were scattering kisses across my neck and up to my jaw, and then his exploration moved towards my mouth. 'The exact same words could be said by me.'

Leaning back, he nodded sombrely. 'After Celia I never thought I would meet someone who could tempt me to lower my guard again, and yet here we are.' Bobbing his head forwards, he placed a kiss on the tip of my nose. 'You've achieved the impossible.'

'Here we are indeed,' I agreed, snuggling closer and letting the intimacy and emotion of the moment warm me from the inside out. I'd never even thought I'd share my bed with a man for more than one night, let alone consider sharing my life with one, but where Marcus was concerned, I couldn't think of anything I'd like more. 'I think we've saved each other,' I murmured contentedly, remembering back to the night at Robyn's wedding where I'd jokingly said to Marcus that he and I were perfectly imperfect for each other.

Turned out that I'd been spot on. We *were* perfectly imperfect, and apparently rather skilled at making the impossible a reality.

Chapter Ten

Natalia

The skin on the back of my neck tingled deliciously, almost making me shudder with pleasure, and even though I wasn't looking in his direction, I just knew that David was now down the other end of the bar watching me. It was like a sixth sense, some strange awareness of him that my body linked with to tell me when he was near, and when he was looking at me.

Pressing 'Start' on the glass-washer, I stood up, readied my confidence and then turned toward the other end of the bar. Even though I'd been certain I'd had an observer, I still pulled in a tiny, shocked gasp at the power I found in his crystal blue eyes. So yes, I'd been right. David was watching me, and more than that, he was giving me *that* look again. The one I'd noticed appear over the last few days since our increase in conversation. I'd never seen it before then, but it looked decidedly like interest, and it was making something crazy inside me think that there was a chance he was attracted to me too.

David's gaze lingered on me for another few seconds and then he sent a wink my way and picked up a tray of drinks to deliver. I watched him walk away, my eyes grazing down his figure and very much liking what they saw. Grey shirt rolled up at the sleeves, leather waistcoat, soft blue jeans, and biker boots . . . what wasn't to like? A crush like this on my boss was hardly ideal, but with all the winks and lingering looks from him, I was starting to believe he did like me too. If he did, could he be tempted into more than just a scene at the Club, or a one-night stand?

People at work had told me he had a reputation as a bad boy and sleeping around with the clientèle, but since working here I'd never personally witnessed any evidence of it. In fact, everything I'd seen was the opposite – I'd seen him politely knock back several girls who had tried it on with him. He was either very discreet with his pick-ups, or the rumours were simply incorrect.

Nibbling on my lower lip as I watched him begin his return journey to the bar, I decided there was only one way to find out. I needed to ask him.

He started to work on fulfilling another drinks order, loading a tray with three pints of lager and a coke, but we weren't that busy so I decided to grab my chance before he walked away again and my confidence deserted me.

Summoning my courage, I walked down the bar just as he went to turn away from me.

'David . . . wait.'

My words caused him to pause, and he glanced over his shoulder curiously before calling over another barman to take the drinks. Once the tray was dealt with, he gave me his full attention and I felt my heart race at the energy in his gaze. I could get lost in his eyes, I really could.

Now I had his attention I panicked. How the hell did I

broach this subject? I worked for him, I could hardly just come out and ask him if he liked to fuck the customers, could I?

'I ... um ...' I felt like my cheeks were being pumped with heat by the second. This was such a stupid idea! My brain was frantically trying to think of a way out of my self-inflicted predicament when I finally decided to just try and push forwards with it. Over the past few weeks, it had become blindingly obvious that I really liked him, so why not try to find out if he perhaps liked me too?

'I was just thinking, you know ... seeing as we've been getting to know each other recently and I've told you a bit of my history, maybe you could, you know, tell me about yours.' Gah! It was fluffed, and stumbled, but at least I managed to get some words out and not just stand here like a gawping idiot I suppose.

David smiled, and nodded. 'Of course, but I've had a pretty normal life really, there isn't much to tell.'

I raised an eyebrow and smiled. 'You're the owner of a sex club, I'd hardly call that normal!' I laughed.

Leaning forwards, he grinned at me. 'Well yes, I guess there's that. It's nowhere near as exciting as your tale of living as a sub for a few years though.' My eyes opened wide with self-consciousness, but David almost immediately calmed my panic with a sweet wink. 'So, what did you want to know?'

I wanted to know if he still slept around and moved from woman to woman with wanton abandon, but perhaps I shouldn't dive straight in with that question. 'Uhh ... when did you buy the Club?' I was genuinely interested in learning more about him and was quite pleased with how easily the question had come to me.

He gazed around the room with obvious pride in his achievements, as well he should have. This place might be a sex club, but it was an amazingly well-run establishment. 'When I was twenty-four.' Crossing his arms over his chest he smiled and shrugged. 'I got lucky. My grandparents were Londoners born and bred, they lived quite local to here, and happened to know the previous owner of this theatre building.'

I glanced at our regal surroundings: large wooden stage, pillars, high ceilings, chandeliers and sculpted patterns in the plaster work. It was a fancy place. 'Back in the seventeenth century this area of London was mostly lived in by aristocracy. This was originally a theatre were the local rich people came to spend their money.'

I felt my shoulders relax as I leant back on the bar and listened to him talk about a subject which he was so clearly passionate about.

'The theatre fell out of use when Soho started to become known for the development of its red-light district. Suddenly the rich people didn't want to be associated with the area anymore.' David smirked, his lips curling into an amused smile. 'We still have a few monied visitors on our books though, not that they'd openly admit it. I'd finished my business studies and was looking for a venue to invest in. Initially I'd been thinking of a bar, but when my grandma mentioned this place was up for sale I decided to change direction slightly.'

David didn't exactly strike me as a vanilla guy, he had a 'rough around the edges' vibe, so I guess if you were buying a building in Soho then something to do with sex made sense. 'I still got the bar I'd always wanted, I just did a little diversification with this part.'

'I think it's worked out pretty well for you,' I observed. He clearly loved what he did, and he did it extremely well.

David chuckled. 'Yeah. I was a single guy owning the coolest new bar in town. It was fun, plus it certainly had its benefits,' he added with a sly smile. I assumed this was a reference to him bedding some of the customers, and it gave me the perfect opening to bring up the topic I wanted to ask him about. Before I chickened out, I spoke, hoping like hell to keep my voice light and casual. 'So, do you still use it for those . . . err . . . "*benefits*"?'

David tilted his head as he watched me, his eyes sparkling with amusement at my clumsy attempt at digging for gossip. He leant forwards onto the bar, so he was now much closer to me, so close that his delicious scent invaded my nose and made my skin tingle with that all-consuming awareness of him again.

'Are you trying to ask if I still sleep around, Natalia?'

My cheeks may have felt red before, but they must have darkened by at least three shades at his question. I could tell from the twinkle in his eye that he was teasing me, which helped me relax slightly, but this was still horrifyingly embarrassing.

'Errr . . . I . . . I . . .' I couldn't get my words out! Speak woman! 'Well . . . um . . . do you?'

David didn't answer me immediately; instead he stared at me so intensely that I swear his gaze felt like it was burning all the way through me. Finally, he broke the link by briefly dropping his eyes as he shook his head. 'No, I don't.' He let out a dry chuckle and winked at me as he ran a hand through his hair. 'I'm too old for that shit.'

He could easily be lying, but somehow, I didn't think he was. From out of the blue, my brain decided that now was the perfect time to tell him how I felt. It was probably a really bad idea, but suddenly I didn't care. If it all went wrong and he knocked me back, then fine, I could quit and never have to see him again. This was only a part-time job on the side, I'd still have my main income to live on.

I prepared myself to speak, but just as I was about to drop my bombshell a young guy approached the bar and asked David for a glass of wine. Gah! I stared daggers at the unsuspecting man and felt an almost overwhelming urge to smack him around the face with a drinks tray for his untimely interruption.

Continuing with his task, David served him swiftly with a polite smile as he paid. Obviously unaware of my impending announcement, he started to clear some empty glasses from the bar and then turned to walk away towards the dishwasher. God dammit! If I was going to do this, then I needed to do it now before my chance passed or my bravery waned.

'David ... hang on.' I paused to wait for him to look at me, and at my words David glanced across at me again. I licked my lips to try and moisten my parched mouth and then forced the words out. 'The other day when Sasha and Robyn were here ... when you heard me tell them there was someone I had feelings for ...' I saw my words trigger interest in his gaze, but now he was a little distance away I felt calmer, so I pressed on with my confession. 'It was ... well ... It's you.'

Bam. Just like that. My secret was out now. There was no turning back.

I let my words sink in and watched in fascination as his eyes widened briefly before he swivelled his big body to fully face me. He put down the glasses he was holding and then frowned, but it seemed to be more of a look of confusion than anything else. I didn't want him freaking out or being polite to save my feelings, so I quickly held a hand up and then dropped my eyes away from the intensity of his stare.

'Before you say anything, I want you to know there's no pressure, or expectation on my part. I just . . . well, I just wanted to tell you.' Brushing some hair back from my face I kept my gaze lowered, not daring to look at him to see what he was thinking. 'I feel a really strong connection to you . . . I can't really explain it properly, but I felt it right from the first day I started here. We met, and something just . . . clicked, I guess.' Shrugging, I knew I probably sounded ridiculous so continued to analyse his scuffed biker boots as if they were the most fascinating thing I had ever seen. 'I know the chances of you feeling anything for me are probably slim to none, but . . . well, seeing as I'm in a rare chatty mood today I figured what the hell.'

My words suddenly ground to a halt as the reality of what I had just said crashed into me. Oh, god. What had I done? I'd imagined this conversation in my head many, many times, but I'm not sure I'd ever actually considered doing it for real. Now that I had there was no taking it back.

Around us, the Club was throbbing with its usual dance music, but it felt muted, like a bubble of heavy silence was surrounding David as I waited for him to say or do something. I half expected him to laugh out loud and throw me out. Whatever his reaction, it was too late to take my words back now, so I stood there frozen to the spot like a rag doll as the long, tense stillness continued to cloak us.

The quiet was only broken only by the rapid hammering of my heart in my eardrums, and the longer it went on, the more I started to regret my splurged confession. My eyes suddenly realised that David's boots were now stepping closer and I felt my throat start to close up with stress.

'Slim to none?' His words were a quiet rumble, and not what I'd expected at all, but I focused on the weaving in his leather jacket and gave a small shrug in response.

'Natalia. Look at me.' His tone was utterly compelling, and my head took away any responsibility of a decision by immediately raising until my gaze locked with his. David's expression was intent, and not one of amusement like I'd expected.

'Slim to none?' he repeated. This time as he said the words his tone was higher, making it into a question. He obviously expected me to explain why I had said that, so I shrugged and reluctantly tried to vocalise it.

'Well, we don't know each other very well, and I'm really shy, and you're really confident, so I'm probably not your type. You're so ... so ...' *Gorgeous and older and more experienced* was what sprung to mind, but it sounded too over the top, so I settled for something else. 'You're so self-assured I figured you probably go for really confident girls.'

There was another long pause where we just stared at each other, and for every second of our close proximity I could feel my body reacting to his. My skin was overly warm, my pulse rapid, and my hands were actually shaking now. Shoving them in my pockets to hide my tremor, I watched as David's mouth curved into a smile that made my insides fizz with something potent.

'Like you say, we don't know each other very well, because if we did, you would know that I also feel it too.' He felt it too? Could he actually be saying what I thought? He paused and gave a small nod as if to answer my silent question and in response I heard a strange wheezy breath suck down into my lungs.

'That's right, Natalia. When you assumed that you weren't my type, you figured wrong.' David chuckled softly and took another step towards me so that we were now impossibly close, and I had to hold back from reaching out to him to steady my trembling body.

He raised a hand and ever so gently used his thumb on the point of my chin to tip my head back so I was looking up into his eyes. 'The connection between us, it's there for me too, Natalia. And just to clarify things fully, you are *exactly* my type.'

My expression must have looked disbelieving, because David frowned and then lowered his head to place a short, soft kiss on my lips. My body exploded with sensations at his touch. The kiss was chaste, just a mere brush of his mouth over mine, but the shock of the feel of his lips and the light scrape of his stubble sent sparks of pleasure exploding in my body and dancing across my skin. It could only have lasted a second or two, and as he lifted his head I gulped and then swayed on my feet so suddenly that my right hand finally shot out and grabbed onto his wrist for support.

David cast a quick glance across the bar, and upon seeing all the customers settled and happy he guided me out to the back storage room, away from prying eyes. 'You're shy yes, but you're also beautiful, funny and sweet, Natalia. You're the most genuine person I've met in a very long time.'

As he spoke, he peeled my hand from his arm and guided it so it sat on his waist, and then he moved closer and pulled me gently against his chest. Being surrounded by him like this was the most incredible feeling, and I took a second to enjoy it and absorb the scent of him. My hands displayed a bravery I didn't know I possessed as they slid around him and settled on his back, and then my fingers took things a step further as they dipped under his leather waistcoat and explored the feel of the warm cotton shirt and firm skin below.

David's hands did some exploring of their own too, tracing across my shoulders and down my arms before settling on my lower back where he pulled me even closer into his embrace. Our stomachs were pressed together, and with every breath I took the peaks of my hardened nipples brushed against the hard plains of his chest, heightening my awareness tenfold. We stood there like that for an age, absorbing the feeling of each other, and then David slowly pushed back from me so he could gaze down into my eyes.

Raising a hand, he caressed my jaw and then used his thumb to tilt my head up so he could gaze into my eyes. His gaze dropped from my eyes and lowered to my lips, and as they lingered there the electricity between us ramped up again until it was like a tangible presence entwined all around us. The hairs on my arms felt like they were reaching out for him, my skin was heated with anticipation, and my heart was absolutely thundering in my chest.

Our eyes were locked, and all I could think was that I desperately wanted him to kiss me. I'm not sure if I vocalised my request, or if we were just on the same wavelength, because the next second David's head began to lower towards mine.

Suddenly it felt like everything was moving in slow motion. My body stilled, but my heart rate continued at rocket speed as the anticipation between us grew and grew.

His lips lowered towards mine and then stopped just short of touching. Our breaths mingled, his minty and spicy and causing me to lean in and try to press my mouth to his. He denied me though, bobbing his head just enough so that he danced around my lips, our mouths still fractionally apart as his not-quite-kiss built the expectation between us to crazy levels until a small, frustrated moan actually escaped my lips.

David chuckled and then finally gave me what I had been desperate for. He closed the remaining gap, his lips touching mine, brushing gently and exploring the shape of my mouth before his tongue dipped inside to twirl with mine.

It was a while since I'd kissed anyone, but wow, David's kiss was incredible. I could have happily stood there kissing him all night, but before we'd even properly got started there was a bang behind us as one of the bar staff came crashing through the door from the bar and then immediately slammed to a halt upon catching us in our compromising position.

'Oh! Uh ... shit ... sorry, boss ...' David lifted his head from mine with an amused smile on his lips, but as I tried to pull apart with embarrassment, he tightened his grip and kept me firmly wrapped in his arms. I saw the poor lad's cheeks heat when he realised what he had interrupted and he started to shift nervously on his feet. 'I ... err ... the ale is finished, I need to change the barrel.' More embarrassed fidgeting followed, and then he scratched at the back of his neck as he started to edge backwards towards the door. 'Uh ... shall I come back later?'

David kept a firm grip on me, but shook his head. 'No, go ahead, we're coming back out front now anyway.'

Disappointment seared through me. No! We'd barely even kissed properly! It couldn't be over already! David looked down at me and smiled softly, before leaning into me and whispering in my ear. 'To be continued later. Deal?'

This was all going so well that I felt like I was floating. I tried to reply, but my throat was so tight with excitement that I had to clear it before my words would come out. Reaching up, I brushed my lips across his neck before whispering my reply. 'You definitely have a deal.'

Chapter Eleven

Sasha

As I snuggled deeper into Marcus's arms I could hardly believe the events of the evening so far. Even with both of our hang-ups and issues we'd both just committed to saying 'I love you'. The utterly incredible thing for me was that I truly meant it. I knew Marcus pretty well by now, and judging from the wideness of his eyes and pulse pounding in his chest, he had meant it too.

Marcus cleared his throat, and then shifted me on his lap so he could look into my eyes. 'So yeah, as I said earlier, I don't want to tie you up tonight.'

After our deep and meaningful conversation, I'd actually thought that sex might take a bit of a back seat tonight, but as he gave a thrust of his hips so I could feel that he was still hard below my bum I realised I may have been wrong.

Marcus nodded his head slowly. 'You'll have to bear with me, but I want to try.'

Cupping his jaw, I stroked it gently, desperate to make sure that he didn't feel anxious. 'You have no reason to be nervous, Marcus. We can just take it slow and enjoy ourselves. I'll limit the amount I touch you, and if you want to stop at any point you just have to say so.'

Nodding gratefully at my sentiment he placed a soft kiss on my lips. 'I trust you implicitly, Sasha.' Given all that he had gone through, his words meant a great deal to me and I felt my chest tighten with emotion.

It seemed crazy after all we'd shared so far, but instead of him acting nervous it was me that found myself with trembling fingers. Seriously? Me, Sasha Mortimer nervous about sex? It was hardly a sentiment I could compute, but I guess being with Marcus was just so important to me that this meant way more than any casual interlude I'd ever had in the past.

It was fair to say that as soon as Marcus started to kiss me again my promise of *taking things slow* pretty much shot out the window as our mouths collided with a pent-up passion that bordered on explosive. We did however manage to successfully focus on my other statement of *enjoying ourselves,* because god, did I enjoy being with this man.

As Marcus continued to kiss me, I tried to make sure he would feel at ease. I slightly spread my arms, not so wide that I was near his trigger of the bedside cabinets, but just enough that he wouldn't feel confined or worried about my touch. With all the pillows and duvet rumpled up around us I was too cramped for space to do it properly. My elbows couldn't move where they needed to, and my hands were trembling too much to shift the cushions, so in the end I gave up and settled for trying not to startle him with any sudden touches.

Raising his head, Marcus smiled down at me and gave a small chuckle at my clumsy attempt at spreading my arms wide. He glanced around us and then grinned. Taking me completely by surprise, he scooped me into his arms and strode through to the lounge. The fire was still flickering in the wood burner and he lowered us down onto the soft rug in front of it, obviously deciding to remedy the space situation.

'More space here,' Marcus mumbled as he returned to lean over me and continued to kiss me eagerly. I did indeed have more space, and once I had my trembling fingers under control, I was more successful at spreading my arms out and digging my fingers into the deep pile of the rug.

At first, I did well at not touching him, but as Marcus leant over and captured one of my nipples in his mouth, I impulsively reached up a hand and slid it through his silky, wild locks. As soon as my hand dug into his hair Marcus's body stilled above me and I felt anxiety twirl in my system.

'Shit. Sorry,' I blurted, quickly withdrawing my hand; but as I looked at him, I saw to my surprise that he was smiling.

'Don't be. It feels good.' Marcus let out a groan and a shudder of pleasure. 'Go for it. Touch me.' He closed his eyes, seemingly giving me permission to explore, so I did, lifting my hand and raking it through his hair again. It felt silky smooth to touch, and as always flopped about wildly, doing its own thing. Slipping my hand from his hair to the nape of his neck, I lightly encouraged his mouth back down to mine.

Although I was completely immersed in kissing Marcus, and enjoying every second, I could feel my body becoming impatient. The evening had been a series of highs, and there had been so much kissing and touching that I was incredibly turned on. An ache of desire was settled in my lower abdomen and spreading through me like a wildfire, demanding that I do something about it.

I began to squirm, trying to press myself more fully against Marcus, and carefully allowing my hands to explore his amazing body. My nails dug into his shoulders as I encouraged him to speed things along, and he didn't tense at my contact, or flinch at all, and a rush of happiness at this amazing development flooded through me.

Marcus left my mouth and took several minutes exploring my body, his warm hands and lips seeming to touch or kiss every single part of me until I was almost crying out for him to make love to me.

Finally, when I honestly felt like I was about to burst with desperation his hand slipped to where I wanted it the most – straight between my legs to the point of my desire. I let out a long, low moan of sheer pleasure and relief and arched myself keenly towards his touch. His finger circled my clit several times before sliding lower and dipping inside me.

He groaned. 'So tight, Sasha. Fuck.' He cursed, starting to move his hand rhythmically in my wetness.

My nerve endings felt like live electricity was coursing through them, and almost as soon as he had touched me, I felt like I was right on the edge of orgasm. 'Marcus, I'm not going to last long,' I warned him in a desperate whisper.

Marcus chuckled but after teasing me for a few more seconds he shifted himself above me and I felt the thick head of his cock nudging at my entrance, where his fingers had been just seconds earlier.

Instead of immediately pushing inside of me as I so wanted, Marcus hovered there instead, and I glanced up at him desperately. 'Please, Marcus. Now.'

'Touch me. I want your hands on me as I take you.' Now that

I could do. I skated my hands up his back, tracing the firm muscles with pleasure. My nails dug into his back to encourage him, and finally Marcus obliged me by pressing his hips forwards and joining us in one smooth movement.

Marcus was well endowed in the groin department, and the thickness of his cock always filled me to the brim and touched me in all the right places deliciously. His contact on my g-spot tonight when I was so turned on almost sent me straight over the edge. Thankfully, it seemed that Marcus was just as excited as me, because he noticeably started with a slow pace whilst we both regained our control.

We wouldn't win any awards for stamina tonight, that was for sure, because it seemed that all of our confessions and intimacy had turned us both on and primed us ready for our climaxes. Staring deeply into my eyes, Marcus began to increase the speed, his hips thrusting faster and deeper and sending us towards a dizzying peak that suddenly burst for both of us at the same time, causing cries of gratification to escape from us before we collapsed onto the rug in a satisfied, contented pile.

I had just had amazing sex with Marcus, and he had let me touch him anywhere and everywhere. This was something I'd dreamed of since we'd met. Now it had finally happened, and because of the enormity of that realisation it had felt like possibly the most emotionally and physically incredible moment of my life.

Chapter Twelve

David

Marcus sipped his beer, but continued to watch me over the top of his glass with slightly narrowed eyes until I couldn't take it anymore. 'What the fuck is it, man? You've been staring at me for the last ten minutes! Have I got something on my face?' I wiped a hand over my mouth and scratched at my stubble, but I couldn't find anything that shouldn't be there.

'No, there's nothing on your face. But there's something different about you. I just can't figure out what.' He placed his pint down and cocked his head to the side as he continued to stare at me. His attention was really starting to piss me off. I glanced down at myself, but there was nothing different to usual.

'You've not cut your hair, and your stubble is still scruffy as hell . . . Is that a new jacket?' he asked with a frown.

I snorted out a laugh. I didn't even need to look at my jacket to know the answer to that question. 'Mate, your observation skills are shite. This is the same sleeveless leather jacket that I've worn to work almost every day for the last ten years.'

He frowned as he looked at my jacket and then shrugged. 'I can't work it out then.'

Oliver joined Marcus at the bar and nodded a greeting to me. He looked his usual slick self, suited and booted in a navy three-piece. Other guys would wear his outfit and look like they were trying too hard, but Oliver's suits were like his trademark. I poured him his customary glass of whisky and slid it across to him. 'Can't work what out?' he asked as he shrugged out of his suit coat and started to roll up the shirt sleeves.

Marcus shook his head with a frown. 'I dunno, it's weird, I feel like there's something different about David tonight, but I can't work out what.'

Oliver paused with his shirt sleeves and turned his gaze upon me. He might be my mate, but he had one seriously intense stare and I felt my stomach tense as the urge to step backwards away from his scrutiny almost overwhelmed me. I could see exactly why he made a good Dominant, that intensity of his was quite something.

His eyes narrowed, and then after a few more seconds of staring a knowing smile curled his lips. 'Did you get laid?'

'Nope.' I felt my cheeks start to heat though, because he was pretty close to the mark. I'd been in really good mood since my encounter with Natalia last weekend. We had hoped to continue where we'd left off that night, but that night shift had really dragged on, and she'd been working her day job all week so we hadn't had the opportunity to get together again since. We'd talked every day though, our conversations making me feel like an excited teenager, and we both had some days off coming up soon so I was planning on taking her out then.

'It's a woman then. You're seeing someone? Or interested, at least.'

How did he manage to do this? He'd always been a great judge of character and had an uncanny knack of reading people, which had come in useful over the years when assessing new applications for club membership. It wasn't quite such a nice feeling when his skill set was being used on me though. Echoing my thoughts, I rolled my eyes and crossed my arms over my chest. 'How the fuck do you do that?'

Oliver smiled smugly. 'It's a unique talent.' He commented drily before going back to arranging his shirt sleeves into intricately neat folds at his elbow. 'So, who is it?'

Oliver was feigning nonchalance with his sleeve rolling, but Marcus was openly grinning at me in curiosity. Bastards.

Was nothing private anymore? For fuck's sake. Rolling my eyes, I sighed and gave in. They'd no doubt find out soon enough from the girls, anyway. 'Natalia.'

Both of my mates smiled with apparent pleasant surprise, but I couldn't miss their raised eyebrows. 'Yeah, yeah, she works for me, I know. I'm not taking advantage of her. It's not like that, we haven't slept together.'

'How is it then? Do tell,' said Marcus, barely containing his glee at the gossip appearing before him.

I shrugged, trying to look casual, but no matter how hard I tried, I couldn't keep the shit-eating grin off my face. I was happy. Really bloody happy, and as much as I wanted to play it cool in front of the guys I couldn't seem to stop smiling. 'I liked her since she started, and obviously she's really pretty, but I wouldn't have tried anything because she works for me.' I paused and recalled how excited I'd been last week when she'd told me she liked me. The fact that she'd been brave enough to make the first move had been such a turn-on. 'But last week she told me she liked me.' My shoulders jerked in a shrug. It sounded so simple and insignificant, and yet it meant so much. 'I wouldn't usually associate romantically with a staff member, but this feels different somehow.'

Oliver threw his head back and laughed. 'Associate with a staff member . . . is that your polite way of saying "I wouldn't usually fuck a staff member"? Because it certainly never used to be an issue for you. From what I recall, back in the day you shagged your way through the clientèle, and that must surely have included the staff too.'

I glared at him, feeling slightly self-conscious. 'Yeah, yeah, whatever. I know I was promiscuous back then, but you're wrong – I never messed around with any of the staff.' Grunting, I dismissed his remark with a frown. 'Besides, this is different. It's not just a casual thing.'

Oliver lost his cheeky grin and instead gave me a curious look. 'Thinking of following in our footsteps and actually try-ing out dating, are you?' I couldn't deny that the dating game had worked out pretty well for both Oliver and Marcus recently. Oliver was now a married man, and so happy that it was almost sickening, and things between Marcus and Sasha actually seemed to be settling really well too. If I wasn't careful, I was going to end up as the old single man left on the shelf.

'How long has it been since you dated?' Marcus asked curi-ously. How long? I'd slept around, and experimented with a lot of crazy shit, but been on a date? It had been so long since I had done anything that could be classed as 'dating' that I actually couldn't remember. Scratching my chin, I grimaced as a vague recollection of a series of dinners and sex with a blonde girl entered my mind. 'Probably back in my early twenties, I guess.' It said a lot about the relationship that I couldn't even remember her name. 'That was around the time I bought the Club though, and I guess it just kinda took over my life.'

'You certainly haven't allowed yourself to be lonely or have an empty bed though,' Oliver remarked sardonically.

Rolling my eyes, I shrugged his remark off. 'I was no worse than you, and you damn well know it.' I didn't fuck the clients anymore, but for many years there had been a handful of the original members – whom I now deemed friends – including Marcus and Oliver, and we would regularly indulge in some form of delicious depravity with various women who willingly volunteered. None of us had been the marrying kind back then, all happy with the freedom of singlehood and the relaxed agreement had suited us all.

Recently though, it had tailed off. Oliver had met Robyn, Marcus had started to obsess over Sasha, and I had just lost the love for it, somehow. I was busy, and I was older, and I guess mindless sex with strangers had started to lose its appeal.

'How long's it been since you got laid?' Marcus asked with a wicked grin.

I tried to think back and frowned when I struggled to recall when it had been. 'Six months? Maybe seven?' Jesus, that was a pretty big dry streak for a guy as sexual as me.

Marcus slapped a hand onto the counter and almost choked on his beer. 'Hell, man, you better have a few wanks before you bed her, otherwise you'll come before you even get your trousers off!'

'Thanks for the advice, Marcus,' I replied drily. I recalled

Natalia's description of her sexual experience and suddenly realised the implications of it. Lifting my hands, I ran them through my hair and then let out a disbelieving chuckle. 'Damn. I'm nearly forty-three and I think I'm about to bed a virgin. How the hell did that happen?'

This time it was Oliver who coughed in surprise. 'A virgin?' He placed his drink down and then raised his eyebrows in surprise. 'She obviously younger than you, but not that young, surely?'

Shaking my head, I leant back on the bar. 'No. She says she's technically a virgin, in terms of actual intercourse, but she's had other experience.' I could see their intrigued stares, so trying to stick to the basics I gave them a quick update on Natalia's past living in Russia as a sub, and how it had limited her experiences, and as I finished, I saw them both nodding in understanding.

'So, she's submissive *and* experimental,' Oliver observed with a smile. 'Now I see why you're so interested – that will suit you down to the ground, my friend.'

The smug-arsed grin returned to my lips as I nodded. 'That's what I thought when I found out,' I chuckled, but then shrugged as my face sobered again. 'It's more than that though, honestly. I feel such a good connection with her. We've been speaking on the phone every night and the time just flies by.'

'You're well and truly hooked.' Oliver tipped the last of his whisky back and then held the empty glass out to me. 'Well, this calls for a toast, but I appear to be dry.'

I rolled my eyes, but took down the bottle and topped him up regardless, before pouring myself a generous shot too. 'What are we toasting then?'

Oliver paused as he considered it, and then he grinned. 'To the three of us being under the fucking thumb!'

It was very early days for me and Natalia, but even though the idea of being with a girl in a serious relationship would have scared the crap out of me when I was younger, I had to say, it sounded pretty bloody good to me right now.

Chapter Thirteen

Natalia

As I approached the building I paused and gazed up at its glass and pale grey marble frontage. Checking the address on my phone again I shrugged; it seemed I was in the right place, but the exterior was so neutral it could have easily been offices or even a hotel. Moving to the entrance I saw the security door and intercom system and it seemed that it was indeed apartments.

I used the keypad to enter the code that David had given me and then as I pushed the glass door open, I entered and saw that the inside was just as swanky as the outside: soft lighting, pale grey carpets and a series of oak doors lining the corridor.

Taking in my surroundings, I made my way down the corridor until I saw the lift doors. I wasn't a massive fan of lifts, and if stairs were available as an alternative I would always opt for the extra exercise. Skipping the shiny silver doors, I went in search of the stairs and then began to climb two floors before emerging into a corridor almost identical to the one downstairs.

Apartment 3C. There seemed to be six doors on the corridor and a quick glance left showed flats D, E and F so I turned right and made my way to the final door. I felt nervous, but excited. I was at David's place, and I couldn't wait to see what the evening had in store for us. I ran my fingers through my hair and then straightened my shoulders before tapping my knuckles to the door.

Almost instantly I heard movement behind the door, as if he had been waiting for me, and I smiled, wondering if David had been as keenly anticipating our meetup as I had. I heard the lock turn, but then, instead of the door swinging wide as I had expected, it only opened a fraction.

Frowning, I looked through the gap and saw a sliver of David's face, grinning broadly. 'Evening, gorgeous.'

Despite the weirdness of his not opening the door properly, I couldn't stop a smile spreading on my lips. 'Hi.'

David's gaze roved down my body and then back up to my face. 'Take off your jacket and drop it on the floor.' As soon as he'd spoken the door closed again and I was left standing in the hallway in confusion. What the heck?

As I frowned at the closed door, I heard a crackle, and then David's voice floated through the air from the small intercom next to his door. 'I'm watching. Don't keep me waiting, Natalia.' His voice was soft, and I could tell from his tone that he was smiling, but the hint at a domineering instruction was enough to send a flutter of excitement through my body and an instant flush to my cheeks. Without hesitating further, I shrugged off my leather jacket and let it fall to the floor as instructed.

There was a small noise as the door shifted slightly in its frame, and I imagined David now leaning on the other side with his face close to the intercom screen as he watched me. The idea that I may be the cause of his excitement was a potent turn-on for me. The crackle of static started again as he pressed the speak button, and then his voice caressed me again. 'Next, kick off your shoes.'

A small smile fluttered to my lips and I stared straight into the intercom screen as I complied and kicked off my shoes one by one.

'Very good, Natalia. Now, I wonder, jeans next, or your top?' My eyebrows jumped in surprise and I gave a quick, nervous glance down the empty corridor. Exactly how far was he planning to go with this?

The sound of him chuckling through the speaker at my reaction warmed my skin and somehow seemed to fill me with bravery. Before I could overthink it, I took hold of the hem of my shirt and peeled it up over my head so I was left standing in my bra and jeans.

'Fuck, Natalia!' David's voice was now gruff and thick with arousal and I couldn't help but giggle.

'Touch your breasts.' His voice sounded strained, and as I raised my hands and cupped my lace-clad breasts, I imagined that he was probably standing behind the door with a raging hard-on now. Just as I felt like I had the upper hand in this little scene, David spoke again, bursting my bubble and filling me with nervous self-consciousness.

'Just think, babe, my neighbours could be watching you right now through their intercoms. If they are, I bet they're enjoying the show. Aroused because of you. Touching themselves. They want to touch you too, but they don't dare open their doors and scare you away.' My pulse was thundering in my veins now and my eyes darted towards the two doors behind me. The residents wouldn't be at their doors, there was no reason for them to be. Was there? What if they *were* there . . . what if they really were watching me?

'Jeans off. Now.' His words broke my frantic thoughts with a jolt, and I licked my lips, wondering if I could really do this. Stripping in his hallway was all fun and games until someone actually opened their door on the way to the shops, or a trip to the cinema, and then it would just be me stark naked and freaking out in front of a complete stranger.

A further crackle of the intercom, and then David's voice came across again, this time deeper and sounding more serious. 'Natalia, I'm waiting.'

His sterner words had my submissive nature bursting to get back to the surface, but it had been so long since I'd taken that role that I was hesitant. Back when I'd lived with Vasili and Zoya in Russia it had been second nature for me to hand over all control to them. I'd responded to their commands without hesitation, putting aside my fears and allowing them complete responsibility over what we did. Over what *I* did.

My first submissive experiences with Vasili and Zoya had been brilliant. I'd been lucky, they were very respectful Doms and had taught me well. Thanks to them I knew that despite outward impressions, submissives actually had all the power. If I said stop, then the play would stop immediately. They took control of me, but only because I allowed them to.

Submission was probably a bit like riding a bike . . . I might feel a bit rusty now, but with a bit of practice I was sure I'd slip right back into it. I'd loved the freedom it had given me, the pleasure, the total escapism — and I just knew that I would experience that with David.

It was quite liberating really, and the more I thought about it the more I realised how much I missed it.

In one of our late-night phone conversations this week I'd confessed to David that I wanted to sub for him. I hadn't quite expected it to be like this, stripping in a corridor, but nonetheless, I'd asked for it, and he was delivering. If I was going to do this, I may as well do it well, and decided to dive back in with gusto, and reached down to pop the button on my jeans. Remembering that David was watching I raised my eyes to the camera and then took a step back to make sure that he'd been able to see me fully.

Staring straight at the camera I bit down on my bottom lip and then slowly lowered the zip. Slipping my hands into the waistband I found the material of my thong and decided to shock him by taking both off at the same time.

With a wiggle of my hips I shimmied the material down my thighs before adding in a teasing twist and rotating away from him. I continued to remove my jeans and thong, sliding my hands down to my knees and then lower so I was bending over and he'd have a full view of my naked arse.

'Jesus Christ ...' David's choked words whispered through the intercom before I heard him clear his throat in an apparent attempt at regaining his composure. 'My little teaser. Turn around again, I want to see your beautiful face.'

I immediately followed his command, fluttering my eye-lashes at the camera as I discarded my jeans onto the floor beside me. 'You know what to do next, gorgeous,' he instructed me huskily, and he was right. I did. Without lowering my gaze from the camera I dropped the last of my self-consciousness as well as the last of my clothing, shedding my bra and adding a little drama by swinging it around on my fingertip with a giggle before adding it to the pile on the floor.

It felt like I had been standing in the corridor naked for hours, but in actual fact it had probably only been a minute or so. It was long enough for nervous tingles to run up my spine, and also long enough that aroused moisture was pooling between my legs. Finally, though, I heard the click of the lock and the door opened fully to reveal David standing there with a hungry look on his face and impressive bulge pressing out in the front of his jeans. Hmm ... what a sight.

Without saying a word, he dropped to his knees and placed a kiss on my stomach. His hot lips caressed my skin and I struggled to supress a shudder of desire. He smiled up at me and then scooped up my clothes. With my belongings bundled under one arm he stood and gently took hold of one of my wrists before guiding me inside the apartment.

The door was slammed shut and my clothes were lobbed away in a flash and then the next second I was encased in his strong arms and pressed against his hot body as his lips sought out mine with a throaty groan.

'You are so fucking sexy.'

His kiss was so hot it was almost consuming me. Wow. He had obviously *really* liked my striptease. My hands roved over his broad back, fingernails clawing at the material of his shirt, wishing I could rip it from his body. As if he read my mind, David stepped back and roughly grabbed the hem of his shirt before dragging it over his head. I heard a soft ripping sound and I think a few buttons pinged off but then I was distracted by his naked torso. The lighting in here was bright and illuminated every ripple of muscle. There were a lot of ripples.

He really did have a great body: broad shoulders, flat stomach, and bumps and dips of his six pack which I wanted to touch and kiss. With the scattering of hair on his chest, his muscled body, and his rough and ready stubbly looks he almost reminded me of a sexy-as-fuck werewolf in the fantasy books I liked to read.

My daydreaming was broken as David tossed the shirt aside and it fluttered to join the haphazard pile of my clothes, and then he pounced forward, his strong hands finding my hips and pressing me back against the wall, pinning me just where he wanted me.

His mouth found mine, nipping at my lower lip, exploring the shape of my lips and then twining his tongue with mine. He was by far the best kisser I'd ever experienced, and I felt dizzy from the pleasure swirling around my body as his mouth continued to consume me.

Just when I felt completely lost to his pleasure, David broke the spell and stepped back, breaking the contact between our bodies. He left me feeling giddy and I had to clutch at the wall to try and keep my wobbling legs upright.

David's chest rose and fell several times, as if he were composing himself, and then I watched as his eyes dragged down my naked body and his nostrils flared. I felt completely exposed to him, but at the same time completely relaxed. It was quite a weird sensation, because apart from with Vasili and Zoya I'd never felt comfortable being naked in front of anyone. I guess that even though we were new to each other, David put me at ease somehow.

'On the floor, beautiful,' he murmured. My gaze jumped to his, and I saw his eyes full of dark intent and naughty promise.

Ohh, this could be fun. Using my experiences from Russia I fell to my knees and looked up at him.

'Fuck, you are glorious.' He shook his head. 'That is a very tempting position, but right now I want you on your back.'

I nodded and followed his command, lowering myself to the soft carpet and making myself comfortable.

'Arms out, touch the walls if you can.' I did as he said, and found that the hallway was wide enough for my arms to almost be at their full extent. David leant over me, bending down and trailing his fingertips up the delicate skin under my arms. I nearly squirmed from the ticklish sensations, but thinking that he might be looking for me to stay still I subdued my urges and instead just stared up at him with a soft smile.

'Very good. Keep those hands there.' David growled his praise, and I felt it resonate right through me. My submissive side had burst right back to life, and practically purred its happiness; I adored the fact that I was pleasing him.

Standing up, he positioned himself by my feet and then crossed his arms over his chest. 'Now, legs spread too. Touch the walls if you can.'

I'd done ballet as a kid, so had always been quite flexible. This wasn't too much of a challenge for me. I did however draw on my experience with Visali and Zoya and slow down my actions, moving first one leg and then the other, making it more like a show for him. I remembered how much they had liked that kind of thing, and I hoped that David might enjoy it too.

I was now spreadeagled on the floor, and as I hoped, David seemed to really like my attempt at seductive presentation. As well as the wolfish smile that had spread on his lips, I saw his cheeks flush a very satisfying shade of red as he watched my performance and then finally settled his gaze between my legs.

He looked at me long and hard and then with a soft curse David tipped his head back so he was staring at the ceiling. From the rapid raising and lowering of his chest it seemed that he was trying to get control of himself. I heard his breathing intensify until it whistled through his teeth and then he lowered his head until our eyes met again. The hunger in his stare was unlike anything I'd ever seen before, and it was such a turn-on that I felt a rush of moisture pool between my legs.

From the determined set of his jaw, it seemed that David was now well and truly back in control of himself. Cocking his head to the side he continued to watch me as he lowered his hands and popped the buttons of his jeans until his fly was straining open and I could see the navy cotton of his boxers below.

Dropping to his knees David flashed me a wink before lunging down between my legs and wasting no time running a hungry lick along my inner thigh. My control may have been good earlier, but there was no controlling my reaction to his hot tongue, and my back arched up off the floor and a pleasured cry flew from my lips.

The sharp, delicious rasp of his stubble followed his tongue, brushing the tender skin of my inner thigh, and then, before I could get a grip of my skittering heart rate, the rubbing moved across to my clit and I found myself disobeying his order and moving my hands down to desperately grab at his hair.

One of the many things I loved about David was his stubbly jaw and his rough and ready look, but I had had no idea just how good it would feel between my legs. It was tickling and arousing me in all the right places, almost painful, but boy did it feel good.

A chuckle from between my legs sent his warm breath fanning across my sensitive skin, and then the stubbly teasing was replaced with a hot mouth as he tongued urgently at my opening and then moved higher to suck my clit into his mouth. Holy mother of god! He was getting straight to the point, wasn't he? It didn't seem to matter that he had essentially skipped all foreplay, because my body was clearly more than ready for him to target my most sensitive of areas, and my fingers dug deeper through his hair until I was clawing at his scalp like a wild animal.

'Ебать!' My desire crazed brain flew back to my native Russian and I quickly pursed my lips to stop more curse words escaping. There was no way I could have prevented that one though, because David had used so much pressure with his tongue on my clit that he had nearly sent me spiralling straight into an orgasm.

Lifting his head David gazed up and me and raised his eyebrows. 'You appear to be going against my request, Natalia.'

I was so entwined in his spell that I didn't move my hands immediately, and instead just stared down at him like a zombie as I tried to process his words. One of his hands pressed into my inner thigh to part my legs wider, and the other trailed up my stomach, across my chest, and then cupped my left breast before rolling the nipple between his fingers and tugging. *Hard*. It was hard enough to make my core clench with desire and caused yet another curse to leave my mouth. 'Ебать!'

He then removed all contact with me, so I was left gasping and panting on the floor. 'Hands back on the wall.' His voice was stern, but there was still a softness to it and after sucking in air for clarity I managed to get my fuddled brain to comply and pressed my hands back to the cool plaster of the walls.

Instead of dropping his head back down and carrying on David gave me a curious glance. 'What does that word you said mean? It was Russian, I presume?'

I couldn't help the chuckle that slipped from my lips as I nodded. 'Yeah. I guess the closest translation is "Fuck".'

Content with my reply David gave a nod and then dropped his lips back to my hot core. My earlier thoughts of no foreplay dissolved, as he spent what felt like hours teasing me by licking, sucking and nibbling at me until I was almost sobbing from the desperation to come. I fought the urge to grab him again by shoving my hands against the walls so hard that I was surprised that the plaster didn't crack from the pressure.

The burning heat of David's body suddenly disappeared as he stood up and rapidly shed his trousers and boxers. He was now completely naked, completely aroused and staring straight down at me as he rolled on a condom.

What a sight. He really was glorious.

As soon as the protection was on, he dropped back down over me and began to crawl up my body, his lips and teeth leaving a hot trail across my skin. He finished his teasing trail, finally lifting his face to mine and our eyes had only just met when I felt the solid, silky tip of his erection pressing against my opening.

'You OK, sweetheart?'

He seemed to be asking for my permission, which was sweet, but frustrating as heck, because I was beyond desperate for him to be inside me. 'Yes! Please, David, fuck me.'

He blinked once at my crude request, and a second later he

surged upwards, his palms falling on either side of my head as he caged me in and plunged into me in one long, hard stroke that sent me halfway to heaven.

A noise somewhere between a scream and a gasp left my throat as I desperately struggled to adjust to the feel of all of him inside of me so swiftly. He wasn't small, that was for sure! I might not exactly be a virgin, but I wasn't far off, and I had to wiggle my hips a few times before I felt my body relax and give the extra room I needed to allow him fully inside me.

David sensed my struggle and paused for me while our bodies adjusted to each other. He was big, and I was tight, but by god did he feel incredible. I could see a sheen of sweat on his brow as he struggled not to move, so when I was comfortable, I gave a small nod of permission and with a heated curse he started to move again.

His moves were slow at first, letting me settle to the new feelings and rubbing me in all the right places, but it wasn't until my hips started to bump and grind up against his in a desperate plea for him to move me closer to climax that he started to move more purposefully. Over the next few minutes, he built the rhythm until he was burying himself inside me in deep, fast, and hard thrusts of his glorious cock that had me rapidly spiralling towards a climax.

Everything about our short relationship had been intense; from our lingering looks to the hot, searching kisses, but this was full on and frantic, even by our standards. His hips were pumping in and out at a frantic rhythm and my hips were just as desperate, our moves making it plain that while long drawn-out encounters could be fun, we were both more than ready to find the climaxes at the end of this sweet ride.

'You can let go of the wall.' His words were a mere grunt, but my hands immediately fell from the wall and gripped at his shoulders so I could better time my hips with his thrusts. Holding on for the ride was about the only thing I could do, because he was like a man possessed; but then, just when I thought I could take no more, I felt my body flare with a rush of heat and fly into a huge climax, my muscles gripping him as I threw my head back with a cry and dug my nails into his back to ride out my orgasm.

David let out a deep growl above me, his cock thickening as he continued to drive deep inside of me, and then he yelled, his hips bucking as I felt him come inside me in a series of hot, throbbing spurts.

His body sagged above me, but David caught his weight on his arms so I was caged beneath him, but protected from being squashed as we continued to pant and recover ourselves.

After a minute or so, David pushed himself up and looked down at me with flushed cheeks and a shit-eating grin on his face. Without saying a word, he got onto his knees, scooped me into his arms and stood up. After dropping a kiss on my forehead, he carried me through the apartment past several closed doors until he nudged one open and entered. We moved into a darkened space, but he was obviously very familiar with the layout because he negotiated it with ease before bending and placing me on a surface that was so soft it almost enveloped me into its snuggly depths.

A second later the room was illuminated with a soft glow as David turned on a lamp and I saw that we were in his bedroom. 'Make yourself comfy, I'll just grab our clothes.'

David disappeared and I took the opportunity to look

around the room. Pale grey bedcovers and a super thick duvet were my current nest, and the rest of the room was done out in a similar colour scheme and matched with a lovely set of wooden furniture which looked like it might be handmade. It was fairly sparse of personal items, but there looked to be a few photographs on a far dresser, and a painting of the London sky-line on the far wall which was so large it almost took up the entire space.

David came back in with a bundle of our clothes under one arm and two bottles of water in the other hand. I noticed that the condom was gone, and then blushed when I realised he was still semi hard. Oddly enough, even though we were both still stark-ers, I didn't feel remotely self-conscious in front of him. Somehow this man put me completely at ease. 'So, this is your place, huh?'

David put our clothes on a chair and then walked to the bed where he handed me one of the bottles and placed the other on the bedside table. Instead of answering my question he leant onto the mattress and placed a lingering kiss on my lips. Hmmm. His mouth was gentle this time, and instantly re-ignited the lust I felt for him. Our connection really was electric because he had barely touched me and I felt like my core was on fire. Just as I was considering dragging him down onto me, he separated our mouths and climbed into the bed beside me.

Chuckling at my lust-struck expression he arranged my body so I was under the covers with him and then nodded. 'Technically yes, I own the apartment, but a couple of my friends rent it from me.'

Someone else lived here? My eyes widened. We'd just had sex on the hall floor! 'This is someone else's flat? My god! They could have walked in on us!'

'Here, drink.' David cracked the seal on my water bottle and held it up for me with a wicked grin. 'And yes, they could have walked in. Would that have bothered you?' I managed a small sip of water and then placed the bottle on the bedside table. Would it have bothered me? I pondered the question, and found that, actually, the idea of being caught was sending a thrill of excitement through me.

'I see that blush on your cheeks, Natalia. It excites you, doesn't it? The idea of someone watching us?' I'm not sure why, but it almost felt wrong to admit it. Biting down on my lower lip, I gave a small nod, and in response saw that David's smile broadened. 'After your little striptease in the hall I could see how much you liked the challenge. I saw you glancing around the corridor too, but you didn't look nervous, you looked excited. I think perhaps you and I are perfectly matched with our liking for a bit of risk, hmm?' he added in a lower, more alluring tone that sent delicious tingles running across my skin.

My inner submissive demanded that I answer his question truthfully, so with a nod I smiled. 'Yes.' He kissed me, it was brief, and chaste, but almost felt like we were sealing a deal of some kind. 'So . . . is this their bed?' I asked, unsure whether I should be aroused at the naughtiness, or horrified by the idea that we might be in someone else's bed.

David laughed. 'I'm not that bad. Don't worry, this is my bedroom.'

I was confused. He owned this place, someone else lived here, but he had a bedroom too? 'So, what is it, you flat share this place? Is that right?'

'Not really. I have a bigger place of my own a bit further

away, a house to myself. But I have an agreement with Daniel and Elle that I can keep this room for when I'm working late as it's so close to the Club. That's why I bought it in the first place. They pay slightly lower rent on the understanding that I can come and go as I please.'

I was struggling to afford to even get on the property ladder in London with a small flat, and yet David owned not one but two properties! The sex club business was obviously a profit-able one.

'So how come we're here tonight? Did you not want me to see your house?' Suddenly a sickening thought settled in my stomach and I scrabbled to sit myself up. 'You're not married, are you? Is this your fuck pad?'

I watched his reaction carefully to look for any trace of deception, but David simply threw his head back and laughed. 'No. You have my word I am not married, Natalia. Never have been. Ask any of the regular patrons of the bar, they'll tell you that I'm the long-term bachelor of the place.' He smiled lazily across at me and then frowned. 'I won't lie to you, Natalia, I've not got a perfect past. I like sex, and I've had a lot of it, but I've never been interested in dating.' He cocked his head and gave me a soft smile. 'I may be changing my view on that recently though.' His words made my heart flutter crazily and my mind whirled as it got more than a little carried away with the idea of a relationship with him.

David cleared his throat and then leant in close to my ear. 'The reason we came here tonight . . . I wanted to use the com-munal hallway. I've always fantasised about making a woman strip for me in public . . .'

Oh. I'd just lived out one of his fantasies. God, I hope he'd enjoyed it. 'Did it live up to the expectation?' I asked quietly, worried that it might not have been everything he'd imagined.

David's hand slid under the duvet and gripped my thigh, teasing and massaging me until I let out a quiet moan.

'Fuck, yeah. You looked incredible stripping for me. You are so sexy.'

His words bolstered my confidence and I raised a cheeky eyebrow. 'And did your fantasy involve fucking me hard on the hall floor afterwards?'

'Ha! No.' A roar of laughter ripped through his body. 'I was just so turned on that I couldn't hold back.' David fell back on his pillows as he continued to chuckle and then, suddenly, he looked worried as he leant up and stared down at me. 'Shit, I'm such a selfish prick ... are you OK? Was I too rough?'

I was more than OK. It had been amazing, and so I smiled to try and reassure him. 'I'm great, it was incredible, David.'

He still didn't look certain, and then he slid a hand below the sheets and gently cupped me between my legs. He didn't stroke me, his hand simply held me, as if protecting me. 'From what you told me, that was kind of your first time, Natalia, and I lost control and took you hard.' His brows pinched together and I could see he was beating himself up. 'Are you sore?'

I laughed and shook my head. 'Only a little, and I'll let you in on a secret ...' I leant closer to him and nipped on his earlobe before whispering to him. 'I like a little pain.'

Leaning back to look him in the eye, I grinned. 'It was amazing, stop worrying. I loved every second.' As if reinforcing my words, I gave a small thrust of my hips to push my groin into his hand and then moaned with pleasure as I felt the press of his fingers.

He growled gruffly and then gently began to circle his finger in my slickness. 'Fuck.'

Fuck indeed. What a night. I grinned against his warm skin as I snuggled closer and let utter contentment and arousal wash over me.

Chapter Fourteen

David

I smiled to myself as I pulled on my jeans. This evening had certainly been a memorable one. Seeing as it had been our first night together, I'd been unsure whether Natalia would be up for stripping in the hall, but as soon as I'd issued my first command and seen her shocked expression morph into one of aroused intrigue I'd known she'd enjoy it. She had been perfect. Teasing, brave and so fucking sexy it made my cock ache to be inside her again. My groin gave a lurch in my jeans just thinking about it, and I grinned – I think it was fair to say we had both *more* than enjoyed it and were both keen for more. There was no rush though; this was for the long term. Besides, I had Natalia here all night, so perhaps after some dinner I could satisfy my body's craving for her again.

Grabbing a T-shirt, I pulled it on and pondered what I could rustle up for us to eat. Perhaps just a simple pasta dish. I knew I had some cooked chicken and veggies in the fridge and there was always pasta in the cupboard.

Just as I was thinking through my recipe, I heard a shriek from the corridor outside and frowned. Natalia had nipped out to use the toilet five minutes ago, but what on earth could have made her jump? Hurrying to the bedroom door I pulled it open and then immediately laughed. Natalia was hovering in the bathroom door wide eyed, and standing in front of her, half blocking the corridor, were Daniel and Elle, my tenants.

My *stark naked* tenants.

Daniel held up a hand to apologise, but made no effort whatsoever to cover his nudity which made me chuckle even harder. 'Sorry. We were going to grab a shower. We didn't realise anyone was home.'

The whole situation seemed hilarious to me and Dan and Elle were completely relaxed and acting like nothing unusual was happening at all; but I could see from Natalia's eyes that she didn't know where to look and was obviously thrown by their sudden appearance, not to mention their state of undress. To make matters even more comical, Elle then leant around Daniel and held out a hand to her.

'Hi! You must be with David. I'm Elle, and this is Dan.'

To give her some credit, Natalia blinked rapidly but then quickly recovered her poise. Even though she flashed me look that seemed to scream *'What the heck is going on?'*, she still politely took Elle's hand and shook it. 'Um, yeah. Hi. I'm Natalia.'

'Natalia. That's a pretty name. You have a little bit of an accent too. Where are you from? Croatia?'

These guys were pretty much naturists. If they were in the house, chances are they'd be naked, so conversations like this were a bit of a norm for me, but apparently it was a fairly new experience for Natalia, because her cheeks were now flushed with colour.

'Er no, Russia.' She swallowed loudly and then took a side-step which had her almost brushing across Elle's breasts as she did so.

'Yum. You smell lovely too,' Elle commented, taking a big inhale as Natalia squeezed past her and then, flashing me a wicked grin, Elle added, 'Chanel Allure and fresh sex, what a combination.'

I laughed and rolled my eyes. She was such a flirt.

I hadn't thought it was possible for Natalia's eyes to open any wider, or her cheeks to flush more, but she was now bright red and had eyes like dinner plates. 'I … uh … I'll … um … I'll let you get in the bathroom.'

'Nice to meet you!' Elle cooed, before grabbing Daniel's hand and dragging him into the bathroom.

Natalia was watching their retreat with shocked fascination, so I leant in close to her ear and whispered. 'They shower with the door open too.'

She pulled in another shocked gasp and then shoved at my chest to get me moving. I couldn't help but laugh. Perhaps I should have warned her about my nudist housemates, but where would the fun have been in that?

'Are you OK, sweetheart?' Sweetheart? That was at least the second time that the endearing name had slipped from my lips and I frowned. A pet name? Was it a little early in our relation-ship for that kind of thing? Would it freak her out? Before I could dwell on it too much, I saw Natalia give a small smile in response to the title and my shoulders relaxed. 'So, that's Daniel and Elle,' I continued mildly, taking her hand and directing her to the kitchen.

'And little Daniel. Don't forget about him,' Natalia retorted with a roll of her eyes. I chuckled, glad she was seeing the funny side to it. I knew she wasn't a prude; she worked in my sex club for god's sake, she'd seen all sorts going on in there, but it was always slightly shocking to see nudity when it was out of context like this. 'They're very relaxed with their bodies. And their sexuality.'

'I'd never have guessed,' she replied drily with a smile, before walking to me and slipping her arms around my waist. Now she was closer I could smell her scent too, and Elle had been spot on — soft perfume and hot sex. A perfect combination in my opinion.

'You say they are relaxed with their sexuality too?' she asked curiously.

'Yes,' I nodded, 'they used to be performers at the Club, so they're both very relaxed and open sexually.'

'But they're a couple, right? In a relationship?'

'They are. They've been together years.'

'But they have other partners? Is that what you meant by open sexually?'

Shrugging, I pulled her closer and then leant backwards onto the kitchen counter to get more comfortable. 'Yeah, but they are always there together. They like to play with others, and experiment, but generally they're always both involved.'

I could see her thinking and wondered if she was going to put one and one together and ask me some probing questions.

'Do you join in with them?' I was still learning her expressions, so it was hard for me to judge her reaction, but I was fairly sure it was curiosity on her face, and not jealousy or envy. Either way, I would never lie to her, so hopefully the truth wouldn't put her off.

'Not recently, no,' I murmured, watching her face intently. 'Not for a while.' It wasn't because I hadn't wanted to, I'd just been so bloody busy that sex had taken a back seat.

She gave a small nod and then cocked her head, her eyes twinkling with curiosity, and what looked decidedly like interest. 'But you used to?'

I paused, unsure how to answer. Was she upset at the idea of me playing with the guys? I couldn't decide if she was jealous or the complete opposite ... She looked curious. Was it possible she liked the idea of me being with them sexually? Or was she perhaps contemplating all of us experimenting together? Hmm. Perhaps my girl had a wilder side hidden beneath her quieter front.

Hedging my bets, I went for the truth, but kept it as casual as I could. 'Um ... yeah, on occasion.' She considered my answer and then to my relief gave a small smile. 'Does that bother you?'

'No. Not at all.' Her head shake came immediately, and I could see from the curiosity in her eyes that she was genuine in her answer, which further relaxed me, not to mention turned me on.

Sliding a hand around her waist I pulled her against me so we were pressed together from the hips downwards and decided to lay another truth on her. 'Would it shock you if I said I really liked the idea of fucking you in front of them?'

Natalia's hands gripped at the front of my shirt as she gasped softly and then I watched with pleasure as her cheeks flooded with a flush that seemed to me to be one of arousal. It was perhaps too much for her today, she had only just met them, and we'd only just begun our sexual journey together, but my girl was definitely interested, and that was enough for me.

Clearing her throat, Natalia smiled up at me. 'I already told you I like experimentation too. That sounds like fun,' she added with a wiggle of her eyebrows.

My trousers suddenly felt far too tight for me and a chuckle rose in my throat at how Natalia just kept surprising me – could this girl be any more perfect for me?

Chapter Fifteen

Sasha

Making myself comfortable on my stool I narrowed my eyes and watched Natalia more carefully as she worked behind the bar with David and another younger bartender called Ian. Natalia had always been shy, but since she'd started to integrate into our friendship group she'd been opening up to Robyn and me and we all now regularly messaged for catch-up chats.

Marcus and I had been having dinner last night when he'd dropped a bombshell and let slip that David had said that he'd started to date Natalia. It had been a complete shock for me, and obviously as the self-appointed gossip of the group I'd decided I needed to follow up on it as soon as possible.

'Natalia and David?' Robyn whispered. 'Are you sure?' So far Natalia hadn't confided any gossip to me or Robyn, so we'd decided to come down to Twist for a drink to have a look for ourselves.

'I don't know, she's not told me anything herself.' I shrugged as I watched Natalia and then turned to Robyn. 'But Marcus said that David was looking like the cat that got the cream the other week, and when he and Oliver pressed him on why he was so happy, he'd confessed that things were developing between Natalia and him.'

'He's a bit older than her. Mind you, that hasn't stopped Oliver and me, I suppose,' Robyn pondered, sipping her drink. 'I do remember she once said she was attracted to the whole biker image, so I guess David fits that.'

I glanced at the man in question and nodded. He did indeed. Stubbly beard, chunky leather boots, jeans, shirts and a leather waistcoat that on some guys would look ridiculous, but on David looked good. He didn't ride it very often because he lived close enough to walk to work, but I also knew that he owned a bike – a Ducatti – which, if Marcus's drooling had been anything to go by when we'd seen it, was obviously a rather nice bike.

'And when we had drinks with her the other week, she told us there was someone she liked,' I added conspiratorially. 'Maybe it was David all along!'

'That's true!' Robyn murmured, watching the bar through narrowed eyes.

I chuckled to myself as I thought about what we must look like – both sitting here across the bar but staring at David and Natalia like a pair of unsubtle private detectives on a stakeout. All we needed were sunglasses, a couple of beige raincoats and some binoculars and we'd be all set to feature in a low-budget spy film.

The customer at the bar walked away with her drinks and I watched as Natalia grabbed a cloth and quickly started to wipe up a small spill. David walked behind her towards the till, and to most observers there would have been no interaction to be seen. To me, however, and apparently Robyn, judging from the small squeak she'd just made beside me, there had been plenty, and as David made his return journey past Natalia, I watched it again more closely: just like before, as he walked behind her, he stalled just slightly, then smirked, and continued on his way. Natalia's response to him pausing behind her was to jump, and then flush as a smile burst onto her lips. Her head turned to follow him as he walked away, and then he looked over his shoulder and flashed her a wink.

Tiny interactions, but if you were really looking for them, they seemed blindingly clear, not to mention intimate and very telling.

'I'd place money on the fact that he just squeezed her arse. What do you reckon?' I concluded with a smug smirk as I sipped my wine.

Robyn was nodding beside me with a grin on her face. 'Yep. One hundred per cent.'

As we continued to watch, Ian disappeared out to the back store cupboard, leaving David and Natalia alone. Almost imme-diately, David cast a quick glance around the bar and then darted towards Natalia. As soon as he was beside her, she leant in close to him and seemed to whisper something that made David grin wickedly and then briefly nuzzle into her temple.

'Did he just kiss her on the head?' Robyn hissed.

'Looked that way, didn't it?'

I couldn't see properly from here, but it seemed that he now had a hand laid on her waist, and Natalia's hand flitted up the buttons on David's shirt and rested momentarily on his chest as they shared a heated stare. I raised an eyebrow at the obvious heat and connection between them and then laughed out loud as Ian came back to the bar and interrupted their moment, causing them to jump apart like startled cats.

'It looks pretty conclusive to me,' I declared, turning to Robyn. 'You can practically feel the heat between them from here.'

Robyn nodded with a grin. 'I know! Looks like great chemistry between them. If they aren't together, they will be soon!'

'They're together,' I declared, certain of it from the evidence I'd seen. 'Or at least sleeping together.' You didn't get chemistry like that with a friend, that was for sure. Looking to Robyn with a huff I feigned irritation. 'I can't believe she hasn't told us! The cheek of it!'

'She is a very private person, I guess. And quite new to us as friends, so maybe she wasn't sure how to tell us.' Robyn laughed and then levelled me with an amused stare. 'Or maybe she hasn't told us because she didn't want you giving her a grilling on all the juicy details!'

I held up my hands as if wounded and then laughed. 'Me? Pushing for gossip? Never . . .' I knew that my fake lie wouldn't stick for a minute with Robyn.

'Natalia probably remembers the other week when we had drinks and you were asking me all about my honeymoon . . . and I mean ALL about it. The poor girl was probably trying to avoid the embarrassment of one of your inquisitions!'

Laughing, I raised my hands and pretended to frame my face as if proud. 'I am pretty out good at them, aren't I?' I wasn't going to deny it, I was an out and out gossip hound. If I wanted to know some exciting details then why not just ask? Life was too short not to, and so much more fun when there was sex to talk about!

Just then the subject of our conversation began to walk in

our direction and I wiggled my eyebrows and grinned at Robyn. 'Let's confirm our suspicions, shall we?'

Oblivious to the fact that she had been the focus of our conversation, Natalia reached our side. 'Hey, girls! I didn't know you were coming in today.' She was smiling fondly at us as she approached, and I chuckled to myself as I wondered just how quickly I'd be able to morph her expression into one of embarrassment.

'We just thought we'd pop in and see you ... and David,' Robyn commented mildly. Her mention of David caused Natalia to pause and then fidget slightly on the spot and I felt somewhat giddy at the prospect of the gossip we were about to expose.

'How is he today?' I asked casually.

Natalia looked at me with wide eyes, and then flashed a quick glance towards the bar where David was busy serving a customer. 'Ummm, he's good, I guess.'

She seemed confused by our opening lines so I gave up trying to be subtle and instead raised my eyebrows several times. 'You guys are hot with a capital H!'

If possible, Natalia's eyes widened further at my words and then I watched as a blush spread across her cheeks and down her neck. 'Um ... what ... what do you mean?'

I spluttered out a disbelieving chuckle and shook my head. 'Don't try and play it coy with us, kiddo. We've just witnessed some seriously steamy chemistry between you and Mr Boss Man.'

Natalia's nervous swallow was so loud that both Robyn and I heard it and laughed. Bless her, she looked like a deer in some headlights, but her cheeks were reddening and a smile was beginning to stretch at her mouth, so I knew she was loosening up.

I patted the seat beside me in invitation and then urged her on with an impatient shake of my hand. 'Don't leave us hanging! Spill the beans!'

She flopped into the seat and then shook her head. 'We're being professional at work. How the hell did you guys guess?'

I spluttered on my glass of wine and then smirked. 'Professional huh? We saw him grab your arse a minute or so ago!'

Natalia buried her face in her hands and then started to giggle. 'You saw that? Oh my god!'

'No one else would have noticed, it's only because we were watching for it,' Robyn confessed, obviously trying to put Natalia at ease. 'Marcus let slip to Sasha that David had told the boys that you and him were getting together. We were just excited for you, so we came down to see for ourselves.'

'I didn't tell you guys yet because it's really new. I wanted to wait and see if he was actually going to stick around.' Shrugging, Natalia finally gave in and nodded. 'But he has! And so yeah, we have started seeing each other. It's only been a little while though.'

Yes! A confession! I had so many questions lined up that I barely knew where to start. 'Who approached who? And have you slept together yet? And if you have, is it as smoking hot as it looks like it would be?' I was about to fire off a load more questions when Robyn laughed beside me and placed a hand on my arm to stop me.

'Give Natalia a chance to breathe!' Turning to her, Robyn smiled softly. 'Don't listen to her, you don't have to tell us anything if you don't want to.'

'She bloody well does! I want deets!' I declared with a laugh that made Natalia giggle too and then reach forwards to pinch a swig of my wine before starting her confession.

'I've liked him for ages, but he was my boss so I wasn't going to do anything about it.' Brushing a hand through her hair she cast a quick glance at David and caught his eye. I could see him evaluating our group, and probably the intrigued expressions on mine and Robyn's faces, and then a knowing grin spread on his face as he clocked what we were talking about – him.

'Something changed between us the other week, I'm not sure what it was, but suddenly the chemistry between us was just crazy. I had a suspicion he liked me to, and so one night on a whim I just told him.'

'Wow! That's so brave!' Robyn said gleefully.

Natalia shrugged, but looked pretty darn proud of herself. 'Yeah, you guys know how shy I can be, so I was really nervous! I still can't believe I did it, but I just came out and told him.' She laughed and then shrugged. 'But it worked out pretty well because he said he liked me too, and then things have just gone from there.'

'And . . .' I prompted, rolling one of my hands in front of me, hoping to prompt her into giving out some more details.

She laughed, but I could see from her relaxed shoulders and smile that she was quite enjoying sharing her exciting news with us. '*And* . . . So far, it's amazing. We have such a strong connection, and when we talk time just flies by.' She bit her lip and then, after seeing my expectant face, Natalia rolled her eyes and leant in closer. '*And* . . . we had sex for the first time this weekend and it blew my mind!'

'There it is!' I declared triumphantly. 'I knew it! Tell us more!'

Natalia cast an amused glance at the bar, which was starting to get a little busier. 'I'm supposed to be working!'

'Well, you better talk quickly then, hadn't you?' I teased, not wanting to be beaten on this.

Shaking her head in apparent defeat she leant in closer. 'You both know I'm submissive,' she stated. 'Well, David quite likes to take control, which makes us a perfect match. We've only spent one night together so far, but he . . .' She paused and then her blush deepened to a blood red. 'When I arrived at his flat, he wouldn't let me in. Instead, he made me strip in the communal landing area for him. Every piece of clothing! It was hot! Then he dragged me inside and shagged me on the hall floor!'

Woah! Well, that wasn't a boring first time, was it? It certainly beat a tale of a dull ol' missionary position. 'Holy fuck balls!'

The queue at the bar was bigger now, and Natalia stood up. 'That's all I have time to tell you!'

'Woah! No, you don't, I need more details!'

I made a quick grab for her wrist, but Natalia danced back, just out of my reach and laughed. 'Sorry, girls, gotta go!' Throwing us a teasing glance over her shoulder she made her way back to the bar, laughing loudly.

As we watched her go Robyn smiled fondly. 'Look how relaxed and happy she is. She looks like a whole new woman.'

I couldn't disagree. Natalia looked utterly content. I just couldn't believe she'd left us hanging like that. Pulling out my phone, I scanned my diary, we needed to schedule in a cocktail night with her pronto so I could dig for more dirt!

Chapter Sixteen

Natalia

When David called me earlier and asked if I wanted to meet tonight, I had barely been able to contain my excitement. It had only been a few weeks, but things between us were going so well that I frequently felt like pinching myself to check it was real. When we were apart, I wanted to be with him, and when I was with him, I didn't want him to leave. I couldn't get enough of it all. Thankfully, even though I'd been dubious whether David was the type to do more than a one-night stand, I'd been pleasantly surprised by just how keen he seemed to keep seeing me.

When we'd agreed our date tonight David had suggested taking me to his house and cooking for us. I hadn't seen his London house yet, and he'd said it would give us plenty of privacy to have a nice relaxing weekend together, seeing as neither of us was working tomorrow.

On a last-minute whim though, David had changed his mind and brought me to the flat that he shared with Dan and Elle instead. I was a little disappointed, because I wanted to see his other house, but maybe we could go there tomorrow, and besides, I couldn't deny a tingle of excitement ignited in my belly as we entered the flat again tonight.

Biting on my lip, I felt a flush sweep across my skin. My excitement was because our conversation from our first night about having sex in front of the others had been lingering. I wondered if it was on his mind too and, if so, whether it might have affected his decision to come here instead of his house.

After we had entered and hung our coats in the hall David turned and landed a lingering kiss on my lips. My eyes fluttered shut as his tongue explored my mouth for far longer than I had expected, and a contented sigh rose in my throat.

'God, woman, you taste so good.' Lifting his head, he chuckled and then flashed a wink at me as he led me further inside.

'Make yourself comfortable in the lounge, I'll get us some drinks,' he murmured, dropping another kiss on my lips and landing a spank on my arse which made me gasp and earned me a chuckle and wiggle of the eyebrows from David.

Walking into the living room I stalled on the boundary as I saw that one sofa was already occupied – Daniel and Elle *were* here. I'd been over several times since first meeting them, but they'd never been home. That illicit tingle started in my belly again, and I felt a flush sweep my cheeks. The lights were off, so they wouldn't have seen my blush, but the room was cast with the cosy glow from two lamps. Music was playing softly in the background, and the TV was on but muted, with some black and white film playing that they didn't seem to be watching.

'Join us. Don't be shy,' Elle said with a friendly smile.

I smiled back and, summoning my courage, I entered and took a seat on the opposite sofa. 'Hey, guys.'

Elle grinned at me, and Daniel gave a nod of his head in greeting. 'Evening.'

It felt a little weird to be sitting in silence with people I barely knew, so I turned my attention to the television and tried to work out what film it was.

A few minutes must have passed and then I heard a soft moan filter through the music around us. Turning, I frowned as I glanced around and then I paused in surprise as I realised that they were now making out. They were kissing passionately; Dan was exploring Elle's body with a gentle slide of his fingers, and Elle's hand was reciprocating by massaging Dan's knee and gradually working up his thigh towards his groin.

My lungs seemed to cease functioning as I watched in aroused fascination. I wasn't sure if I should leave the room, but they clearly knew I was in here and obviously had no issue with my presence, so I found myself perversely stuck in my seat and unable to look away. His hands now rested on her hips and gripped the hem of her T-shirt before slowly beginning to peel it up her body. As the material moved over her head I saw that she was braless, and a small aroused gasp left my lips as Daniel swooped forwards and captured one of her hard nipples in his mouth.

'Ебать!' I cursed softly as I squirmed in my seat and had to squeeze my thighs together in an effort at easing the burning sensation that was now coiling in my core. I couldn't deny the fact that watching them was turning me on and causing my pulse to rise to dangerous levels.

I clenched my teeth to stop myself moaning as I watched Daniel's hand slide up under her skirt. From my position opposite them it was suddenly very clear that Elle wasn't wearing any

142

underwear at all. The moan I'd been holding in escaped as my eyes were drawn to her soft, pink pussy, and I had to clench my teeth to stop further noises escaping as Daniel sunk a finger inside of her wetness and began to slowly slide it in and out.

Oh my god. I couldn't quite believe this was happening, but I couldn't drag my eyes away either.

I had always been shy, painfully so, but I'd also known from a young age that my sexuality was very fluid. I guess some people would label me as bi-sexual, because I'd had attractions to both men and women over the years, but I'd never bothered labelling it. I liked who I liked, and my time with the couple in Russia had only strengthened my understanding of how pleasurable I could find both sexes.

I hadn't been with a woman for a very long time though, and watching Elle's soft body flex and arch as Daniel continued to work her was making me horny as hell. As he upped the one finger to two, I found my own right hand dropping between my legs and pressing against my pulsing clit through the material of my dress. Tingles of pleasure exploded from my brief touch and I was shocked at just how close I was to climaxing simply from watching two virtual strangers get it on.

Dan suddenly turned his focus from Elle and stared across at me with a grin. My hand was between my legs and he'd just caught me in the act! Dan flashed me a wink and then returned his focus to Elle just as she started to moan loudly. The flush in her cheeks was now spreading down her neck and seemed to indicate that she was close to climaxing, and then as Daniel upped the pace of his hand I watched in rapt fascination as Elle arched from the sofa, her hands clawing at the material as she threw her head back and gave in to the power of her climax.

My hand was now moving of its own accord, rhythmically moving against my core and my body was rapidly heating up. In my peripheral vision I saw movement to my left and ripped my hand away as I looked across in shock and saw David standing at the doorway. Fuck! What was I doing?! Clearly from the expression on his face I hadn't moved my hand quickly enough, and David had gotten a good eyeful of me touching myself. My cheeks erupted with heat and I tried to leap from my seat only to have David swiftly cross the room and sit beside me on the sofa, pulling me back down with him.

He placed our two bottles of beer on the side table and slid his arm around my shoulders before using his free hand to pick up my right hand and place it back between my legs again.

'Carry on. I'm sure Daniel and Elle are thrilled that you are finding their little show so arousing.' My eyes widened in mortification at his words – he hadn't even whispered them, so Daniel and Elle would definitely have heard him – and then I cast a self-conscious glance across at the other couple, only to find them both watching me with heavy lidded eyes and smiles on their faces.

'We like to be watched,' Elle confirmed with a smile, her cheeks still flushed from her recent orgasm, and her body still open for both myself and David to look at.

'And it would appear from your squirming that you like to watch,' Daniel added in a teasing, gravelly tone.

I could barely believe this was happening, and as much as I should probably be feeling a bit shamed by my arousal, the feeling never came. Instead I was just flooded with desire and a heady feeling of delicious naughtiness as I gave a shy shrug and then nodded.

Daniel whispered something to Elle, and after flashing him a huge grin she slid from the sofa and moved towards me before dropping to her knees and placing her hands on my legs.

I tensed as I realised her intentions. The idea of her touching me turned me on, but how would David feel about it? Looking him in the eye, I found my man smiling softly at me, apparently rather enjoying how this was all playing out. Clearly no issues there then.

Elle placed her fingers on my knees and started a gentle massage on my bare skin. The feel of her soft touch was a complete contrast to David's firmer one, and more arousing than I had expected. I still hadn't fully relaxed, but then a warm breath fluttered by my ear, and I realised David had shifted even closer. 'Relax. Enjoy yourself, baby.'

My eyes flashed back to Elle, and with her cute blonde pixie cut, sparkly blue eyes and kissable lips I couldn't deny that I found her attractive and so I gave a minute nod of my head to say I was OK with her touch.

As soon as she had my permission Elle's hands pushed my legs wider apart and then started to massage me again, tracing light circles on my skin and moving higher and higher until she came to the hem of my skirt. Pushing the material up around my waist she lowered her lips and kissed a trail up the sensitive skin on the inside of my thigh and then she curled her fingers into the waistband of my knickers and began to pull them down.

I couldn't believe I was doing this, but my hips rose to help her remove my underwear anyway, and then once my panties were gone, she looked down at my pussy and licked her lips. Leaning forwards she blew across my heated skin, and the feeling was so arousing that I tried to close my legs to quell the rising sensations in my system, but David and Elle were having none of it, and between them spread my legs wide again.

David decided to join in and leant down and placed a kiss on my shoulder, and then began to unbutton my shirt while still keeping hold of my thigh with his free hand and kissing my neck. He was quite the multitasker, wasn't he?

Elle began dropping kisses on my inner thigh again, working her way closer and closer to my sex and driving me wild with the need to buck my hips upwards and force myself into her face. I couldn't though, not with the way that I was being held open, and so I dropped my head back instead and let out a long moan as her lips finally made contact with my clit.

I was being flooded with attention by them both, and it felt incredible. David succeeded in opening my shirt, and upon finding me braless underneath immediately lowered his head and sucked one of my hardened nipples into his mouth. I let out a moan as he sucked again, harder and sharper, and arched my back as best I could. Elle decided to take this opportunity to lower her head and run her tongue around the hard nub of my clit again, alternating between using the flat of her tongue and the point to run teasing, delicious circles as she moaned her appreciation of my taste.

My eyes rolled back in my head and the lids fluttered shut at the persistent flicks of her tongue on my throbbing clit. This whole scene was so erotic, but god, her tongue felt incredible. Elle teased me on and on by licking a trail from my clit to my soaking entrance over and over again, before finally sucking my clit into her mouth and flicking her tongue across the little nub of pleasure until I was sure I was going to explode into the most powerful orgasm of my life.

Elle's tongue was like hot silk as it worked against me, soothing the bone deep ache to come, and combined with David's attentions to my breasts was rapidly sending me to such a high level of pleasure that I had to grip onto the arms of the sofa to try and keep myself from squirming.

One of my hands lowered and slid though Elle's pixie cut, tangling in the short hair and loving how soft it felt between my fingers. The temptation to grip harder and force her face even closer to my needy clit was almost overwhelming, but I held back, just, and let her lead the pace.

The feel of Elle's soft touches against my slick skin was such a turn-on that I knew my climax wouldn't be long now. To be honest this whole scene was so erotic I was amazed I'd lasted this long. As Elle upped the pace and strength of her sucking again, treating my clit to the exact pressure it needed I felt my climax start to break forth and I twisted my fingers into her hair and jerked Elle's face forwards onto me.

I felt her laugh at my keenness, but all thoughts were lost as my orgasm tightened in my system and then burst over the cusp, capturing me in a series of spasms so powerful that I almost couldn't catch my breath.

My head fell back on the sofa, and my eyes flickered shut as I enjoyed the sensation of Elle licking away the moisture between my legs and David scattering kisses on my shoulder and jawline. Her touch was so much gentler than that of a man, but still so sure and confident. Her tongue was greedily licking at the tops of my thighs, occasionally circling my clit again and sending a little aftershock of pleasure zapping through my system, which she would soothe by lapping at me with her talented tongue.

There was a soft smacking sound, and I forced my heavy lids to open so I could glance down to see Elle licking her lips and gazing up at me with a sweet, sexy smile on her face. Her mouth was glossy with my moisture, and the sight was such a turn on that I instinctively reached down and dragged her to her knees before leaning in and kissing her.

My tongue trailed across her lips and then dipped inside to deepen the kiss. The taste of my own musk mixed with the sweetness of Elle's mouth, and even though I had just come, I found myself just as horny as I had been before.

'Jesus, you two are so fucking hot.' David's voice was strained beside me, and as I glanced across, I saw that he now had his cock in his hand and was working it with slow, firm strokes of his hand. I hadn't felt the sofa move, but it occurred to me that Daniel was now sitting to the other side of us, also with his cock in his hand and his eyes glued to Elle and me as we continued to kiss and touch each other. This was turning into quite an orgy!

Elle's kiss was a teasing temptation that I didn't seem to be able to get enough of. Her lips hovered over mine, close enough that I could feel the heat of her breath feathering across my skin, but just out of reach when I tried to lean in and join our mouths. David often used a similar technique on me, I had termed it his 'not quite kiss', and I loved it. Moaning in frustration I tried to reach her again, flicking my tongue out, but finding empty space again. Opening my eyes in surprise I found Elle grinning at me gleefully, clearly loving her tease. Her eyes were filled with desire and a wicked glint, but then I suddenly realised just how much of my attention she was getting and hastily glanced across at David to check that he wasn't irritated.

To my complete surprise, David's eyes remained glued on Elle and me, his face flushed with desire and his hand now moving faster with sure, firm stokes. Daniel was in a similar state, his erection bobbing in his lap as he palmed it and worked himself towards a climax. The guys certainly seemed to have enjoyed watching us, and as I soaked up the eroticism of the whole scene an idea occurred to me. I shifted myself so I was on the floor next to Elle and then took hold of her hand, guiding it towards Dan's cock. At the same time, I took over from David, curling my palm around his erection and continuing with the firm up and down movements.

Once both of us were pleasuring our men I leant forwards and captured Elle's mouth in a kiss. I heard Daniel let out a hiss of pleasure, and as David's cock jerked in my hand I knew he was also watching us and enjoying the show.

This was multitasking at its finest. We kissed each other as we jerked our men off. The taste of my own musk still lingered on Elle's lips, and even though our mouths were coming together in a soft, sensual meeting of passion, both of us ensured that our focus also remained on the rhythm needed to bring the men to orgasm. I could feel David's erection swelling in my hand, his hips were now jerking off the sofa with each of my moves and I knew he was close.

Pulling back from Elle we shared a stare and then both turned our attention to the guys. Both looked to be on the verge of a climax, and as we knelt between their legs and increased the speed of our hands just a fraction they started to climax almost simultaneously. Dan was the first to go. Letting out a yell he jerked his hips upwards and started to climax just as Elle bobbed her head down and captured the head of his cock in her mouth, sucking his climax to a finish and licking up every last drop with contented moans as she did so.

I turned my eyes back to David and saw him grinning down at me as his hips rhythmically thrust up and down in my hand. Leaning forwards, he pulled me up and captured my mouth in a searing kiss. Our tongues twined desperately and as my hand continued to work him hard and fast, he groaned and I felt the hot wetness of his release oozing over my hand and shooting up onto my bare breasts.

One of David's hands tangled in my hair and he separated our lips with a groan before resting his forehead on mine. He was panting hard, and I had to say that I felt just as exhilarated by the whole experience.

'Fuck, that was incredible,' Daniel wheezed, before collapsing back on the sofa with a chuckle and pulling Elle up so she was cradled in his arms.

It certainly had been incredible. What a start to the evening. One thing was for sure, I wouldn't complain about coming to the flat in the future if David suggested it!

Chapter Seventeen

Natalia

The shower water ran down my body, refreshing me and washing away the dirt of the day. It felt like it had been a long week at work, and I sighed with contentment and then closed my eyes and tipped my head back to let the warm soothing water douse my face and breasts. With all its extra jets and different settings this shower really was amazing, and the perfect way to start the weekend off in style.

'Umm. What a sight.'

I'd been so lost in my thoughts that I hadn't heard anyone enter the bathroom and my eyes flew open in pleasant surprise when I heard David's voice. I had thought I was the only one in the apartment, but as I blinked several times to clear droplets of water from my eyelashes it was obvious that I had been wrong. David was standing at the door to the large shower area wearing a smirk and absolutely nothing else. He was stark naked, very excited and now prowling forwards towards me with a very promising look on his handsome face.

'Sneaking in and showering without me, hmm?' he murmured as he reached my side and ran his gaze slowly down my body. Even though I was standing under lovely warm water the predatory feel to his stare made goose pimples pop up all over my skin as anticipation rushed through my body.

'Hey, you. I didn't think you were home yet.' It felt strange calling the apartment that he shared with Elle and Dan 'home', but it was how he always referred to it, so I suppose it had just worn off on me.

David stepped into the large shower to join me. Settling his hands on my waist he then began to massage my skin with firm circles of his palms. It felt so good that my eyes fluttered shut, and a groan escaped my throat as his hands began to move across my body.

Our work schedules hadn't aligned at all this week, and I'd been so busy with my day job that I'd even had to take leave from my shifts at the Club so I hadn't seen him since we'd bid goodbye to each other last Monday morning. Even with some phone calls to placate us, the week had still felt like an age.

After several moments of massaging me his hands disappeared and I opened my eyes in confused disappointment to find him squirting some shower gel onto his palm. He was going to wash me, was he? I smiled, deciding that I was probably going to quite enjoy this. David started off chaste, washing my shoulders and arms with smooth, soapy movements of his hands while I simply stood there and let him pamper me.

'I've missed you,' he confessed gruffly. His words thrilled me, and I grinned. As his hands reached my collarbones, he paused for a second and used one bubbly hand to lightly grip my throat and tip my head back. The action caused me to gasp, and my body instantly ignited with desire for him. He lowered his mouth towards mine and gently kissed me, the lightness of his lips matching that of the hold he had upon me.

His kiss deepened, and as his mouth began to become more insistent, his grip on my throat also increased. I could still breathe, but the feel of his hold on me was oddly thrilling.

Finally, he pulled his head back with a low growl. 'I could easily lose myself in your kiss,' he murmured, before topping up his handful of shower gel and continuing with his task. My legs, feet, stomach and back were all washed thoroughly, and as lovely as it felt, it was glaringly obvious that he had left out all my private areas. It may be a simple wash in the shower, but with the power of the connection between us I found myself overwhelmingly turned on and could feel my body vibrating with the need for him to give me some relief and touch me where I needed it the most.

David's eyes were now heavy lidded with desire, and as he cocked his head and flashed me one of his trademark lopsided smiles he finally put me out of my misery and began to soap my breasts. The feel of his slick fingers passing over my hardened nipples was so good that it caused me to let out a moan of pleasure, but that feeling was nothing compared to his next move as he lowered one hand and slowly slid it between my legs.

Pleasure pulsed through my system as he ran his fingers over my needy clit, and then as his fingers pushed deeper between my legs David groaned, and leant forwards to place a desperate kiss on my open mouth. 'Christ, Natalia.' Leaning back slightly he took hold of one of my hands and guided it towards my groin. 'Feel how fucking wet you are for me.'

I licked my lips and then kept my eyes glued to his as I slowly slid a finger between my legs. My breath caught in my throat as

I brushed my clit, and then I continued to explore my swollen pussy with gentle movements of my hand that had me clutching at David for support with my free hand. I was so wet my fingers were slipping through my folds with ease, and even though we were in the shower and covered in shower gel I was certain that the slickness between my legs was all of my own making.

I gave David a coy smile and shrug. 'It's not my fault that you turn me on so much,' I whispered.

David's eyes seemed to flash with some sort of pride, and then he tangled a hand in my hair and laid a dizzyingly hot kiss on my lips.

As our mouths continued to kiss, and our hands explored each other, I suddenly heard a noise behind me that made me jump. David glanced over my shoulder and then looked down at me. 'Don't worry, it's just Elle grabbing something.'

I cast a quick look behind me, and sure enough Elle was sorting through the bathroom drawer, apparently oblivious of the pair of us getting it on just a few feet away. I let out a small snort of laughter at how little these guys bothered with boundaries and personal space, but was quickly distracted as she left the room and David once again began kissing me.

His lips worked across my jaw and onto my neck where he licked and sucked, and I once again found my head tipping back in pleasure. One of David's hands was in my hair, and the other gently teasing across my belly so I sucked in a shocked gasp when I suddenly felt a hand grip my breast firmly and then roll my nipple.

My eyes flew open and I saw David staring down at me intently as his fingers continued to caress me. Beside us now, and completely unheard by me, was Elle, naked, groping my breast and grinning at me seductively. What the hell?

'OK, sweetheart?' David murmured huskily.

As I glanced at Elle again, I felt a curl of desire in my belly as I recalled what she had done to me last weekend and couldn't deny that there was something about experimenting with her and Dan that I found really compelling. There was no denying that I found them both attractive too, and that the session we'd shared on the sofa had been amazingly hot.

Glancing back at David, I tried to assess how he was feeling. Was *he* really OK with this? He certainly seemed it, and I guess for someone who had enjoyed threesomes and more for most of his adult life it was probably fairly normal. His eyes were focused solely on me though, and were heavy lidded with desire as he waited patiently for my answer.

I flashed another glance at Elle and in response she gave my nipple another gentle squeeze that sent a pang of desire straight to my core. I felt my cheeks heat as I took in the cute, sexy smile on her face and decided to take a leaf out of David's explorative book and just enjoy the moment.

'I am. More than OK.' Deciding I really should double check that this wasn't going to jeopardise our relationship in any way I looked up at him. 'Are you?'

He raised his eyebrows and then let out a laugh. 'I'm in the shower with my beautiful girl watching her cheeks flush with desire as another stunning woman turns her on.' He glanced down at his raging hard-on and then wiggled his eyebrows. 'I'm in fucking heaven right now.'

Both Elle and I laughed, and then the atmosphere around us all just seemed to relax. While David continued to kiss me, Elle moved in behind me and pressed her soft, warm body against mine as she reached around me and continued to play with my breasts. My body was so alight with sensations I felt dizzy, but it was such a powerful feeling that all I could do was surrender to it and allow these two gorgeous people to make me the centre of their attention.

After several minutes of making out, I felt Elle shift away from me and then David began guiding me backwards until my shoulders touched the wall of the cubicle. The cooler tiles made me suck in a gasp, but the contrast of my red-hot skin and the cold just seemed to heighten the moment.

Opening my eyes, I found Elle and David both standing before me. Elle smiled at me and then leant in for a kiss. Her kiss was so much softer than David's, more intimate somehow, and as her tongue pushed inside my mouth I let out a soft whimper of pleasure. David's hands reached down to my left thigh, and then carefully lifted my leg and helped me position my leg so it was propped on the marble seat in the shower. My weight was now mostly on my right leg, and with my left knee bent and raised so my thighs were spread wide, giving them both easy access to my throbbing core. Shower water still rained down on us, and even though I knew the water was hot it felt cool compared to the intense heat burning between my legs.

Without saying a word, Elle slid a hand down my body and immediately inserted two fingers inside me. Breaking the kiss, I let out a shocked gasp at her sudden move and then groaned as she circled them and spread me with scissoring movements that each seemed to brush against my g-spot with perfection. Even over the pounding of the shower water I could hear the sound of my own juices as she continued to move her fingers in and out of me.

'You are so wet!' she whispered, apparently delighted at how aroused I was, and she wasn't wrong! I was so turned on by this whole situation that I felt deliciously close to orgasm already.

Elle leant forwards and placed a quick peck on my lips before lowering herself to her knees before me. I smiled at David who was still tucked in close to me, and leant up to kiss him as Elle continued to explore me with her fingers. My kiss was juddering, because each time Elle touched at a sensitive spot my muscles jerked and twitched. David was now palming his cock and giving slow, sensual slides with his fist as he watched me, and as much as I wanted to take over and pleasure him, I wasn't sure I could focus on that at the same time that Elle was touching me.

Glancing down, I saw Elle kneeling before me and staring almost longingly at my pussy with her mouth hanging slightly open in desire and her cheeks flushed a pretty pink. Jesus. The look on her face was such a turn-on that I felt my core clench around her fingers and knew that I had just soaked her hand with another lot of my arousal. Elle glanced up at me with a knowing smile and then firmly pushed her fingers deeper, in a move that had me clutching at the wall for support. This woman had clearly had way more experience of pleasuring women than I had, and my god did it feel good.

As her fingers started to work inside of me with greater speed, she lowered her face and I felt my clit give a huge pulse in anticipation. The point of her tongue zeroed in on my clit and with the first brush sent a huge jolt of pleasure through me that made me cry out hoarsely. Her tongue began to rhythmically circle my clit, her free hand digging her nails into my inner thigh and causing just enough pain to add to the amazing feelings swirling inside of me.

157

David's hands continued to caress my breasts, but as I began to thrash around under the attention of Elle's skilful tongue he used one hand to press on my belly so I was pinned to the wall and unable to escape from the pleasure she was giving me. The sensations were so powerful that my legs were shaking now, my whole body trembling from the electricity shooting around my skin, and as such, I was glad of his support. Without it I genuinely think I would have slithered down the wall into a boneless pile on the shower floor.

With my leg raised up and to the side Elle had my pussy perfectly parted for her. The position gave her enough room to continue using the fingers inside of me while also lavishing attention on my clit with her mouth. It was sublime and, combined with David now sucking and nipping one of my breasts, I could feel my arousal soaring rapidly.

So much attention was being focused on me and my prime pleasure points that I wasn't sure I'd ever been this turned on before. A glance down didn't help cool my ardour either, because the sight of Elle on her knees with her face buried in my pussy was so sexy that I just had to reach down and caress the back of her head. My touch caused Elle to briefly pause and look up at me, and I groaned at what I saw; her face was glowing with pleasure, cheeks pink and eyes wide and lusty, but it was the sight of my juices coating her mouth, nose and chin that made me groan out loud.

'You two are so fucking hot,' David growled, before capturing my mouth in a kiss which broke the eye contact with Elle and let her get back to the task she was so clearly loving.

It felt like between the two of them I was completely smothered in pleasure. Their tongues and fingers were everywhere, exploring, caressing, probing and driving me wilder and wilder by the second.

I was aching to orgasm now, and with the way Elle and David were simultaneously upping their efforts I knew it wouldn't be long before I did. That low down ache started in my core, building and swirling, tightening my muscles and making my entire body shake. I tried to hold back for as long as I could, but as Elle sucked my clit into her mouth and gently bit down on it, I couldn't stop the sudden tide that swept up upon me. My entire body bucked and thrashed from the power of the climax that tore through me. I yelled, flailed, and bucked, wringing out every drop of my orgasm by greedily grinding myself against her face until my body sagged forwards, stopped from hitting the ground only by David as his arms encircled me and pulled me against him.

David let out a loud groan and then I felt a surge of heat on my thigh and realised he had just climaxed on me. He tilted my head back with one hand and stared me deep in the eyes as I felt his cock continue to bob against my leg. I smiled at the blissed out look on his face and decided that my expression must surely match.

'What the hell is going on here?' The shout from the doorway caused me to stiffen and tuck myself deeper into David's arms as I looked across the bathroom and saw Dan standing in the doorway in his work suit with his briefcase still hanging from one hand.

Oh shit! My eyes flew open wide, panicked by what he would be seeing, and what we had just done with Elle, and wondering how Dan was going to react to it. Would he class this as cheating? It seemed that these guys were really open in their sexual antics, so it was hard to tell how he would respond.

David turned off the shower, leaving the room sounding eerily silent as no one said a word. Panic began to grow inside of me until it was twisting uncomfortably in my stomach as I stared at Dan with apprehension. Suddenly, he threw his brief-case down, and the clatter in the otherwise silent room was enough to make me squeak in shock. His hands then raised to his neck where he promptly ripped off his tie and proceeded to pull his shirt off over his head.

'You guys could have fucking waited!'

What? I was so tense with shock that it took me a few moments to realise what was happening, but in front of our very eyes Dan was now proceeding to undress, stripping off his trousers, boxers and finally socks.

'Am I too late, or does anyone need a little extra fun?' he asked, advancing on the shower cubicle whilst palming his siz-able cock with a grin.

This all seemed completely surreal to me, but beside me David laughed and then Elle stood up and joined in too.

'Well, your girl has just very thoroughly seen to my girl, causing me to get a little over excited,' David explained with a chuckle, 'but I think Elle would probably rather like your atten-tion to help finish her off.'

'Is that so?' Without further prompting Dan scooped Elle up and cradled her in his arms whilst gazing down at her lovingly.

Elle leant up and kissed him and my mind immediately focused on the fact that she had my juices spread all across her face. The idea of him tasting me on her made my cheeks flush with another surge of heat, but I watched in fascination as he nuzzled her face and neck.

'Baby, I'm horny as hell, please make me come,' she murmured.

Dan lifted his head and winked at David and me before turning away. 'My girl has laid down her demands and I shall obey,' he announced, before striding out of the bathroom in the direction of their bedroom.

'You said they only ever did sex with other people if they were both present. Is he going to be annoyed with her?' I asked, genuinely worried that I'd been so caught up in the moment that I'd forgotten what David had told me about them weeks earlier.

'Nah. He didn't seem bothered. Besides, I'm sure he's having his fun now,' David commented drily as we heard a squeal of excitement echoing out from their bedroom. He pulled down a towel with a grin and wrapped it around me. 'Let's get you warm and dry and we can relax in bed.'

As we dried off, I cast my mind back over the last twenty minutes and could barely believe what had just happened. It had been incredible. Clearly David had thought so too, because if you discounted the kisses I'd shared with him, then neither Elle nor I had touched him at all and yet he had come from simply watching me have oral sex with another woman.

When we were both dry, David took my hand and led me to our bed.

'We can snuggle for a bit and then I'll make us some food,' he murmured as he tucked us both under the sheets. 'Did you enjoy that?' he asked, his voice curious.

I nodded as I nestled into his arms, but as I did a troubling thought crossed my mind. 'I did, but can I ask you something?'

'Of course. Anything.'

'Would you ever join in with Dan and Elle without me? Or anyone else for that matter?'

I felt David's chest rise and fall as he let out a small chuckle, and then he placed a kiss on the top of my head. 'No, because you are what is important to me. If I'm having sex you need to be involved.' His words were strong and immediate, giving me the gut feeling that he was telling the complete truth. 'I quite liked her joining in, but only because I can see from your reactions and questions that you're curious. Have you enjoyed the times that she and Dan have taken part?'

I wasn't going to lie to him, I had really enjoyed it, and that fact must have been very clear from my responses. 'I have, but similarly for me, it's special because you are there. I wouldn't want to do that if you weren't involved.'

'Glad to hear it. It sounds like we both have the same outlook on that then,' he agreed, dropping another kiss onto my hair.

As I snuggled contentedly into his arms, I smiled to myself. This was yet another sexual encounter that I could add to my list of 'firsts' since being with David. I grinned and snuggled closer into his embrace. He hadn't been kidding when he'd said he was sexual and experimental. Seeing as I had loved everything we had so far done together, I guess that meant I was too!

Chapter Eighteen

David

I'd spent the last hour thinking back over yesterday's shower encounter and as a result I was grinning like a teenager who had just gotten laid for the first time. My satisfied smile dropped from my lips though, when an alarm began to sound in the office behind me. It wasn't the fire alarm or burglary alert though; this particular alarm was one I dreaded hearing – it was the distress alarm, triggered if something was going down in one of the private rooms that shouldn't be. Fuck.

I immediately dropped the cloth in my hand and ran towards the private rooms and the security panel at the head of the corridor. In my rush I almost ran into Tom, my head of security.

'Which room?' I demanded, my eyes frantically scanning the panel for a flashing red light.

His eyes were wide, and I'd place money on the fact that his heart rate was just as elevated as mine. We trained for situations like this, but it still didn't help calm you when it actually happened. 'Panic alarm in room two.'

Room two was just behind him, and I frowned. 'Why the fuck are you standing out here then? Get in there!'

'I can't get in.' He shoved his shoulder against the door and I heard a dull thump as it immediately knocked into something heavy. 'It's blocked somehow.' He grunted, giving it another shove.

For security precautions our rentable rooms just had latches, not locks on the interior, so this was extremely worrying news. Presumably some furniture had been pushed in front of it. Damn!

I watched again as Tom banged his shoulder unsuccessfully against the door. 'Who booked it?' I asked in frustration. We had a fairly exclusive clientèle, and only our top spenders could afford the luxury of renting one of our rooms from us so I knew them all by name.

Tom scowled at the door and then sent me an anxious glance. 'That's the thing, it's not booked . . . it should be empty.'

His news made my stomach flip with sickening nerves.

What the actual hell was going on?

It was at that moment that we heard a pitiful female wail emanate from within the room, followed by a cry for help. A red mist rose before my eyes and I felt a kick in my stomach as adrenaline flooded my system. Whoever this was breaking the rules in my club was going to be in serious fucking trouble.

'Stand back.' My voice was barely more than a growl, but Tom heard me and quickly took a side-step. Using the entire width of the corridor I let out a yell and launched myself forward, aiming a stamping front kick at the area just below the door handle. The door didn't shift much, but the frame splintered by the latch. Stepping back, I repeated my kick, this time with every ounce of my power and saw the door shift open about a foot. There was a rumble as something heavy slid across the carpet behind it, so I repeated the action one last time with a roar of anger.

Whatever dickhead was taking advantage in there wasn't just hurting a woman, which was bad enough, but he was risking my entire business. Club Twist worked because our strict rules of practice meant our customers were always safe. Consent was a must, and a safe secure environment was promised, neither of which seemed present at the moment.

The door slid open a fraction more and so I threw my shoulder against it, forcing it back more until I could squash my body through the gap. My shirt snagged on the splintered wood, and I felt it rip at the skin of my torso, but I didn't care, I was a man on a mission. Snarls of frustrated anger were tearing their way from my throat, but finally I managed to force my way inside.

My eyes frantically scanned the room and as they did my stomach dropped to my boots. It wasn't just any female in here in distress, it was Natalia. *My Natalia*. Fuck. I'd thought the voice had been achingly familiar. What was she doing in here with him? Whatever it was, she clearly hadn't consented, and my stomach lurched so violently I felt bile rise up my throat and I had to focus on the situation to try and avoid throwing up from the anger thumping around my body.

Momentarily I felt frozen to the spot. As much as I wanted to fly into action I just couldn't seem to get my legs to move. My eyes were functioning just fine though, and they flicked around the room in horror as I tried to take in the scene before me. Natalia was pressed into the corner of the room, her shirt half torn away from her chest and tears streaming down her face as she fought with a man before her. My gaze focused on him and I instantly recognised him as Richard Lincoln, some high-flying London banker who'd been a member here for at least three years. He'd never caused trouble before, not even anything minor, so this was a real turn up for the books.

'Red! Red!' Her words brought me out of my trance and my blood turned to ice as I realised that Natalia was sobbing the Club safe word over and over but being completely ignored by Richard as he carried on pawing at her and trying to shove his hand up her torn skirt.

Another roar flew from my lips as I launched myself forward and began to tackle the big male. He might have a few pounds on me, but I'd been working out and easily managed to overpower him. Looping my arms under his, I dragged him backwards and then spun, literally throwing him across the room. His body flew through the air like a rag doll, and I saw Tom give me a surprised look as Richard collided into a wall and crashed to the floor with a grunt. He was a big unit, so I was fairly surprised myself, but I was too wound up on adrenaline to dwell upon my apparent super-human strength.

'What the fuck, Richard?' My blood was pounding in my ears, muscles bunched and ready to continue what I'd started by smashing his fucking face in. How the fuck dare he?

I was wound up and ready to fight, but then I heard the sound of Natalia behind me, still sobbing. 'I told him no ... I said "red". I said the safe word ...' Her words faded off, replaced again by quiet sniffles as tears continued to stream down her cheeks.

I was torn; go to Natalia and help her, or teach this miserable low life a lesson.

'So what if you said the safe word?' Richard yelled, craning his neck and trying to look around me to glare at Natalia. 'She's been flirting with me from behind the bar for weeks. Talking to me every Friday night but never doing more than that. She's a fucking prick tease. Why the fuck flirt with someone in a sex club if you don't want to have sex?'

Given the situation he was in, I couldn't believe he even had the balls to speak out, let alone try and blame Natalia for this. Talk about digging yourself deeper into a hole.

'I wasn't flirting . . .' Natalia sobbed from behind me. 'I was just being nice . . . It's my job . . .' Her words were broken and filtered with gasps as if she were struggling to breathe. I glanced over my shoulder at her and my heart clutched at the sight. She looked like a deer caught in the headlights. Her eyes were wide and glassy, her body was pushed into the corner as far as she could go, and as she continued to cry, she clutched at her ripped clothing in a vain attempt at hiding her body.

Every fibre of my being was ready to pound him into a pulp, and even though I knew it wasn't the best course of action I really fucking wanted to. This wasn't *just* a sex club; yes you could probably come here most nights and find a willing partner – emphasis on the word *willing* – but Twist was so, so much more; it was a place for opening people's eyes to sexual freedom, a place for safe exploration of hidden desires, a little luxurious haven of beautiful erotic adventure hidden in the London backstreets.

It was not just a sex club.

And it was absolutely not somewhere where behaviour like this was accepted.

I was so angry I could barely see straight. She was my girl and I hadn't been there to protect her. Beating him to a pulp, as tempting as it might be, would probably get me arrested, which wouldn't help anything, so with a huge attempt to muster some self-control I spun away from him and glanced at Tom. 'Call the police.'

'They're already on their way,' he confirmed quietly, still blocking the exit with his big body.

Turning to Natalia, my heart clenched painfully at the tear-stained state of her. She flinched at my movement, so as I stepped closer, I kept my movements deliberately slow so as not to scare her. 'Can you tell me what happened, sweetheart?' I asked softly as I crouched down beside her.

Her tears had started to dry now, but her eyes were still like saucers and there was still a definite tremble in her hands. 'He dragged me in here . . .' He had dragged her? What we were developing together in our relationship was amazing, and I wouldn't for a second have believed that she would have gone with him on her own accord, but to hear her say it made me feel sick to my stomach.

She had been reduced to a terrified heap, and a million miles away from the strong woman I'd come to know, and a fresh urge to stamp on him rushed over me. Her wide eyes sought mine. 'I . . . I've spoken to him before when serving him drinks, but I wasn't flirting. He was a customer, he seemed nice, and it's my job to talk . . .' She paused again, this time swiping at her cheeks with the back of her hand to clear the remaining wetness. 'He was different tonight when he came in though . . . angry somehow. I didn't feel comfortable so I served his drink and moved to the other side of the bar.' She took a deep breath and I heard it stutter in her lungs.

Seeing her in so much anguish was too much for me and so I carefully reached out and took hold of one of her hands.

Given her current terror I'd half expected her to flinch away from the contact, but Natalia did the exact opposite, grabbing onto my hand as if it were her lifeline and squeezing it with crushing force.

The contact seemed to calm her somehow, and she tore her gaze away from Richard and looked up at me instead. 'Just now I went to the toilet. When I came out, he was . . . he was waiting for me in the corridor and then he dragged me in here. He was too strong for me.' Her eyes began darting around the room, her fear obvious. 'He said he was going to . . .' her eyes closed and when they re-opened, I saw the glassiness of her returning tears. 'He said he was going to have me, even if I didn't want it.' She swallowed loudly and then jerked her head towards the red button on the wall above her. 'I managed to press the button . . .' Her words dried and she looped her free arm around her legs and hugged them as if trying to make herself even smaller.

I'd heard enough. It was very obvious what had occurred in here, and if Richard chose to argue against it, he wouldn't stand a chance. We had CCTV in all the corridors so her story would be simple to validate, not that I needed proof, her wretched state was evidence enough.

'Do you want to press charges?' I asked softly.

Her eyes flew open with concern and she rapidly shook her head. I'd guessed as much. Privacy was pretty important to anyone who came here, even the staff, but I still wanted her to know the option was there. 'I think you should consider it. His behaviour is not acceptable. I'll help you; we can do the process together.'

She nodded nervously, but I suspected it would still take some persuasion to get her to go through with it. Gently letting

169

go of her hand, I stood up and spun towards Richard. As soon as my eyes landed on him, I once again wanted to smash the living shit out of him for hurting her like this. I would have been angry at him for hurting any woman in my club, but the fact that it was Natalia meant that my anger was so heightened that I was almost struggling to see straight.

I pointed at him, trying to throw the venom I was feeling through the stabbing of my finger. 'The police will be dealing with this, but just to make it clear – your membership is revoked, lifetime ban, don't ever show your face here again.'

'What the hell? So, I lose my job *and* my membership in the same fucking day? Over a floosy of a barmaid?'

Floosy? Calling my girl names was the last straw and I was standing upright and advancing on Richard with red mist descending over my eyes before I'd even properly thought it through. 'How dare you!' I was towering over him in seconds, yelling down at him with a voice like thunder. I'd never been this angry in my life. My right fist raised to hit him, but suddenly a strong grip landed on my wrist.

Glancing sideways, I saw Tom holding onto me with a grim expression on his face. 'David. He's not worth it,' Tom growled, his deep tone snapping me out of my rage and making me cast a glance towards Natalia, who was still sat on the floor and still looking utterly terrified. I looked back at Richard with a snarl. I was so close to kicking out my rage on his worthless body, but Tom was right, me ending up in prison for GBH wouldn't help Natalia, and that thought was the only thing that stopped me.

'I've paid thousands of pounds into this place over the years! You'll regret this, David!' Richard started ranting and swearing but I blocked it out. He was clearly drunk, and it sounded like his shitty day might have caused his out-of-character behaviour, but it was no excuse for trying to hurt an innocent girl. If he'd needed an outlet like that he could a booked a session with a consenting partner who liked it rough, and taken out his bad day within the constraints of a rule-driven, consensual, safe scene.

'You just wait, David! You and your fucking Club are finished!'

At that moment two police officers entered the room and Richard began yelling even louder. Behind me I heard a scared sniffle. Turning to Natalia, I quickly crossed back to my girl and crouched down beside her to pull her into my arms. She'd need to speak to the police, but before that I desperately wanted her to feel safe again.

'Can I get you out of here, sweetheart?' Her eyes darted to mine and she nodded immediately so I didn't waste a second in scooping her into my arms and standing up.

'Tom, help these guys get him out of here.'

Striding from the room with Natalia clutching at my shirt I wondered where the heck I should take her.

I wanted to take her home so we were far away from here, but the police would need to question us. My office would be OK even though it was in a bit of a state at the moment because it was nearing tax return time and everything was an absolute sea of paperwork, but that would involve walking through the busy bar to get to it. Glancing down I grimaced; Natalia's clothes were torn and she was clearly a wreck so that was not going to happen.

I had a private room upstairs, but I never used it so it was no doubt dusty and damp. It wasn't ideal, but the only other option would be to go into one of the other rentable rooms, and I very much doubted that Natalia would want that. She was trembling now, and clinging to me and I once again felt an overwhelming protectiveness for her. Supporting her weight on my right knee I freed an arm and quickly pulled out my phone to send a message to Tom, saying I'd be on the top floor.

Walking down the corridor I tapped in the code beside the door that opened the staff staircase and began the climb up. There was a floor of private rooms, which my staff could use if they needed a rest during a shift, or a sleep afterwards, but we rarely used them. They were for solo use only, my rule being that we all had to keep business and pleasure completely separate. If one of the staff wanted to entertain a guest, they could have one of the rentable rooms when they were off shift, but the staff quarters were exactly that, a place to sleep after a long night shift and nothing else.

My room was on the very top floor. It was near the old projection gallery that the theatre had had fitted when it had tried to diversify and become a cinema of sorts. Funnily enough, even though I was the boss, I'd still stuck to the rules, and in all the years I'd owned this place I'd never once taken a woman up here. Richard had way overstepped the laws of the Club so it seemed that several rules had already been broken here in Club Twist tonight. Making a dismissive noise I rolled my eyes and headed towards the final staircase that led to my private quarters – I may as well break another.

Chapter Nineteen

David

I kicked open the door to my private room and my nose wrinkled as I was immediately hit by the smell of stale air and dust. This was why I hadn't wanted to bring Natalia up here, I very rarely came in here, so it was musty, but it was quiet and private. Looking around I was thankful that at least it was relatively tidy, even if it wasn't the freshest space. With Natalia still in my arms I walked to the windows and threw them open wide to let in some air.

As soon as I'd bought the flat around the corner this room had become almost redundant to me. Why stay in a pokey hole like this when I had the luxury of the flat a three-minute walk away? I suppose I'd just kept this room out of habit, but I was glad of it today. Glancing around, I refamiliarised myself with it. It was basic, but useable; there was a bed, desk, chair and wardrobe, and that was about it. I kept a change of clothes in the cupboard in case I spilt things over myself at work, but even those hadn't been touched in months.

With a cool evening breeze fluttering through the open window, I walked to the bed and carefully lowered myself down onto it. I could still feel fury burning in my system over the events of the past half an hour, but for the sake of my girl I needed to box that up for the time being. After taking a second to get my emotions in order I looked down and carefully adjusted Natalia on my lap, realising to my surprise that she had fallen asleep in my arms.

It must have been a reaction to the fear and stress from Richard's attack, so I did my best to make her comfortable and then gently brushed back the hair that had fallen over her face. Her tears had dried now, and apart from her ripped clothes and a small frown on her face there was no trace of her earlier distress.

I felt my heart ache for her. How could I feel so much, so quickly? My gaze traced her features and I felt a smile curve my lips as just how pretty she was.

As if she could somehow sense me watching, Natalia's eyes suddenly flickered open. I felt my cheeks heat in embarrassment at being caught watching her, but after her earlier terror I didn't want her to freak out at my close proximity, so I quickly smiled down at her reassuringly.

'Hey, sweetheart.'

'Hey.' She still looked a little nervous, or perhaps she was in shock, but that was to be expected after Richard's appalling behaviour.

'How are you feeling?'

I saw her expression briefly clouding over as she thought over the events of the evening. 'OK, I guess.' She licked her lips, and I couldn't help the flicker of desire I felt as I watched her tongue dart across. 'It was crazy. I swear I didn't come onto him, David.' She shook her head and then reached up to cup my jaw. 'I didn't flirt with him. I'm with you, I would never cheat on you.' Her green eyes were suddenly serious and pleading, as if she desperately needed me to believe her, which of course I did.

'I know that, sweetheart.' I reached up and gently brushed my knuckles over her cheek. Her eyes closed and she leant her face into my touch, a tiny gesture that somehow meant so much to me.

'It's my job to be nice to the customers. He obviously took it the wrong way.'

'Honestly, you've done nothing wrong. I've worked with you for long enough to know that you are extremely professional with our guests.' My voice was gruff with emotion and I had to take a second to clear my throat before continuing. 'I'm so sorry this happened to you. I should have done something.'

Natalia stiffened in my arms and then rapidly sat up. 'You did do something! You kicked your way in there and saved me.' Her green eyes were flashing with feeling. 'There's nothing else you could have done. He's never behaved badly before, neither of us could have known that he was going to flip like that.'

Even though she was right and there was no way of knowing what Richard was capable of, the guilt I felt was inexplicable. There was nothing I could have done to change what had happened, but it had happened in *my* club to *my* girl, and that knowledge was still sitting on my chest like a heavy load.

Maybe I needed to up the security checks for members at the Club; but Natalia was right, even with enhanced checks I doubted that Richard would ever have raised any red flags before today.

'Hey. Come back to me.' Natalia's voice was soft and as it broke through my pondering, I realised I was miles away, staring at the wall as I thought it all over.

I needed to box up the mix of emotions that Richard had stirred and instead focus on making sure Natalia was OK. I forcibly relaxed myself and then flashed her a wink. 'Sorry. I'm here.'

Natalia's cheeks flushed, and I felt just a little smug that it was me who had caused that reaction in her. Her gorgeous green eyes were twinkling up at me now, and I felt her body relax. The fact that she still felt comfortable with me after what she'd just gone through with another man made me feel ridiculously protective over her, and my arms tightened around her just a little more.

In response Natalia rested her cheek on my chest and let out a contented sigh. 'This feels so good. So right,' she murmured softly, her words sending a spreading warmth through my body.

I bent my head forwards and I placed a kiss on the top of her head, lingering for a second or two to absorb the sweet scent of her hair. She was right; we had been together nearly two months now, and it had been amazing. Having her in my arms always felt so good and so right. As ridiculous as it might seem for a man of my years, I was pretty damn excited about what the future might hold for us too, and instead of dwelling on Richard and all that had happened today, I allowed myself to get lost in dreams of Natalia instead.

Chapter Twenty

Sasha

I adjusted the phone so it was propped on my shoulder and used my free hand to apply a slick of red nail varnish to one toenail. 'So, drinks tonight then, yeah?' I prompted, hoping to get a positive response.

'Ummm . . .' Before she had even answered I knew what Natalia was going to say. 'I think I'm busy with David tonight.'

I frowned and shook my head, knowing that she wasn't telling the truth because it was David himself who had asked me to try and persuade Natalia to go out. In the four weeks since Richard's attack on her, Natalia had barely been outside, and had refused to see any of us socially. She still saw David regularly, but had understandably been left with some major insecurities.

With some convincing from David, Natalia had pressed charges, and Richard had been charged with common assault and released with a fine to pay. David had wanted a charge of attempted rape to be pursued, but because Richard had no previous history with the police and there was no physical evidence to support it, the prosecution had managed to get the lower charge, much to the disbelief of us all.

I'd gone to the courtroom to support Natalia on the day of his trial, and Richard had seemed genuinely remorseful, blaming it on too much to drink and the stress of losing his job, but Natalia was still living in fear that he might reappear to finish the job at any moment.

Now that she was barely going out, David was worried about her mental state, as was I, so I was now on a mission to help her start the healing process.

'Sorry about that,' she added lamely.

Sighing, I rolled my eyes. Perhaps I needed to start being a little firmer with her. 'Nope, you're not seeing David, I spoke to him earlier and it was he who suggested we meet up.'

There was a silence down the line, but just when I thought Natalia was going to make another excuse, she surprised me. 'Ummm. OK then. Drinks it is.'

Huh. Well that had turned out to be easier than expected, now I just needed to plan where we were going to take her.

After some discussions with Marcus and David, we'd decided on a girly night out to ease Natalia back into the swing of socialising. I had gotten the whole gang together to support Natalia as I'd figured she might feel safer in a crowd. Robyn was joining us for drinks tonight, and to boost numbers I'd also contacted Stella and Rebecca to invite them. We were well overdue a catch up with them both, and they had been thrilled to come too.

Instead of just meeting for drinks, I decided to do something a little different that might help to keep Natalia's mind occupied, so I'd booked us onto a cocktail-making class at one of the coolest bars in Soho. We were out in public, but we also had the benefit of a private room to ourselves, which would make Natalia feel safer.

We were now ensconced in the room at the rear of the bar complete with our guide for the night, Joshua, who had instantly told us all to call him Josh, and then plied us all with a porn star martini to 'stir up a shot of fun' to start the night. Over the next hour it became clear that Josh was well versed in not only cocktail-related puns – which he used a lot of – but was also very skilled in teaching the mixology of cocktails too.

Switching stools with Rebecca, I slid closer to Natalia and gave her a nudge in the ribs. 'See, this isn't so bad, is it?' She was silent for a second, so I couldn't decide if she would feel irritated that between David and me we had kind of forced her into coming out tonight. 'Or are you loathing every second and hating my guts right now?' I was thick skinned and preparing myself for a frosty reaction, but to my surprise, Natalia turned to me, raised her glass and smiled.

'Of course I don't hate you! This has been so much fun.' She chinked her glass with mine and drank. 'Thank you for helping me snap out of my crazy streak.'

After joining her in her drinks toast by taking a sip of my martini I shook my head. 'You weren't being crazy, you had a hell of an ordeal, it's no wonder it left you shaken up.'

Natalia nodded and sipped her drink. 'I . . .' She paused and gave a self-conscious shrug. 'It hit me a lot harder than I first thought,' she admitted quietly. 'I've been seeing a therapist.'

This was news to me. Since the attack on her at the Club I had kept in close contact with both Natalia and David, but neither had mentioned a therapist. It made complete sense that she might need that kind of support, but I had no idea why she was looking so embarrassed about her confession.

'Hey, why are you looking like that? Therapy is nothing to be embarrassed about. We all need a little help sometimes.' Back when my parents had died in close succession, I had been a mess, and my aunt had persuaded both me and my brother to see a counsellor. I was just as stubbornly willed then as I am now, so it had taken quite a bit of persuasion, but in the end, those sessions had been the best thing I'd ever done.

'Ruth, that's my therapist,' Natalia explained, 'she's helped me understand that I've probably been overreacting with my worry. Rich . . .' Natalia paused, frowning, and swallowed hard before starting again. '*He* was normally an OK guy.' She shrugged. '*He* was drunk that night because he'd lost his job, and I just happened to be in the wrong place at the wrong time, that's all. It wasn't like he was stalking me or is likely to try and come after me.'

I noticed how she was unable to say Richard's name, but I decided not to bring it up. If that was one of her coping strategies, then that was fine by me. 'No, exactly, that's true. It doesn't excuse his behaviour, but I agree, I think it was a moment of madness, a freak one off.'

From the corner of my eye I saw Josh approaching with the book of cocktail recipes in his hand, completely unaware of the serious nature of our conversation, so I paused and turned to him with a smile.

'You girls look like you're having a deep and meaningful, so I'll just leave this here.' He slid the recipe book towards us with a wink. 'Give me a shout when you've picked what you want to make next.'

'Thank you.' Natalia took the book and started to flick through the pages and Josh left us to ourselves again.

'And after the warning the judge gave him, I'm sure he'll keep his distance from you and the Club from now on,' I said, feeling certain that my words were true. David's background checks for the Club were extremely rigorous, and after Richard's attack he'd got his security team to go back and review them thoroughly. They had, and there was nothing in Richard's past that indicated he'd ever be a risk. This had been a fluke loss of his sanity, and unfortunately Natalia had been on the receiving end of it.

Natalia returned her attention to the drinks menu and flicked to the page showing the cocktail slammers – small cocktails made in shot glasses and perfect for downing in one gulp, and in my experience, almost guaranteed to get you drunk faster. 'So, what do you say we move this party on to the serious drinks?' she suggested keenly.

Seeing as Natalia seemed genuinely OK now, I decided to leave the topic of Richard there for now. Nodding, I laughed and peered over her shoulder at the list of drinks that we could experiment with making next. 'So, what do you fancy? Fruity or creamy?'

'Fruity first, creamy after!' she announced joyfully.

Predictably, as the evening progressed, we did less and less learning and more and more drinking. The major success, however, wasn't the cocktail recipes we bagged up to take home, or the new drinking games we had learnt, but the fact that Natalia had enjoyed herself. She'd been visibly nervous at the start of the night, but was now sitting in a booth with a cocktail in one hand and a grin on her face. I could already sense that tomorrow would be a hangover day, but that was fine by me because Natalia was content and relaxed, and for the first time in weeks she had ventured out of the house.

Sitting back, I downed my latest concoction and then grinned at our gathered group of happy girls. Mission accomplished.

Chapter Twenty-One

Natalia

'Hey, gorgeous.' Hearing David's low, sexy voice down the phone made me smile and I clutched the mobile to my ear as I chucked my bag on the bed and kicked off my shoes and wiggled my toes in relief.

'Did you have a good night with the girls?'

Smiling, I nodded, even though he wouldn't be able to see it. 'I did. I'm a little tipsy.'

David chuckled. 'I'm glad you had fun.'

I looked at the huge, empty king size bed and pouted. 'What time will you be home?'

'At the end of shift. An hour or so. But first, I have a little gift for you.'

'Really?'

'Mmm-hmm. Well, it's sort of a gift for both of us really.' There was an odd note to his voice which triggered my curiosity and my eyebrows rose as I wondered what on earth he could have bought for me.

'Are you feeling up for a little fun?' From his tone it was very apparent that the 'fun' he was referring to was of the sexy variety and I frowned, again looking at the empty bed. 'But you're at work.'

'I am, but I have a plan. So, what do you say? Are you up for it?'

I didn't know what the 'it' was, but I was tipsy, horny, and always up for fun where David was concerned, and so with a smile I nodded. 'Sure.'

I heard a satisfied sigh down the line. 'Excellent! Hang up the phone but take it with you to the lounge and you'll find the little gift I've left for you.'

Well and truly intrigued, I walked to the lounge and opened the door. At first, I didn't notice anything out of the ordinary; there were no gift bags on the dining-room table, or any obvious packages laying around. As I passed my eyes over the room again, though, my gaze halted abruptly as it came to the coffee table, and then a shocked giggle escaped from my throat.

Surely *that* wasn't my gift?

Sitting proudly on the coffee table was a sizable navy-blue dildo. My eyes widened as I tilted my head and stared curiously at the new ornament adorning our room. As I stepped closer, I saw a small bow tied around its shaft and another laugh escaped my throat – it would appear that this was indeed my gift from David.

'Turn and look at the TV, gorgeous.'

The sound of David's voice echoing through the empty room made me jump out of my skin and a small shriek escaped my throat as I obeyed his command and turned towards the television. My eyebrow quirked as I immediately noticed that there was a new addition to this part of the room too . . . a shiny new webcam was mounted on top of the television and there was a red light illuminated on it.

'Hey, gorgeous. You look beautiful tonight.' He could see me, but I couldn't see him? That didn't seem very fair.

'Hey, you. If I turn on the TV can I see you too?'

'Unfortunately not, I didn't have time to set up that kind of connection.' I could hear a few faint noises across the audio and tried to picture where he was. As if reading my mind, he spoke again. 'I'm sitting at the desk in my office watching you on my laptop. So, are you too tipsy for a little fun, or are you intrigued by my gift?'

The fear I'd been left with since Richard's attack had faded during my night out, and I laughed, the cocktails in my system making me feel carefree for the first time in weeks. I eyed the dildo and then grinned towards the camera. 'I'm not that drunk, and yes, I'm definitely up for some fun.' I trailed a hand up my body, starting at my thigh, tracing over my hip, across my breast and then lingering at my neck, giggling when I heard David groan.

'Fuck, baby, you've got me turned on and rock hard already.' There was a low hum down the line and then his next command, which surprised the hell out of me. 'Now, I'd like you to undress and then think of me while you play with yourself and get yourself turned on.' I heard a knock in the background and then David tut. 'Someone is at my door. Don't let me down, start with you task, gorgeous. I'll be back shortly.'

A click echoed through the room and I stared at the red dot to see if it disappeared, but it didn't. 'David?' There was no reply from him, so I could only assume he'd muted me, and as I started to undress, the room around me felt thick with silence.

I placed the last of my clothes on the sofa and then bit on my lip as I started to follow his instruction to play with myself. The

185

unexpected events of the last ten minutes had already got me quite excited and as I slid a hand down between my legs I found that I was already slick with moisture.

I let out a moan that sounded really loud in the silence of the room, and I glanced around again anxiously. I might have had alcohol in my system for bravery, but I wasn't entirely sure how I felt about this whole situation. It was definitely exciting, but the thought that Elle or Daniel could walk in at any moment and catch me was also making my stomach swirl with anxiety. It was late, so were they here in bed? Or still out partying?

Mind you, seeing as I'd had a few shared experiences with both of them now would it really be so bad if they saw me doing this? They'd probably pull up a chair and enjoy the show, I thought with a laugh. The anxiety in my tummy started to swirl and transform into further arousal at the thought of being watched.

Was David watching me yet? Or was he still busy with who-ever had knocked on his door? I had no idea, and even though I could see the red light on the camera was on, there had been no further sounds from the audio device since David had com-manded me to undress.

Moving to the coffee table, I sat on the end and looked at his gift for me ... his 'little surprise'. It was actually rather large, and as I looked at it again I wondered how it would feel inside me. The thought of impaling myself upon it while he watched sent a further flood of moisture between my legs and I felt my core clench with the urge to mount it.

Removing the small pink bow, I leant down and touched the base of it, finding that it was suctioned to the table and stuck firm. Hmm. Was I supposed to use it there? It was perfectly lined up with the webcam, so it seemed so. As I continued to toy with my nipples with one hand, I trailed a finger up its length, admiring the ridges which I knew were in place to add to my pleasure.

'Do you like it? Did I pick well?' David's voice echoed through the speaker and I jumped before turning and glancing at the camera with a shy smile.

'It's nice.' Was nice an appropriate word for describing a dildo? God knows. I rolled my eyes and then looked at the camera again. 'I feel a bit self-conscious . . . I wish you were here. I want to see you.'

I heard David let out a groan and suspected that even though he'd set up this whole scenario he wanted to be here too. 'You have no reason to feel self-conscious, you look utterly beautiful.'

My cheeks flushed at his compliment and I smiled.

'I can see you are gloriously naked now, but did you also do as I asked?'

I nodded, and then, just for effect I slipped my hand between my legs and swirled it in my moisture before removing it and holding it up for him to see.

'Fuck . . .' David cursed and I grinned at the obvious effect I was having upon him.

'Now climb on the table and straddle the dildo, gorgeous.'

My core clenched greedily at his instruction as I climbed onto the table. As well as the dildo, David had also left some small rubbery mats on either side, which were padded and comfortable and in the perfect position for my knees. I rolled my eyes again. How very thoughtful of him!

I positioned myself above the dildo and then sunk down until the tip brushed between my legs. Lowering further, I felt the head press just between my lips and then rocked back and forth. I continued to repeat the motion while looking up and towards the camera.

'Fuck, Natalia.' David's voice was hoarse now, and I smiled at the obvious effect I was having on him. 'You are so damn sexy.'

Reaching down, I trailed my hand across my belly, through the small thatch of curls at my groin and then lower still until it slipped through my moist folds. I was so wet! I circled my fingers again and again in the slickness and then wrapped my hand around the shaft to lubricate it with my own moisture.

With my eyes firmly fixed to the little red light on the camera I started to lower myself fully down onto the shaft. A long, strained moan left my lips as it stretched me, filling me up and feeling strange in its size after so long of being used to David's unique shape. Finally, I felt the large base of the dildo and knew that I was fully seated upon it. It wasn't as large as David but still filled me in ways that felt really good.

David let out a strangled noise over the audio and I imagined him sitting in his office at work with a raging hard-on pulsing in his jeans, or was he perhaps touching himself too? Running a strong fist smoothly up and down his erect shaft in time with my moves? The thought was such a turn-on that I moaned.

I circled myself on the shaft and it hit against all the right places inside me. I was still greedy for the feeling of stimulation on my clit though, so I lowered a hand and started to circle my needy bud with a finger. My eyes were heavy lidded with arousal, and I felt almost desperate to drop my head and close my eyes, but I knew David was watching me, so I didn't.

Even though I was performing this for David, I couldn't help but get caught up in the pleasure of the moment and soon I found myself humping the shaft with enthusiastic, deep plunges of my hips. Every time I fully impaled myself I heard the sound of my buttocks slapping onto my calve muscles, and along with my heavy breathing and soft moans I imagined it must sound quite erotic to David as he listened and watched me.

'I wish you were here,' I panted. 'I wish this was you inside me ...'

There was a noise down the line like David was scraping his chair backwards across the floor. 'Fuck, baby, I wish I was too.'

There was a mirrored wall to the left of the television which was usually half hidden by the dining table, but I realised now that David had shifted the table away to the side so I now had a perfect view of myself sat astride the dildo. He'd thought of everything, hadn't he?

I paused and looked at my reflection. My hair was long and flowing free, my body shiny with a layer of perspiration, and my position ... well, I couldn't deny that it was quite a sexy sight. Every time I lifted my hips the shaft of the dildo became visible and it was visibly wet from my juices. As I lowered down again my eyes fluttered with pleasure and my muscles tensed and ripped as my body accepted the length over and over again.

I focused my attention back on the camera and let out a soft moan as my pussy gripped the shaft. I sped up my moves, greedily slamming my body down on the shaft over and over sending jolts of pleasure through my body and quickly spiralling towards orgasm.

Before I fully lost myself to the sensations, I remembered that even though I was on my own in the room, I wasn't fully alone – David was still watching me and I decided to up the performance for him. Moving my hands to my breasts I fondled them and sucked in a sharp gasp at just how sensitive my nipples were. Tweaking the tight buds again I bit down on my lower lip and let my head drop back in ecstasy.

'David . . . I'm so close.' My words were a whisper, and met by a gruff exhalation of air through the speaker from David.

'Fuck!' he growled, and I wished I could see his face and how much he was enjoying the show. 'This was such a bad idea! I need to be there with you.'

I continued the movements of my hips but slowed the pace just enough to bring myself back from the cusp of orgasm. 'Shall I come for you?'

There was another frustrated grunt down the line which made me giggle, and then I heard David clear his throat as if attempting to regain his composure. 'Yes baby. I want you to come for me. Imagine I'm there with you. There inside you.'

My core tightened at the thought of him here with me and I nodded slowly, hoping I still looked seductive and in control. Keeping my eyes on the camera I rocked my hips back and forth, and then while one hand continued to caress my breast I reached down with the other hand and began rubbing my clit. The little bundle of nerves was so swollen and sensitive that it sent electrifying shockwaves rippling across my skin as I circled my fingers across the slick nub.

'I'm almost there,' I panted. My body was nearly out of my own control now as it desperately sought the release it was pining for. 'This is you deep inside of me.' I rolled my head forwards as a wave of desire shot through me and my hair fell down around my face and shoulders like a curtain. Knowing that he'd want to see my face as I climaxed, I lifted it back up and nodded towards the camera. 'I'm yours, David. Yours.'

My body was vibrating now, muscles tense and wanting,

breasts bouncing with each sharp movement of my hips and my eyes felt wild as they desperately tried to focus on the camera instead of rolling back in my head like they wanted to.

'Come, baby.' David's voice was strained, but more in control than earlier and I wondered if perhaps he'd been touching himself too and had calmed his ardour with a climax. 'Come.'

As on command, my body flooded with further moisture and a million sensations rushed through my nerve endings as I rapidly approached my peak. I continued to pump my hips and rub my clit and then suddenly my pussy clenched violently around the dildo as I smashed into my orgasm with a scream. The thick shaft filled me, hitting every spot to perfection and I almost fell forwards from the power of my climax, but knowing I was being watched I forced my body to stay upright, riding out every last twitch of pleasure and moaning David's name over and over.

Finally, my pleasure began to ebb, and I was left sitting astride the dildo in a sweaty, panting mess. I could feel a trickle of sweat running down my back, and as I lifted my head I saw in the mirror that my cheeks were flushed with desire, my skin glistening and my hair was now a wild mass upon my head. All in all, I looked thoroughly well fucked.

My cheeks reddened further as my gaze roamed over my reflection and I saw that the insides of my thighs were shiny with the moisture from my climax. Looking down I gasped and then giggled with embarrassment – I was so wet that I had made a small puddle on the tabletop.

'Jesus, Natalia.' I could only assume from the tone to his voice that David had also spotted my mess.

Sleepy and dizzy from my lust, I grinned lazily at the camera and then slowly began to lift myself from the dildo. I was still panting hard, my breasts swaying and I imagined David's gaze greedily focusing on them as he watched me. My legs felt wobbly as I climbed from the table and then I sat on the edge again to steady myself. The room smelt of sex, my own unique scent filling the air around me and screaming of the pleasure I had just given myself.

'That was fucking incredible to watch.' David's voice was hoarse. 'You look worn out.'

I giggled and then sighed with a mixture of exhaustion and bone deep contentment. 'I am.'

'Go and tuck yourself in bed; I'm going to arrange cover and come home early. You'll be in my arms in no time.'

My ears perked up at his statement. 'Is that a promise?' I tried to look sultry and sexy as I spoke, but in my currently sweaty state I probably didn't succeed.

David growled and the sexy sound reverberated across the audio and sent a delicious shiver down my spine.

'It certainly is, baby.'

My core clenched with anticipation and I laughed at his ability to affect me so powerfully when he wasn't even in the same building as me. I stared into the camera, hoping to look seductive and not exhausted. 'OK. See you soon.'

His promise reinvigorated me, and with the thought of his arms wrapped around me in the very near future I quickly collected up the dildo and rubber pads and made my way to the bedroom to grab a restorative nap before he got home.

Chapter Twenty-Two

Marcus

'We're meeting everyone at eight o'clock, yeah?' I threw the question over my shoulder as I attempted to persuade my hair into some sort of style. Looking in the mirror, I watched as the chunk that I had just smoothed down immediately popped back up again.

I caught a glimpse in my reflection of Sasha as she strolled across the bedroom behind me, putting in an earring. 'Yup. We'll leave in ten minutes.'

I was really looking forward to tonight. It wasn't unusual for us to go out on a Friday night, but Sasha had arranged for a whole gang of us to meet up tonight, including my closest friends Oliver, Nicholas and Nathan who I hadn't seen for ages.

Nicholas, Nathan and I had been inseparable in our younger years, always out clubbing and getting up to mischief, but since Nicholas had settled down with Rebecca and Nathan with Stella, we now met up far less frequently. I guess that was just how life went. Our group had morphed slightly; children had come along for some, and although we were all still in contact, my closest socialising friends were now Oliver and Robyn, so I was really excited about catching up with Nicholas and Nathan.

Although I was looking forward to seeing my old friends, the main purpose of tonight was stage two in Sasha and David's 'Get Natalia Better' plan. Poor Natalia had really struggled with her confidence after she was attacked at the Club a couple of months ago, but after the success of their girly cocktail night last week Sasha had decided to build on Natalia's blossoming confidence with a surprise gathering at Club Twist. David and Natalia were both working tonight, but David had secretly arranged for them to finish their shifts early so they'd be able to join us from nine o'clock.

Using my palm, I tried again to calm my crazy hair. I had my father to thank for this haystack on my head, but whereas he chose to shave his head nowadays to avoid the Gordon Ramsay jokes, I wasn't quite ready to say goodbye to my locks just yet. As if taunting me, another clump of hair bounced back up at a quirky angle and I let out a sigh of defeat.

Sasha had once described my hair as 'Wild' and said it looked like I'd just been 'thoroughly well fucked', a look she apparently loved. Admitting defeat, I turned from the mirror with a roll of my eyes. Just as well she liked it because there was no taming it tonight.

Leaving the bathroom, I flicked the light off and went in search of my girl. I didn't have to look far. Following the sexy scent of her perfume down the corridor, I came to the lounge and then drew abruptly to a halt as the air caught in my lungs. Wow. Sasha always looked amazing, but tonight she looked drop-dead gorgeous.

My eyes clocked the black high heels she was wearing and then travelled up her toned legs to the red dress that was such a perfect fit it outlined every one of her curves. It skimmed her legs at mid-thigh and dropped just low enough at the cleavage to highlight what was there.

'You look gorgeous, babe.' My voice was husky, and as my eyes trailed across her again, I felt my pulse kick-start and predictably my groin joined in the appreciation by beginning to thicken in my trousers.

'You don't look so bad yourself,' Sasha purred as she returned the favour and ran her eyes over my attire of boots, smart jeans and a black shirt.

Approaching her, I grinned as she clocked the obvious bulge in my jeans and then widened her eyes as if shocked. 'That's your fault, woman,' I chided playfully as I reached her side and leant down to place a soft kiss on her lips.

'Little ol' me? What did I do?' I really liked the teasing side to our relationship. Things were just so comfortable with Sasha and I loved that.

'You don't need to do anything really. I get turned on just being in the same room as you.' It was true as well. The chemistry between us was so potent that it honestly felt like I spent ninety per cent of my time with Sasha supporting either a semi, or a full erection. Shaking my head, I gave an amused chuckle. This woman really could affect me so easily.

Sasha reached out and gently trailed a finger down the buttons on the front of my shirt. She was still being so careful when she touched me, which I really appreciated, but thankfully, so far, I seemed to be settling to her touch far better than I'd expected. The awful flashbacks of Celia were lessening by the day, and instead of making me tense with paranoia, her touch now made me tense with aroused anticipation.

195

Sasha smoothed the collar of my shirt for me and then smiled. I knew she liked this shirt, which was one of the reasons I'd chosen it, but it was also really comfortable and the perfect thickness so I wouldn't need a jacket.

Making eye contact with me, Sasha wiggled her eyebrows and then lowered a hand to gently cup my erection. A groan rumbled up from my chest and she laughed before wiggling her eyebrows at me. She gave my throbbing groin another squeeze. 'We were very quick getting ready. I think we might have a few minutes before we need to leave, maybe I could help ease this for you.'

Keeping her gaze locked with mine, she slowly undid the zip of my trousers and before I'd even registered what was happening, she had my cock free and in her palm. It jerked upwards as her warm skin enveloped it and I sucked in a deep breath through my nose as she squeezed harder.

'Sasha!' I was so aroused that I could feel it burning through my veins like liquid magma. Before my very eyes Sasha dropped to her knees and gazed up at me with those big beautiful eyes of hers before glancing at my cock and then leaning in to swipe a soft lick across the tip. Jesus. It felt so good that it nearly made me go cross-eyed.

'I think I'd like to practise this a little more. You know what they say, practice makes perfect.' She winked at me and then my body jerked harshly because Sasha set about reacquainting herself with my cock in a very thorough way by running her tongue around the top and lapping at me as if I was the best thing she'd ever tasted.

Since the first night Sasha had given me a blow job and confessed that it was her first ever time, we'd done it several times.

She seemed to love giving me head, and I definitely wasn't going to complain because holy fuck, she was so good at it. I guess we were evenly matched there, because I loved going down on her too. Her taste was incredible, and she was so sensitive to my touch that I always wanted to bury my face between her legs and never leave.

Sasha started to work me with more intent, sucking me back into her hot mouth and hollowing out her cheeks as she worked her tongue up and down my shaft. Her hands joined in, one gripping the base of my cock and working in time with the movement of her lips, and the other dipping between my legs to cup and fondle my balls.

'God, Sasha.' With my cock still in her mouth she looked up at me, her eyes were sparkling with pleasure and her cheeks were flushed.

This felt so good that I wanted it to last for ever; but on the flip side, I was also craving the incredible feeling that I knew would come with my climax. She shifted one hand and began to explore, giving a tentative rub to the soft skin slightly further back behind my balls. As her touch skated across my perineum a burst of intense pleasure shot through me and one of my hands slid into her hair and gripped her head to try and steady myself.

Briefly letting my cock slip from her mouth, Sasha looked up at me with uncertainty. 'You like it when I touch there?' It was so unusual to see my confident girl questioning herself, but this new side to her was also undeniably sweet.

'Yes. It feels incredible.' My words were rough and tight as I tried to maintain my control, but Sasha heard them, and with a smile she immediately sucked me straight back into her mouth.

As her mouth and one hand worked my shaft, the fingers of the other hand slipped further back and began to massage behind my balls again. Holy crap. The triple sensations of her hot mouth, tight fist and massaging fingers was fast driving me towards orgasm. As I felt my balls rising and my cock thickening, I knew I wasn't going to last much longer and my hands tangled in her hair desperately as I tried not to fall over.

Sasha moaned, sensing my imminent release, and moved her efforts into top gear. Her fist was so tight but so slick that it felt like perfection as it slid up and down my length in time with her mouth. From my position above her I could see her cheeks hollowing from the effort she was putting in and finally I had to lean sideways and steady myself on the back of a nearby armchair.

She twirled her tongue around my tip again, pulling her lips up my shaft one last time and adding in a slight drag of her teeth that finally did me in. With a husky moan I exploded into her mouth as my orgasm crashed over me in a series of red-hot waves that made my knees buckle. My climax didn't make Sasha relent, in fact she sucked me into her mouth even harder, lapping up and swallowing everything I had to give, and not stopping until my legs were weak from the power of my climax and I was sagging sideways onto the back of the armchair.

Using my hands in her hair I gently guided her backwards away from me and then fell to my knees with a moan. I kissed her reddened lips with all my might. I could taste myself on her tongue, salty and musky, and I groaned at the power of what we had just experienced. Slipping my arms around her I gathered my girl into my arms and the held her as I tried to get my breath back.

Christ. That had been even better than last time. Basically perfect. A grin spread on my face – perhaps Sasha had been right; practice really did make perfect.

We sat entwined like that for several minutes, and then just as I was getting enough energy back to turn my attention to making Sasha come, she stood up an held out a hand for me. 'Come on, stud, let's get going before we miss our evening out.'

Looking up at her with a frown I shook my head. 'You haven't come yet.'

Sasha grinned down at me. 'We haven't got time for that now.' A curious look crossed her features, and then she bit down on her lower lip, drawing my attention to the area and prompting me to recall exactly what pleasure she'd given me with that mouth just moments earlier.

'But . . . if the opportunity arises at some point in the near future, I've been thinking I'd like to re-enact the encounter we had in that club in Barcelona . . .'

Her words brought me up short and instantly reignited my lust as my mind cast back to our trip to Spain and the very heated encounter we had shared in a dark corner of a nightclub there. It was before we'd been together, back when both of us had felt the intense connection between us, but had both been too stubborn to admit it. We'd had sex, and it had been intense, erotic, and insanely hot.

'Although we can skip the argument afterwards,' Sasha added with a smirk.

I laughed out loud as I remembered what she was referring to – after the incredible sex in the darkened corner of the club we had then argued and both gone our separate ways in a huff.

Pushing to my feet, I tucked my cock back inside my trousers and then pulled Sasha into my arms. 'I'm sure we can arrange that.' My promise hung in the air between us, and as I took her hand and led my girl towards the front door I tamped down my arousal, hoping that maybe, if the chance arose, I could make her fantasy a reality later this evening.

Chapter Twenty-Three

Sasha

I looked around our gathered group and grinned with happiness. Nicholas, Rebecca, Nathan, Stella, Oliver, Robyn and of course Marcus and myself. Just like old times. All we needed now was for David and Natalia to finish work and join us, and then we'd be complete. Some friendships were just so right that it didn't matter if you had some time apart because when you did get back together it was just like you'd never been separated, and that was what this group was like. It felt like I'd seen them all yesterday. To be honest, seeing as my parents had passed away and my brother lived at the other end of the country, these guys were probably more like family to me than my actual remaining blood relatives.

Placing my glass down, I made my way to the ladies' room to freshen up. After a quick trip to the loo and a reapplication of my make-up I re-entered the familiar surroundings of the Club. Skirting the edge of one of the performance stages, I glanced up at the sex show currently in progress and smiled as I recalled how shocked I'd been when I'd first come here. Shocked, but also excited. I'd always had a bit of a wild side, so I guess somewhere like this was perfect for me.

I made my way past the watcher holes; the cosy, candlelit alcoves that edged one wall of the Club. They were private, great for a sharing a drink, and also had a fantastic view of the second stage.

Just as I was nearing the end of the watcher alcoves, I spotted Marcus across the bar, staring my way. The intensity in his gaze was enough to stop me in my tracks. Wow. We still had insane chemistry, but I hadn't seen him looking that focused on me for quite a while.

With my feet seemingly stuck in concrete Marcus began to walk my way. His eyes remained glued to mine, but even without tearing my gaze from his I could see that he wasn't walking, he was *stalking*. My man appeared to be on a mission and that realisation made my pulse jump and skin heat.

With thoughts of our earlier conversation in my mind I started to wonder if Marcus was planning on following through on my earlier request. Was he going to help me relive our heated nightclub encounter? My feet still refused to move, but the thought of another public encounter with him made the hairs on the back of my neck stand up with excitement.

Marcus reached me and dragged his gaze up my body with such force that I practically felt it trail across my skin. Last time we'd had sex at Fantasia, the club in Spain, it had been me that had initiated things; I'd leapt up unto his arms and kissed him, but seeing the look on his face I had a feeling that tonight things were going to be just a little different.

Instead of me starting things, or saying anything, Marcus reached down and took hold of my wrist before pulling me firmly sideways, so we ended up in one of the vacant watcher holes. No sooner had my feet stopped than he had me pressed against the wall and his mouth crashed down onto mine. Hips pressed together, hands explored, tongues twined, and within seconds of his kiss starting my skin felt like it was on fire with desire for this man.

The last time we'd had the encounter like this Marcus hadn't liked my touch on his skin and he'd pinned my hands above my head, refusing to let me touch him throughout the entire episode. I remember thinking that perhaps it was like a scene to him, with his rule being one of no touching, but obviously as things later developed between us I'd discovered that his dislike of contact was traced back, to far deeper issues.

As if reading my mind, Marcus leant back and winked at me before removing my hands from his body and pinning them above my head in one of his warm palms. 'You wanted it just like last time, yeah?' he questioned hotly as his free hand skimmed across my body and then came up to gently grip my throat.

I grinned, loving how this game was playing out, and then nodded at him. It had been frustrating as hell not being able to touch him, but it had also been a wild turn on letting him control me, and so I nodded keenly.

Just like last time, the hold on my throat was arousing me beyond my understanding. His grip was firm, but not hard enough to affect my breathing and the dominant position was making my underwear wet.

He continued to hold my hands above my head as his mouth found mine again, and then his other hand was moving, tracing my jaw, neck and collarbone before cupping my breast and squeezing. My body reacted to his touch as it always did, with my nipples hardening and goose pimples rushing across my skin. He fingered one nub, rolling it through the cotton of my dress and causing a moan to rise in my throat.

Marcus let out a throaty laugh and then with a cheeky wink he leant back and licked his fingers. From the promising look on his face I'd been fully expecting those moistened fingers to find their way between my legs, but to my amusement, he reached behind himself to snub out the one candle that had illuminated our little alcove. I laughed out loud at the surprise move, and Marcus joined me, clearly enjoying his tease.

We were now alone in our little public space, cocooned away from the world in the darkness, so that we felt perfectly private. The beat of the music still throbbed around us and passers-by moved past the alcove, unaware that we were there and wrapped in each other arms.

Now the candle was extinguished, Marcus went back to his exploration of my body, reaching up and popping one of my breasts free from my dress, massaging the sensitive skin before lowering his head and sucking it into his mouth. My back arched as both my nipples competed for his attention, feeling impossibly tight and aching for his touch. I writhed under his contact and gave a tug at my wrists. 'I want to touch you.'

This exact scenario had happened in Fantasia, but back then I hadn't been allowed to touch him. I wondered how far Marcus would go with his recreation of that night, and I didn't have long to find out. The hand that held mine above my head tightened as he shifted his head and stared into my eyes. 'No.'

Hmm. He seemed to be going for an exact replica of that night, and was really was holding me to my word, wasn't he?

Leaning forwards, I kissed his jaw and trailed my tongue up towards his ear, wondering if I could persuade him. 'Please, baby . . .'

He pressed his body against mine, trapping me firmly against the wall with just enough force to stop me speaking. '*No.*' He shook his head slowly. 'You wanted to recreate that night, and that's what we're doing.'

From the wicked glint in his eyes Marcus knew exactly what he was doing to me. He knew that I always wanted to touch him with such desperation that it burnt in my system like an obsession, but he also knew that I bloody loved it when he took control and denied me. Perhaps it was because I was so independent and in control in my everyday life that giving control over to him on occasions like this always felt illicit and turned me on like crazy.

Once I nodded my compliance like a good girl his fingers continued their teasing, and our mouths joined in another frantic kiss. He tasted so good that I just couldn't seem to get enough, and we were both breathless in seconds.

Shifting his body so we had some space between us Marcus ran a hand down my body and began to lift my dress up my thigh with soft, sensuous slides of his hand. Hooking his fingers under the thin silk he pressed inside my knickers and then toyed his fingers across my damp skin before circling my moisture around my clit.

'Holy fuck, Sasha, you are so wet.' Marcus's words were hissed between clenched teeth as he seemed to be struggling to maintain his control.

He wasn't the only one losing control though, because all I managed in response was a groan. As his fingers continued to work me, words became beyond my ability and I was lost in a thousand pleasurable sensations.

The rough scrape of his zipper lowering brought me back to the moment and I bit on my lower lip as I watched him pull his cock out in the dim lighting. It might be dark around us, but it was clear to see that he was just as aroused as I was.

In Fantasia he'd asked my permission before taking me, but Marcus didn't do that tonight. We were both so comfortable together now that it simply wasn't needed. Instead, he stared deep into my eyes as he shifted my knickers to the side and altered his position so the tip of his cock nudged at my entrance.

Placing a brief kiss on my lips, Marcus thrust his hips forwards, impaling me in one hard thrust that banged me back into the wall with its depth and made me cry out. Just that first thrust sent such a powerful wave of pleasure rushing though my body and I knew that it wouldn't be long until I climaxed.

He called out my name in a rough, husky groan so I muffled the noise with a kiss, forcing my tongue into his mouth and sharing the overwhelming sensations with him as his hips started to work back and forth, making me grind against each and every one.

Marcus followed on from his commanding start, leading the pace and leaving me to try my best to keep up. The eroticism of being in public and having sex seemed to have us both ramped up, and I knew that neither of us was going to last long. My climax was already building in the pit of my stomach, and from the jerkiness of his hips I knew Marcus was close too.

As Marcus continued to move within me in deep, hard thrusts I suddenly burst into an orgasm, silencing my cries of pleasure by burying my face in his shoulder and drawing out my orgasm by tightening my leg around his waist and grinding myself against him.

Marcus growled beside my ear, and then I felt his cock expand and hips flinch as he began to come too. A strained rumble rose from his chest and he clung to me as he ground out the remains of his climax and panted hard into my neck.

We stayed joined like that for several moments as we got our breath back, and then Marcus let go of my wrists and gently slid from inside me. With a grin he reached into his pocket and pulled out a tissue that he handed to me with a wink.

'Very prepared of you,' I remarked with a matching grin as I cleaned myself up. 'Anyone would have thought you'd been planning this.'

He shrugged, feigning nonchalance. 'What can I say? I like to keep my girl happy.'

Feeling unusually romantic, I smiled soppily and snuggled into his neck. 'You certainly do that,' I confessed quietly. God, listen to me! I really had fallen for this man hook, line and sinker if I was spouting sentimental crap like that!

'I'm glad.' His arms tightened around me and then he placed a kiss on the top of my head. 'We should get back to the guys, otherwise it's going to be really obvious what we've been up to.'

My skin felt flushed and my hair was probably a right mess now so I suspected it would be pretty bloody obvious anyway, but I nodded my agreement and straightened my clothes as best as I could before heading back to enjoy the rest of our night.

Chapter Twenty-Four

Marcus

I could hardly keep the smug grin off my face as I smoothed down my clothes and made my way back towards our group of gathered friends. Talk about a good night; blow job before coming out, seeing all my old friends again for a great catch-up, *and* illicit sex in the Club! It was certainly on the list of memorable moments since I'd got together with Sasha.

'I'll get another round in. Same again for everyone?' My announcement was met with nods and so I turned towards the bar and signalled David over. Glancing at my watch I saw that it wouldn't be long until he and Natalia could finish working.

'Same again, bud?' he asked, already knowing the answer and starting to pour me a pint of larger.

'Please, mate.' I sipped my beer as he sorted the rest of our drinks. 'You guys ready to come and join us?'

'Yes, nearly. Natalia's been delayed at the cash and carry, but when she gets back, I'll hand over to Lee so that we can come and join you. Should be about twenty minutes, tops.'

His words made a great night even better – now our old group would be complete. 'Excellent!'

David winked at me and then turned to another customer, so I made a few trips to deliver our drinks and then gave them the good news. 'As soon as Natalia gets back from some errands she and David will join us.'

Even Nathan smiled, which made me laugh, because as much as he liked David as a friend, Nathan had always struggled with David's slightly over the top touchy-feely nature. David was a hugger. Considering he was a big, muscly, gruff-looking guy he was the biggest softy underneath it all. Nathan didn't understand it, or particularly like it. He was also steely and tough on the outside, and while he wasn't soft with any of us, I knew from first-hand experience that when he was with Stella and their son William he was a very different guy. He was still one of the strictest Doms I'd ever met, and would certainly never get called a soft touch, but he had definitely mellowed since being with Stella.

Our increased ages weren't the only thing that had changed since the last time we'd all been out together. Our conversations had matured too – instead of discussions about sex shows or the latest new club to open in London, I grinned to myself as Nicolas regaled us with a story of what their twins Ben and Holly had been up to in the last week. He was such a proud dad that it literally seemed to shine from him in waves.

We might have moved on a little in our lives but looking around our gathered group I was filled with happiness. It was so bloody good to have all of us back together again.

Chapter Twenty-Five

Sasha

I was loving this catch up with everyone. We'd been saying we'd do it for months, but I guess life had got in the way. Trying to help Natalia get back out socialising had given us all the perfect prompt to make the effort, and with the amount of fun we were having I was definitely going to pester them all to make it at least a once-a-month occurrence.

'We need to make sure we do this way more often! Next time I think we should . . .' I was midway through my sentence when a noise like a clap of thunder suddenly echoed through the room. I say a clap of thunder, but this was so close and so loud that I screamed and raised my hands to my ears in an attempt at protecting them. The room then juddered with such force that I staggered sideways and felt my insides reverberate from the shock of whatever had caused the loud noise.

What the fuck was happening?

From that point on it seemed like time clicked into slow motion. I felt like I was on the edge of a film production set watching as they created their newest action masterpiece and it was very clear that I wasn't the only one staggering. Stella fell sideways into Nathan, and Nicholas managed to dramatically fling the entire contents of his glass of red wine over everyone as he struggled to stay on his feet.

My friends started to get lost to me then, as a plume of dust exploded into the Club from somewhere, mushrooming out like some crazy optical illusion and causing panic in the dancers now enveloped in it. Parts of the ceiling started to fall like huge, deadly raindrops crashing around us and causing screams of panic to fill the air. The noise of them hitting the floor added to the other loud noises which continued, crashing and pounding their way around me, but they were now accompanied by a cacophony of terrified voices. The screams and shouts were immediately recognisable as those of people experiencing such utter terror and pain that my entire body reeled from the reaction to their obvious fear and exploded with goose pimples.

Chaos ensued. Utter chaos. People started to run and push and shove. I was being tugged sideways and shoved forwards so rapidly that my feet were barely touching the floor anymore. I don't know if the crowd was heading for the exits, or just running in blind panic, because I was now so disorientated by the bedlam around me that I didn't even know where the exits were anymore.

'Sasha!' I heard Marcus scream my name close beside me, and then felt relief wrap itself around me as he gripped onto my arm. We might be in the middle of something inexplicable, but at least we were together. I could just about make out his face through the smoke and dust and saw my own confusion and panic reflected right back at me in his expression.

The lights flickered as they began to fail, and then there seemed to be a second surge of hands and bodies pressing into

211

me, pushing me backwards, away from my friends, and away from Marcus. His grip tightened on my arm, but as the crowd increased their jostling, I felt it start to slip down my arm towards my wrist as we were pulled further apart.

'Marcus!' My voice sounded nothing like the strong, confident woman that I usually was, instead coming out in a high twisted lurch of pure fear. I couldn't lose him! I had no idea what was happening, but I knew with bone deep certainty that I had to hold onto him.

In their attempt to escape, someone slammed into my shoulder, knocking me backwards another step and Marcus's palm slid again, down over my wrist until our fingers joined. I squeezed his hand with all my might, but with people barging us from all sides it was only a few seconds until I felt the last tiny connection with him slip away as our hands parted and terror engulfed me.

'Marcus!' I called out again, but only half my word came out because something heavy hit me in the centre of my back with enough force to knock me to my knees. Stabbing pains erupted in my knees, which felt like I was kneeling on glass, and feet moved past me in all directions. My brain began to register the fact that I might well be trampled to death, and even though the thought terrified me, the heavy weight on my back meant I couldn't stop myself reeling forwards towards the floor.

There was a loud rumbling followed by thumps and creaks and then more dust filled the air like a suffocating cloud. Screams echoed in my ears, feet trampled over me and as searing pain began to shoot through my body everything went black.

Chapter Twenty-Six

Marcus

Something was so tight around my neck that I couldn't breathe, and my hands instantly raised and started to claw at my neck to try and free my windpipe.

Couldn't . . . breathe.

I needed air.

Choking.

Shit! I was choking!

As well as choking, my confused brain also registered that I was moving. My body was on the floor, but I was being dragged backwards over bumpy, sharp ground. What the fuck was happening? My head hurt from trying to think, and then as something gouged into my back I tried to shout, but a garbled noise escaped my throat instead and came out like a strangled wheeze.

'Woah! This one's alive!'

My ears were ringing and the yell above me made me wince. Who was that speaking? And what the hell were they talking about?

Suddenly my body came to an abrupt halt and my shoulders

213

and head were lowered towards the ground until I was laid out flat on my back. The tightness around my neck instantly eased and I sucked in a grateful lungful of air as my hands came up and rubbed at my sore neck. Trying to make sense of what was occurring, I opened my eyes and looked around me. My vision was blurry, and my eyes felt full of grit, but I could make out the sky above me. It was inky black and scattered with stars, indicating that it was night, but beside me I could see bright lights flashing and moving erratically. Rolling my head to the side I saw what looked like a rocky crag, with several men carrying torches picking their way across the edge.

Where was I?

A face suddenly appeared above me and I blinked as I tried to focus on it.

'Are you all right, mate?' It was a man, but I didn't know him. 'Can you hear me?' I could hear him, but I still didn't recognise him. The man speaking was older, maybe mid-fifties, and wearing a luminous jacket that was making my eyes hurt.

'Y . . . yes.' My voice was weak and dry, but when I tried to swallow to moisten my throat all I could feel was grit in my mouth. 'Where am I?'

'London, mate. There's been an explosion in a nightclub. I just pulled you out. Sorry about your neck, I couldn't get a decent grip so I was dragging you by your shirt, must have tightened on your throat.'

I could hear his words, but they were making no sense to me. An explosion? A second person appeared by my side, this time a woman, wearing a green jacket and white bump hat that had green stripes around it. 'Hello there, I'm a paramedic with the

214

London Ambulance Service. I'm just going to check your pulse rate. Have you got any pain anywhere?'

Paramedic? Check my pulse? I was so confused. Was I in hospital? 'My head hurts.'

As she picked up my hand and started to attach something to one of my fingers, I had a vague sense of recollection, but it faded before I could fully recall it. My brain scrabbled to catch what I was being reminded of, but my thoughts were foggy, and it seemed just out of reach.

Just out of reach . . . My mind was desperately prodding me, yelling at me that there was something important that I needed to remember.

Just out of reach. What had I been trying to get? Like a sudden blinding light, my mind cleared and I remembered everything. The Club. The explosion. *Sasha*. Sasha had been just out of reach. We'd been drinking in the Club, then the loud noise had happened and then all hell had broken loose. I'd been holding her hand, gripping on with all my might and then she'd slipped away from me. Pulled from my hand by the surging crowds just seconds before the ceiling had fallen in above her.

'No!' I sat up so suddenly that I banged my head straight into the paramedic leaning over me. Both of us let out a grunt of surprise, but then I refocused and desperately looked around me.

Chaos. All I could see was chaos. Rubble piles, smoke, flames and emergency services were all around me. I couldn't see the Club, I couldn't even see a building anymore, just wreckage. Fuck! Panic and confusion flooded my system so ferociously that I instantly wanted to vomit. 'Sasha! Where's Sasha?'

'Sir, please lie down while we assess you.' The people surrounding me made an attempt at pushing me back down, but there was no way I was going to sit here doing nothing. Ripping the sensor from my finger I tossed it aside and pushed to my feet before staggering sideways.

'I'm fine. Treat someone else, I need to find my girl.'

Chapter Twenty-Seven

David

I felt like I was drowning in a horrific, never-ending night-mare that I just couldn't wake up from.

My heart was pounding painfully in my chest, my hands clenching at my sides and my eyes moving wildly over the scene of chaos before me. Rubble piles, torn metal pillars, sparking wires, flames licking up to the sky, smoke, dust ... it was too much to take in. My hands rose to clutch at my scalp as an almost animalistic wail ripped its way from my chest. My Club. Club Twist ... my life's work was now a pile of stone and flames.

The only godsend in amongst this shit fest of a night was that Natalia hadn't been in the Club when the explosion had happened. With the secret gathering of all our friends having been arranged I nearly hadn't sent her to the cash and carry, but looking at the pile of destruction before me I was so bloody glad that I had.

There were people wandering around looking dazed, customers that I recognised and knew well, but so far I hadn't been able to spot any of my friends. Were they out here somewhere? Had they survived? Or were they trapped? My desperate thoughts were interrupted as a police officer in a high visibility jacket pushed me to the side and ran in front of me towards the Club. 'Sir! Sir! Get down from there! It's not safe! You need to move back!'

Frowning, I watched as he ran to the side of the collapsed building and began waving his arms. Scanning my eyes across the rubble to see what he was waving at, my eyes widened as I settled on a figure crawling across the stone and cables and attempting to dig through the wreckage. The person was covered in dust, dirt and smears of blood, but the mop of wild blond hair was unmissable – *Marcus*. Fuck! It was Marcus, several metres in, and several metres up the devastation, and clawing at a wooden beam as he attempted to move it. He was a good guy through and through and over the years he'd always been the one to have my back or help, so presumably he must be trying to assist people trapped in the rubble.

I ran forwards until I got to a police officer standing by the red and white tape that the fire brigade had set up as a cordon. Upon seeing my approach, he turned to me, squared his shoulders and raised a hand to halt my progress. I ground to a stop and immediately pointed to Marcus. 'That's my best mate, he'll listen to me, can I go in and get him down?' The police officer seemed to be weighing up my statement and then radioed someone before nodding and lifting the paper barrier.

I approached the police officer at the base of the rubble who was attempting to coax Marcus down with no success, and saw the look of frustration on his face. 'Ben says you know this fella. Can you get him to come down? There are people trapped and he's shifting the rubble. It could cause more collapses. He needs to leave it to the experts.'

Following his line of sight, I saw a team of emergency service workers to our left who were hastily dressing in harnesses and hard hats in preparation for a search.

Looking back to Marcus I watched as he chucked another handful of bricks to the side and then heard him call out Sasha's name. My stomach plunged as sickening clarity tore through me. *Sasha*. He wasn't just being a good guy and helping others, he was searching for his girl.

Fuck. She must be missing in this shit storm. My eyes widened at the thought and I took a sharp breath. Getting him down might be a little trickier than I'd first thought then, because if I knew one thing, it was how much Marcus loved Sasha – he would literally do anything for her, including putting his own life on the line.

Grimacing at the police officer, I nodded. 'He's a stubborn bastard, but I'll do my best.'

I stepped closer, as close as I could without disturbing anything, and then called out to Marcus.

'Marcus! Stop!' I saw him acknowledge my call with a brief flick of his eyes in my direction, but then he ignored me, pretending he hadn't heard as he carried on with his frantic search.

Fuck.

The police officer tapped me on the shoulder. 'You can go a bit closer. That path there has already been checked.' Following his suggested route, I began to pick my way closer to Marcus until I was only a metre or so away. He was filthy, and his face was a mask of sweat, blood and determination.

'Marcus.' Again, he ignored me and carried on shifting rocks. 'Marcus. Mate. Stop.'

I attempted to reach out for him, but before my fingers had

even made contact with his shoulder Marcus turned to me with a snarl and batted my hand away. 'No. It's Sasha. She's missing. I need to find her.'

My chest tightened at the pain in his voice, and I nodded grimly. 'I know, and I know you want to help but if she's under here you're putting her more at risk by haphazardly shifting stuff.' He paused at my words and as his eyes darted around. I thought perhaps I was getting through. 'I know it's utterly shit, mate, but you need to leave it to the experts.' Finally, Marcus paused in his digging and looked up at me.

'I was holding her hand . . .' His words were almost unintelligible from the roughness in his voice. 'I couldn't keep the grip. Everyone was pushing. I let her go . . .' Marcus turned his head then and stared down at me with a face tight with tension. 'I let her go, David. I let her down.' When I saw his red-rimmed eyes my heart just about broke for him, but finally, much to my relief, he gave a slow nod.

I held out a hand to assist him. 'Come on, mate, let's get down.'

Chapter Twenty-Eight

Marcus

My fingers ached from digging through the rubble, and my body was battered from the injuries I'd sustained in the explosion, but the pain was nothing compared to the crippling terror that was clutching at my heart every time I remembered back to seeing the ceiling of the Club collapse down onto the bar area.

Collapse down onto Sasha.

She'd been beside me when the first explosion occurred and I'd managed to grab on to her for a few moments, but in the panicked rush to escape people had pushed her away from me. If only I had been stronger, held her better, or pulled her into my arms so I could have protected her.

I paused and squeezed my eyes shut to try and push the horrific images from my mind, but then let out a determined grunt and kept on working. If Sasha was under here, I was bloody well going to find her.

'Marcus.' David had appeared at the bottom of the rubble a minute or so ago and had been trying to get my attention, but I kept my head down, hoping he'd fuck off and leave me so I could focus on my search for Sasha. Bending lower, I hauled at a wooden post, but it wasn't shifting. The back of my head throbbed like a bastard, but I shook it off and gritted my teeth.

From the corner of my eye, I saw David moving closer to me and sighed. He wasn't bloody giving up, was he?

'Marcus. Mate. Stop.' No chance. I didn't even acknowledge his words. I wasn't stopping. Not until I had Sasha out, safe and in my arms. I couldn't even consider any other options at the moment. She had to be OK. My throat started to tighten in terror. *She just had to be.*

My peripheral vision caught a flash of movement as David reached out for me and I instinctively bashed his arm away with a growl. He might be one of my best mates, but no one was stopping me looking for my girl. Suddenly it occurred to me ... maybe he didn't realise she was missing? 'No. It's Sasha. She's missing. I need to find her.'

'I know, and I know you want to help but if she's under here you're putting her more at risk by haphazardly shifting stuff.' His words made me pause. Fuck! What if he was right? If Sasha, and god knows how many other people, were trapped under here I could be doing more harm than good. My eyes flicked towards the emergency crews kitting themselves up ready to start their work and I winced. I couldn't bear the idea of stopping my search, but the last thing I wanted was to make it worse.

'I know it's utterly shit, mate, but you need to leave it to the experts.' His words were filled with regret, but deep down I knew he was right. I dropped my head as my body fought with my brain over what to do.

'I was holding her hand ...' My words were garbled, and overcome with emotion as I recalled Sasha's soft hand slipping from my grip and becoming lost in the chaos. 'I couldn't keep the grip. Everyone was pushing. I let her go . . .' I stared across at David, willing my tears not to fall. 'I let her go, David. I let her down.'

Knowing there was nothing else I could do here, I finally gave a reluctant nod and then looked up at him. David's posture was just as stiff as mine, and his face was covered in dirt and dust and looked just as stressed as mine felt.

Drawing in a long breath, I carefully stood up.

'Come on, mate, let's get down.' He held out a hand to help me.

'I'll come down, but we're not leaving the area,' I clarified firmly as we began to pick our way down through the rubble.

Chapter Twenty-Nine

Sasha

Dust filled my nostrils, scratchy and dry and choking me as my lungs protested at the filthy air. I tried to cough to clear it, but only managed to draw in more grit. The inability to breathe brought instant clarity to my mind, my consciousness leaping up on me as panic and self-preservation filled me and caused my eyes to fly open.

Black.

Everything was black.

I was also lying down for some reason, because even though I couldn't see anything, I could feel a cool hard surface below my body. Blinking again to try and clear my vision, I dragged in a panicked breath only to remember that I *couldn't* breathe.

Fuck this shit! I couldn't see *and* I couldn't breathe?

What. The. Fuck?

My mind raced to try and process what was going on, but then survival instinct kicked in and I pushed my thoughts aside as breathing became the highest priority. Grabbing hold of the front of my dress I pulled it up over my nose and mouth before taking another breath. The hot dust-filled air still coated my mouth in a dry, powdery sensation, but the makeshift filter worked, and at last I was able to get some air to my straining lungs. Jesus, this was fucking surreal.

Now that the initial stress of breathing was temporarily fixed, I squeezed my eyes together and then opened them again in the hopes that my blindness would have passed. I huffed when again I saw nothing, but then, after opening them as wide as I could, I saw what looked like small stars dancing in the distance. This tiny glimmer of hope had me straining all my senses, and as well as the flickers of light, I realised I could hear some muffled noises too.

Tuning in to them, I could make out creaking noises and what sounded like moaning. *Terrified* moaning. Frowning, I tried to shift myself in the direction of the sound, but it was at that point that I noticed the pain in my body and I found myself letting out a wounded gasp of my own.

My leg felt like it was on fire, but no matter how hard I tried, I couldn't move it. The adrenaline and stress coursing through my system must have initially masked it, because fuck me, my left leg was killing me.

Wracking my brain, I thought back over the evening ... the last thing I could remember was ordering some drinks at the bar. The bar. Club Twist ... oh my god! I'd been out for drinks with Marcus! Where was he? Was he hurt too? We'd been standing separately because he'd been getting a round of drinks in, but he'd grabbed my hand as the chaos started so we hadn't been far apart. Our table had been nearer to the entrance, so perhaps he was OK?

'Marcus?' My voice was scratchy and faint, but even when I tried again there was no response.

Desperation flooded me. How had a lovely night out turned into this? What the hell had happened?

Suddenly I had an idea and I reached down in the darkness to see if my handbag was still with me. As my hand came into contact with the soft leather I let out a huge sob of relief – thank god for the shoulder strap! My fingers were trembling, but I began to fiddle with the catch and after what seemed like hours, I managed to open it and retrieve my phone. Praying that it hadn't been broken in whatever had happened to me, I pressed the side button and sagged with joy as the screen lit up with its familiar pale glow. The screen was badly cracked, but I pressed a trembling finger to the torch icon and gasped as the space around me was illuminated.

Instead of seeing the familiar expanse of Club Twist as I'd expected, I seemed to be in a tiny space and was suddenly overwhelmed with a sickening sense of claustrophobia. All I could see was what looked like the rough stone walls of a cave interior, with jagged edges and dark crevices all around me.

Trying not to focus on the confusion of my surroundings I immediately shone the light to my leg and yelped in terror as I saw it trapped below a huge piece of what looked like rock. Blood was soaking my dress and my stomach flipped as I saw crimson pooling on the floor below it as well. Jesus, it looked like a bad wound. My heart was hammering with fear now, which was no doubt just helping my blood loss.

Bringing up my contacts I immediately searched for Marcus's number and pressed call. Silence. There was no ring tone, no nothing, so I pulled the phone away from my ear only to see that I had no signal.

'Fucking fuck!' In my frustration I very nearly threw the bloody useless thing away from me, but common sense prevailed, and I kept a hold of it.

Swallowing hard I tried to control the sickening pain in my leg and used the torch to look around me again. It was like a scene out of a disaster movie. My tiny space was made up of rubble piles, and the air was thick with dust. It felt hot too, way too hot, and my skin was clammy, but perhaps that was just because I was in a small space, or maybe a reaction to my injury?

The loud bang I'd heard when I'd been standing at the bar ... what had it been? A building collapse? I couldn't imagine Club Twist just crumbling of its own accord though, so presumably it had been some sort of explosion.

An explosion. That just seemed crazy. As I continued to look around me, I realised that there was one familiar thing here – beneath the dust and débris below me I could make out the glittery purple marble flooring that surrounded the bar area of Club Twist.

Keeping my jumper pressed over my nose and mouth to filter the air I looked around me again and began to wonder what the hell I should do.

God, my leg hurt. Grimacing, I gave in to curiosity and shone the light down again. I instantly wished I hadn't, the blood on the floor had significantly increased and my stomach flipped violently at the sight.

Swallowing down the urge to vomit, I took a shaky breath. Well, this sucked; I was going to die on the floor of Club Twist. I'd often wondered if my lifestyle of going out and clubbing would be bad for me, but I'd never thought it would be harmful to quite this extent. Rolling my eyes at my inappropriately timed sick humour. I frowned and had another attempt at shifting my leg.

A pained hiss slid through my teeth. Nope. I was well and truly trapped. My leg wasn't going anywhere, which obviously

227

meant neither was I. I desperately tried to control my heart rate, but it was thundering in my chest and pounding in my ears so hard that I felt like my brain was going to explode.

I felt dizzy too. My head was spinning like I was drunk, and lights started to flash before my eyes. Voices and noises echoed through my fuzzy mind in a confusing jumble but I couldn't separate one from another. Just as I was starting to lose hope and feel utterly delirious, I realised through my fog of confusion that the voices might not actually be in my mind.

Was that someone calling out?

Blinking hard, I tried to focus my attention away from the pain in my leg and it was then that I heard the faint strains of various names being called again . . . including mine.

I might be feeling groggy, but that *definitely* hadn't been in my head.

My eyes popped open in hope. I could see that the lights I'd thought had been dancing in my vision were probably torch lights flickering through gaps in the rubble. Oh my god! Someone was there! I might actually get out of here alive!

'Yes! I'm here! Help! Help me please!' At first my voice was croaky and dry from the dust and barely more than a whisper, but I called again, and this time my voice was stronger, as if my body knew that this might be my one and only chance of surviving this ordeal. 'HELP ME!'

'Hey! I hear you!' It was a male voice and I had never been so glad to hear another human in my entire life. 'Stay nice and still for me, OK?'

My head was nodding frantically, even though my saviour wouldn't be able to see. 'OK. Please get me out.'

His voice was distant, but confident, and just what I needed at that moment. 'We will get you out. We just need to do it safely, so you'll need to be a little bit patient. My name's Duncan, I'm with the search and rescue team. What's your name?'

'Sasha.' Swallowing hard I tried again. 'Sasha Mortimer. What's happened?'

'Well, Sasha, you've been in an explosion. Are you hurt at all?'

An explosion? That was so far beyond my life experiences that I couldn't even comprehend it at the moment. I grimaced as my attention focused back onto the pain in my leg, and again I found myself nodding. 'Yeah. My leg. It's trapped under some stone. There's ...' Fear wrapped its icy tentacles around my throat as I thought about what I'd just seen, and I had to fight to force it away so I could speak. '... there's quite a lot of blood.'

'OK. Sasha, try not to worry. Stay nice and still for me; we're going to get you out.'

The relief I was feeling was undeniable, but it was still tinged with worry. How exactly were they going to get to me? I seemed to be surrounded by stone, rubble and other débris; it looked like an impossible task. I dug my fingernails into my palms in an attempt at distracting myself from my predicament and found that as a secondary bonus it actually helped to take my mind off the pain in my leg.

Now I just had to do as Duncan had asked and be patient and wait, which unfortunately had never been one of my strong points.

Chapter Thirty

David

I felt utterly useless as I stood on the dust covered street and watched the emergency services doing their best to help the injured and stabilise the remains of the Club. I also felt remarkably lucky, which was a peculiar sensation, given that my life's work had been destroyed — but in terms of my health, I *was* lucky. I had somehow come through it all relatively unscathed. I had a small cut to my left arm and a lungful of dust and that was it. From the injuries around me that I'd seen on other people, I had gotten off very lightly.

I'd deposited Marcus at the medical muster point to get the gash on his head looked at, and finally seen some of our friends too; Oliver and Robyn were both OK, just sporting some minor cuts, and Robyn had a badly sprained ankle. They were heading to hospital to get it x-rayed, but they were alive, and even better, they'd managed to get through to Nicholas on the phone who said that both he and Nathan had made it out with Rebecca and Stella. They were all OK.

It was a big relief, but didn't dull the fact that Sasha was still missing. If she was uninjured she would have walked out and made herself known by now, so the longer the time stretched on, the harder I had to try to convince myself that she was going to be found alive and well.

The emergency services had now evacuated the entire street and as I glanced in both directions all I could see were blue flashing lights as far as the eye could see. Jeez. I'd overheard a conversation earlier, so I knew this had been declared a major incident, but they must have sent every emergency responder in London here tonight.

Running a hand though my hair I shook my head, still in disbelief at what had occurred.

'David!' I vaguely heard my name being called from a distance but with all the noise around me it was hard to tell who was shouting, or where they were. I frowned as I turned and scanned the scene to locate where the voice was coming from. As I turned and stared down the street that led back towards Covent Garden, I saw Natalia pushing though the cordon and running towards me like a prize sprinter.

She dodged the pieces of rubble and people in her way like a skilled mountain goat picking the perfect path through, and then she was upon me, leaping at me with a sob and clambering up my body until she was held in my arms with her legs wrapped firmly around my waist like a baby monkey. Wow. That was quite some reaction. My arms looped around her, and as I registered that she really was OK and here with me I felt my grip tighten protectively around her.

Her hands cupped my face, tracing my temples and cheekbones and then brushing through my hair as if checking for cuts or breaks. 'Thank god you're OK!' She leant forward and kissed me, but instead of our usual passionate kisses this one was

231

desperate and spoke of far deeper feelings. Feelings of protection and bone deep relief that I was all right. Feelings that I perhaps wouldn't have expected this soon into a relationship, but as I considered it, nothing about Natalia and I was as expected. The connection between us had been phenomenal from the start, so given the stressful nature of this evening it was no wonder we were both feeling a little protective.

As she continued to kiss me, I tasted salt on my tongue and pulled back to separate us with a frown. Natalia's face was covered in tear tracks and she quickly raised a hand and wiped at her face to try and hide them from me.

I very rarely cried, but as the magnitude of this evening sunk in, I too felt my throat start to tighten with emotion. Trying to maintain my composure I cradled my girl against me and placed a kiss in her hair. 'It's OK, sweetheart. We're OK.'

Thankfully, I had always paid out of my arse for buildings insurance, so although I was devastated at tonight's events and losses, I knew for certain that I'd rebuild. There was no way that Club Twist was dying tonight, it would rise from the ashes like a phoenix from the flames; bigger, better and stronger than ever.

Lowering Natalia to the floor, I looped an arm around her shoulders as we both stood gazing in shock at the remains of my club. A heavy silence surrounded us for several moments before Natalia placed a hand on my chest and gazed up at me with wide eyes. 'What happened?'

'I have no fucking clue.' A gruff noise rose in my throat as I shrugged, completely at a loss. 'It was just a regular night. One minute the Club was throbbing with music and happy people, and then there was just a huge boom and...' my free hand lifted and gestured towards the chaos before us, '... well, this.'

Before I could speculate any further, we were approached by two police officers. 'Mr Halton, I'm not sure if you remember us, but we attended your club earlier this year when you had the issue with an assault inside the premises.' At his mention of the attack by Richard on Natalia my arm tightened instinctively around my girl and I gritted my teeth as I nodded.

'Any idea of the cause?' I asked. 'Was it a gas explosion?' Even though I couldn't smell gas and hadn't had any issues with my supply recently it was the only logical explanation I could come up with for the completely random blast.

From his expression, the officer appeared to be as clueless as me. 'It's a possibility. Obviously as soon as the search and rescue side of things is complete, we're going to have our forensics teams here to try and work out the cause.' He shifted on his feet and then glanced at Natalia before looking back at me with a frown. 'We just wanted to ask you if you thought there was any possibility that this might have been deliberate?'

His words played through my mind again and I frowned. Was he insinuating that I might have done this? Perhaps an insurance job like you often heard about? I immediately felt my hackles rise and in response my shoulders rolled back unconsciously, making me taller and broader than before. 'Deliberate?' My word was more like a growl and the officer on the left visibly paled and shuffled backwards.

His colleague obviously had more balls because he stood his ground, even if he did look slightly tenser than earlier. 'Yes. When we were here for the attack on Miss Ivanov I recall the suspect involved making a threat towards you and your club. Something along the lines of "You and your club are finished".'

So, he wasn't accusing me then, but my heart started beating

233

faster in my chest as I realised what he *was* implying. 'You think Richard did this?' I asked, my tone steely.

'We don't know anything for sure at this point, sir, but when my colleague remembered the threat I thought I'd ask you if there had been any further contact with him? Any visits from him? Any more threats?'

'No, nothing.' I shook my head as my brain went into overdrive, trying to process the possibility that Richard might have tried to blow me up. Me, Natalia, *and* my Club full of customers. Surely not? Would he even have the skills or know-how to create something as catastrophic as this?

Grimacing, I looked to Natalia. 'Have you seen him at all?'

Natalia's skin had vaguely paled, but she shook her head. 'No, nothing.'

Apparently seeing my frown, the officer reached out and patted my shoulder to break me from my thoughts. 'It's OK, that's fine. We just wanted to check with you, but try not to overthink it. It's highly unlikely that it was linked to him. We have multiple avenues to pursue and it's just one of them.'

Handing me a contact card, the officers nodded and then left us, and I looked down to see Natalia staring up at me with her ashen face. 'My god ... do you think he could have done it? Tried to blow us all up?' she whispered.

I pulled her against my chest. Her arms instantly slid around my waist and clung to me. 'I have no idea, sweetheart.' One thing was clear in my mind though, if Richard had been behind this then so help me god I wouldn't stop until I found him and made him pay.

Chapter Thirty-One

Marcus

I felt like I was going insane waiting for news on Sasha. The scene at the Club wasn't any calmer now than it had been when the explosion had first occurred. There were still emergency services swarming the area, still injured and dazed people wandering around in shock, and still no sign of Sasha.

I'd called her mobile relentlessly, but there had been no answer, and I was now positioned just off to the side of the chaos in an area for walking wounded, waiting for news about the people being pulled from the rubble.

Five times now I'd overheard mentions of women being rescued alive and I'd been in desperate agony to see who it was that the rescuers appeared with from the rubble pile. All five had been carried out of the destruction, all with different degrees of injury, and all five had frustratingly not been Sasha.

I ran a hand through my hair and let out a growl as I watched a man stagger towards a waiting ambulance. I felt so useless and so helpless that it was killing me inside.

My eyes hurt as I strained them to search across the rubble pile for what must have been the millionth time searching for any sign of life, or clue that Sasha might be nearby. God, I was desperate to see her wild blonde hair appearing or hear the filthy swear words she was so fond of using floating through the air. I felt like the evilest man alive, because after each and every rescue I found myself cursing the survivor as I realised that it wasn't Sasha. I was struggling with overwhelming fear for her safety, and also swamped with guilt, because these other people didn't deserve these injuries either. No one deserved to have endured the hellish night we had, but right now, at this exact moment in time, all I could think about was the possibility that I might never see Sasha again.

My throat contracted as I tried to swallow down a fearful, emotion-laden sob. How would I cope if I never got to see her beautiful face again? Never held her hand and marvelled at how soft her skin was? Never leant in to nuzzle her neck and inhale the sweet scent of her skin that was so delicious, and so alluring and just so her . . . . .

No. No. No. Shaking my head, I cursed and then gave myself a firm talking to. I couldn't allow myself to think like that. I had to stay strong for us both. She was in there somewhere and she *was* going to be OK.

Just as I was trying to focus, I felt my body deny my desire as my legs started to feel weak beneath me. My head started to swim, and I staggered slightly as I reached out to steady myself on a wall. My body lurched sideways as I realised too late that the wall was actually nothing more than a sheet of canvas, hung over flimsy metal fencing and forming part of the structure of the hastily erected medical area that I was in. The canvas gave way, so did the metal, my legs followed suit, and the next thing I knew I was falling as various strangers around me let out shocked gasps and desperately reached out to try and catch me. Their efforts were valiant and appreciated, but I'm a fairly big guy and I slid through their grasps as gravity did its thing and dumped me unceremoniously onto the cold pavement.

The air was forced from my lungs in a loud woosh, and then, with my head dizzy and body weary from the stress of the moment, I found myself content to just lie there for a few moments as I tried to recover.

A woman in a green paramedic jumpsuit appeared in my vision. 'Sir? Are you OK?' She looked just as frazzled as I felt, but I managed a nod and then immediately winced as my head started to throb like a bass drum being beaten savagely.

I still didn't seem to have the energy to move, so I simply continued to lie there while she moved around me examining my head and making several thoughtful humming noises. 'Your head wound is bleeding again,' she finally concluded. I dragged my tired eyes to hers and saw a resolute expression on her face that I didn't like one bit. 'I'm afraid you need to go to hospital and get it checked.'

Her words finally kicked my body into action, and I started to try and push myself upright. 'No. My girlfriend. I have to find her. I have to be here.' I shook my head resolutely and immediately regretted it as I was swept with the urge to throw up. I tried to swallow it down, but as my head continued to thunder with banging pain, I lost the battle and only just managed to turn my head away from the paramedic as vomit erupted from my mouth.

I threw up into the gutter until I felt like there surely couldn't be anything else left in my stomach and then slumped sideways with an exhausted groan, trying to cradle my throbbing head in my arms. I don't think I've ever felt so wretched in my life.

'No arguments, sir. You're going to hospital to get checked out. You probably just have a concussion, but you need a scan to make sure this isn't anything more serious.'

A sob of frustration croaked its way from my throat. 'But Sasha . . .'

'Sasha will want you fighting fit when she gets out, won't she?' The paramedic levelled me with an uncompromising glare and I knew that I wasn't going to win this fight. 'Get the checkup, get yourself sorted and then you'll be in a better state to support your girlfriend. You've already given my colleague your contact details and a description of Sasha. I promise you you'll be contacted as soon as we have any news on her, OK?'

It wasn't really OK; I didn't want to leave here at all, didn't want to leave Sasha, wherever she was, but I felt so poorly myself that I reluctantly had to agree with her – I was no use to Sasha in this state, I needed to get fixed up so I had a clear mind to help look for her, or care for her, or do whatever was needed of me.

Finally, I gave in and allowed myself to be stood up by some helpers and escorted to an awaiting ambulance. My head was spinning wildly, and as I persuaded my aching body up the steps into the rear of the vehicle, I gave one last desperate glance at the remains of Club Twist and made a silent promise to my girl that I would find her soon.

Chapter Thirty-Two

Sasha

Rattle. Bump. Wail.

Bump. Rustle. Wail. I was groggy, but the noises around me wouldn't stop, and they were irritating, interrupting my sleep. I was so tired that my eyes felt glued shut and my limbs were so heavy I could hardly muster up the energy to move. I really wanted to sleep!

Wail. Rustle. Bang.

The wailing was incessant. For fuck's sake, what the hell were my neighbours doing? Let me sleep! Using all the remaining energy that I possessed I peeled open my eyelids, only to rapidly shut them again as blinding lights seared into my head like laser beams. I had blackout blinds in my bedroom, so this made no sense to me at all.

'Why is it so bright?' At least that's what I tried to say, but what I heard come out of my mouth was garbled and nonsensical. What was happening to me?

I felt something grip my shoulder and give a gentle squeeze. 'Are you back with us, love? It's OK, just relax, you're in good hands.'

In good hands? What was happening? Where was I? And come to think of it, if there were people here then why was I lying down? My brain felt so fuddled that I wanted to let out a scream of frustration, but as I tried, a pathetic moan came out instead.

'It's OK, sweetheart, we're sorting some stronger painkillers for you now.'

Her mention of painkillers made me force my eyes open again, and as I stubbornly persevered against the blinding lights, I finally focused my eyes on the woman beside me, who was wearing a green jumpsuit and a kind smile.

As I blinked several times to work out what the hell was going on, I noticed that as well as some sort of uniform, she was wearing a pair of blue latex gloves and one was covered in a smears of dark red that looked suspiciously like blood. Flicking my eyes back to her clothes, I groggily realised that she was a paramedic, and as my unfocused eyes moved around my surroundings, I saw that I was inside the back of an ambulance. We were moving too, judging by the way everything was swaying back and forth.

That explained the bright lights then, and the bumping, which was happening every time we went over a rough bit of road. It made sense of the fucking irritating wailing noise I could hear too, which I sluggishly realised was the familiar sound of an emergency siren rolling itself around the vehicle to alert others of our presence.

'Hello. Can you tell me your name?' The voice was different this time, and I rolled my heavy head to the side to see a man in red looking down at me.

I tried to say my name, but it wouldn't come out. Licking my lips, I tried again, but only managed a weak. 'Sash.'

'Hi, Sash, my name is Ian, I'm one of the doctors from the air

240

ambulance. You've been in a rather nasty accident. Can you remember what happened?'

An accident? Even in my sleepy state his words sent a chill of panic slithering through my system and I felt my heart rate accelerate until it was throbbing in my temples. Had he said Air Ambulance? I'd watched enough documentaries on television to know that the air ambulance only went to really serious accidents. I didn't know why, perhaps it was the overwhelming panic in my system, but I still couldn't reply, I did, however, manage a shake of my head.

'OK, don't worry. We've given you some quite strong pain-killers that might make you feel a bit sick or sleepy, but they can also stop you remembering what happened. You were in a building collapse, you got trapped under some rubble.'

A building collapse?

What building? And where was Marcus? Panic was making it hard to breathe, and I was desperate to fill in the blanks, but my head felt like it was filled with cotton wool. I still felt dizzy, so much in fact that it was a struggle just to stay awake. If I'd been less of a stubborn person I would probably have given in to the urge to sleep ages ago.

He swapped places with the female doctor and took hold of both my hands. 'Can you grip my fingers?'

There were so many questions in my head, but my brain just wouldn't co-operate and let me vocalise them, so instead I lay there and complied with his instructions as he started a series of tests on me. I squeezed his hands, followed his finger with my eyes and then shook my head when he asked if I had pain in my belly, back or hips.

I gave a croaky groan when he poked the side of my chest

and then suddenly started to become aware of an ache where my left leg should have been. I say should have been, because I couldn't seem to move it at all.

Moistening my lips, I tried to speak again. 'Leg.' It came out sounding like 'laaaag', but the doctor obviously understood my slurring because he nodded down at me. 'Yes, I'm afraid you've broken your leg quite badly. There was significant damage to one of the major veins too, which started to bleed heavily when the pressure was removed from it as you were rescued. You've lost quite a bit of blood, but I've managed to clamp the vein and straighten the leg for now. You're going to need surgery today.'

I was groggy, but those words hit home. Surgery? I'd never had surgery before.

'I know it's a lot to take in, so just try and relax. You've got the best doctors here possible, and we're taking good care of you.'

Against my will my eyelids flickered closed. Even if I'd been feeling bright eyed and bushy tailed this would have been a heck of a lot to comprehend, but in my current state it was almost impossible to process.

'Ian, I've just had an updated list through of the people who are missing and there's a Sasha Mortimer on there. Her boyfriend has been looking for her. Could be our girl.'

Marcus! If he was looking for me then he must be OK! I made a muffled attempt at telling them that I was indeed Sasha, but it came out like just another gurgled noise. Happy in the knowledge that Marcus was alive, I let my body flop. I was still vaguely aware of hands touching me as the doctors tended to me, but as the sirens carried on wailing around me, I let the drugs and lulling sway of the ambulance send me off to a deep sleep.

Chapter Thirty-Three

Marcus

I was sitting in the sterile interior of a hospital cubicle staring at the pale green curtain and trying to come to terms with what had occurred tonight. I shook my head in shock before wincing and raising a hand to grip at my still aching head.

An explosion at the Club. It just didn't seem real.

Over the course of the last few hours I'd had a CT scan which had cleared me of any major issues, and confirmed that I had a concussion along with general bruises and cuts. I'd have a headache for a few days, but I'd live. They were keeping me here for observation at the moment, but I'd been allowed my phone and I'd managed to get in touch with David for an update. Miraculously, so far, there had been no fatalities, but there was still a growing list of people missing, and as gut wrenching as it was for me, one of those people was Sasha. David had also informed me that with the exception of my girl, all of our friends were now accounted for, which was a relief.

How could I be alive and here, and her still missing? We'd been standing so close together in the Club that it just didn't make any sense to me. Just as I was pondering this for the millionth time, my phone started to buzz in my jacket pocket. My rush to answer just in case it was Sasha was so desperate that I almost ripped my coat in the process of retrieving the bloody thing.

The number was withheld, but I answered immediately. 'Sasha?' I enquired desperately.

'Mr White?' My shoulders slumped as I heard the male voice that most certainly didn't belong to my gorgeous girl.

'Yes, that's me.'

'I'm Police Constable Ford. Are you still at St George's hospital?'

'I am, yes.' Regardless of the pounding in my head I was now standing up and pacing back and forth in the tiny cubicle. My shoes squeaked on the shiny floor with every step, and I was causing the curtains to billow so much with my agitated movements that I had to force myself to stand still before someone complained.

'Oh, good. We might have found Sasha; we need you to come and identify her.'

Identify her? Every remaining ounce of blood in my body felt like it drained down to my feet as I digested his words.

'I ... I ... Identify her? She's ... she's ...' Bile rose in my throat as I failed to complete my sentence. I could barely even say the word. 'She's ... *dead*?'

I heard a noise down the line like a curse word and then a muffled scrape as someone else seemed to take over the phone. A different voice came over the line, this one female and more mature. 'Hello? Mr White? I'm so sorry about that. My colleague is rather new to this type of incident. My sincerest apologies. We believe Sasha has been rescued from the club and taken to St Georges. She's alive, Mr White.'

Alive. She was alive. A huge breath flew from my lungs that I hadn't realised I'd been holding.

'A search and rescue team dug a female from the rubble some time ago. I'm just in the middle of processing all the missing person's reports and I realised that the description of Sasha matched a woman I'd seen admitted earlier. The reason we don't know her name is because she's on painkillers and rather woozy, so she isn't making a great deal of sense at the moment. She matches the description you gave though, blonde, mid-twenties and clothing matching what you said she was wearing. If you come to the desk in Accident and Emergency and ask for room twenty-three, one of our officers can accompany you to see if it's her.'

I was picking up my belongings and shoving them in my pockets before the woman had even finished speaking. 'Thank you so much. I'll head down now.'

I told the nurse where I was going, and much to her disapproval I then discharged myself and set off for the Accident and Emergency department. My stride down the hospital corridor was so purposeful that my steps were echoing loudly off the walls and causing people before me to scatter in all directions like ants trying to escape a descending footstep that shadowed above them. The forcefulness of my stride was mostly to help clear a path for me through the crowds of other injured customers from the Club and their worried relatives, but was also partly in the hopes that I might persuade my achy body that I really was well enough to be up and about.

Currently it was touch and go. One minute I felt good, and then the next second I'd be woozy and desperate to slump in a chair and rest. I couldn't allow that urge to win though, not now I knew that Sasha might be here in the hospital somewhere.

She *might* be here. It was sketchy, so I was desperately trying not to get my hopes up, but as I finally made it to the enquiries desk in the Accident and Emergency department and joined the queue I couldn't deny the swirling of anticipation in my stomach.

Lifting a hand, I gingerly explored my head as I waited. I now bore a rather fetching bandage that was circled around the top of my head and holding together a three-inch gash to the back of my skull. It had been stapled shut so was no longer bleeding, although even with the painkillers I was on I could still feel it throbbing like crazy.

While I stood there, I gazed down at my hands and slowly opened my fingers. They were red and swollen and covered in cuts and grazes where I'd dug in the rubble. The black shirt I'd had on was long gone, ripped and discarded by the paramedics, but the white T-shirt I'd had underneath remained, albeit with some significant blood stains and tears. Stretching out my spine I winced, I had two deeper lacerations to my back from where I'd been dragged from the Club and my body had snagged on bits of wreckage. All in all, I looked a mess, but it probably made me look a lot worse than I was. None of my injuries was major, not really, and certainly nothing compared to some of the wounds I'd seen on people I'd passed in the corridor.

I tried to be patient and wait my turn, but my chest was so tight with anxiety that all it really succeeded in doing was making me feel dizzy again. At this precise moment I was barely in control of my emotions, and the only reason I wasn't screaming or pushing my way to the front of the queue was because a tiny

246

logical part of my brain kept telling me that everyone here was in the same horrific position as me. All of us were either injured ourselves, or desperately worried about someone else who was injured. Screaming wouldn't help any of us, even if it might well have felt cathartic right about now.

Finally, I reached the front of the line and gripped the countertop for both the physical and emotional support that it offered me as I stared frantically at the man sat behind the desk.

'Hello. My girlfriend, Sasha Mortimer might have been brought in. She was in the explosion. At Club Twist. She's on painkillers. She's blonde. It might be her. She might be here.' I realised as I listened to myself speak that I was making absolutely no sense and so gave the man an apologetic look as I tried to calm myself down.

'Sorry, let me try again. I was at the club in Soho tonight where there was the explosion?' The man nodded his understanding and waited for me to continue. 'Since the blast my girlfriend has been missing, and I just got a phone call from a police officer who said she might have been brought in. Apparently, she's out of it because they've given her drugs, so she hasn't given a name, but he said I needed to come down here and ask to be accompanied to room twenty-three to see if it's her or not.'

The man nodded. 'I see. Just a moment, sir.' He tapped something into his computer and then picked up a radio from the table beside him before briefly speaking into it. 'Someone will be down in a moment to take you.'

I stepped to the side to allow the queue to move up, and then stood waiting for what felt like an hour, but was probably only a minute or so, until a police officer appeared at the end of a corridor and headed towards the reception desk. He spoke briefly to the staff and then approached me. 'Mr White? This way please.'

I nodded keenly, desperate to get moving and see if my girl was somewhere within this hospital. The officer started to walk with me and smiled across at me awkwardly. 'Club Twist, huh? I hear it's a pretty cool club.' I looked down at him, taken aback by the inappropriate nature of his comment. Cool club? Did he realise that the place had been destroyed by an explosion? Not to mention all the people who had been injured.

Looking down at him again I saw that he looked young enough to be my son, if I'd had kids, and judging from his uncomfortable demeanour he was quite shy, so instead of reacting to his thoughtless remark I gave him the benefit of the doubt and focused instead on what I was about to see behind the door we had just arrived at.

The young officer shuffled on his feet and then took the door handle. 'So, um, you just need to tell us if this is your girlfriend or not, OK?'

I nodded, but just as we were about to enter, the door was opened from the inside and a doctor appeared. 'Ah. You must be the potential boyfriend? Perfect timing. Please come in.'

My heart felt as if it were in my mouth as I stepped into the room, and then my step faltered as I took in the shape of a person on the bed bundled in blankets and surrounded by monitors and equipment. I was listening, but also focusing on the mass of blonde hair I could see fanned out on the pillow. One more step and I'd be able to see the face of the person in the bed. One more step.

Swallowing down a lump of fear in my throat I took the step

248

and then felt the most immense sense of relief sweep through my body.

Sasha! It was Sasha! She looked bruised and bloodied, but there was no way I could mistake her beauty. My girl was alive!

She was alive, but looked far worse than I'd prepared myself for. I felt sick to my stomach and I had to grab the side of the bed for support. 'Ignore the wires and tubes; they always make it look far worse than it is,' the doctor said briskly. He adjusted his glasses on his nose and gave me a sober look. 'She was seriously injured though, but considering a ceiling fell on her she's been remarkably lucky. Two breaks in her left leg, one very severe, a broken ankle, three cracked ribs and some general cuts and bruises.'

I wasn't usually one for crying, but as the pent-up stress from the last few hours started to escape my body I couldn't help it and before I knew it I was sobbing loudly. I grabbed Sasha's hand and leant down to place a soggy kiss on her forehead. Sasha let out a soft moan that caused me to jump upright, but as I looked at her face I saw she was still sleeping.

She might be sleeping, but I was an absolute mess. My whole body was shaking and I couldn't stop the tears that were flooding from my eyes.

'I take it this is your girlfriend then?' the doctor enquired gently, placing a hand on my shoulder and giving it a reassuring squeeze.

'Yeah.' My voice was thick with emotion and I coughed to clear it before speaking again. 'Sasha Mortimer. I can give you any details you need. Date of birth, address, that sort of thing.'

'Excellent, thank you. Are you aware of any medications she is allergic to?'

I shook my head, remembering a conversation where we'd both said we had hardly any allergies. 'Good. So far she's responding fine to treatment. The reason she's out of it is because the breaks in her leg are pretty nasty so she's been given ketamine for the pain. It's put her right out of it, but she should be coming around soon enough.'

I stroked the back of Sasha's hand and watched as her eyelids flickered again. 'Is she going to need an operation?'

It took supreme force, but I made myself look away from Sasha for a moment so I could give the doctor my full attention. He was nodding. 'I was just getting around to telling you that part. We've already operated.'

I spluttered in shock. 'You've already operated?' Glancing at my watch I saw that it was nearly eight o'clock in the morning. Where the hell had the time gone? I'd been brought in at what . . . midnight? Given that my head injury was relatively mild in comparison to the far more severe injuries that had been flooding in from the explosion I guess I must have been waiting to see a doctor for a lot longer than I'd realised. 'I thought any treatment she needed would happen later today.'

The doctor crossed his arms and shook his head sombrely. 'Sasha's injuries were severe. She was trapped beneath some rubble, and as the rescue team removed a concrete block from her leg a very significant bleed became apparent in her thigh area.' The doctor pointed vaguely at a point above her knee and then continued. 'The accident had crushed her leg, and the broken bone had ruptured one of the main veins. Luckily one of her rescuers was an off-duty doctor doing a shift with the air ambulance and he managed to isolate the bleed very quickly. I suspect his prompt actions saved her life.'

250

Fuck. I'd nearly lost her. A wheezy breath filled my lungs, but the doctor seemed oblivious to the fact that I was now struggling to breathe.

'She was rushed straight into surgery and we've fixed the vein as well as setting the breaks in the leg. She may need further surgery on them, but we'll know more in a few days when the swelling has gone down.' He glanced at Sasha and gave a small nod. 'Apart from that, everything else will just heal of its own accord.' He looked at me again and smiled. 'As I say, by the sounds of the scale of the explosion I think your girlfriend is remarkably lucky to be alive.'

I staggered towards him and grabbed hold of his hand to shake it, almost collapsing onto him in the process. 'Thank you so much. I literally can't thank you enough.'

He smiled and patted the back of my hand. 'You are welcome. It's just what we do.'

I swallowed a large lump of emotion and then glanced back at Sasha. 'How long until she comes round?'

He wobbled his head back and forth as he considered my question and then glanced at the clock on the wall. 'She had a general anaesthetic during the operation, but I'd say she'll be coming out of it in the next hour or so. She'll be groggy at first, and please don't worry if she can't remember any details of yesterday evening, one of the side effects of the ketamine she was given earlier to relieve her pain is often a short-term memory loss.'

Panicked, I frowned. 'Will she remember who I am?'

The doctor chuckled and nodded. 'Yes. I'm talking about the loss of a few hours, nothing more than that. It's often a blessing as the patient doesn't recall the pain or trauma they went through.' Moving towards the door he gave me one final smile.

'I better get on with the rest of my rounds. I'll be around if you need anything further, but as I'm sure you can understand I'm having a rather busy shift.'

'Of course. Thank you, doctor.'

He left the room, closing the door behind him, and I immediately felt the silence close around me like a calming blanket. Sasha was OK. I was OK. I let out a breath of relief and felt complete and utter exhaustion roll over me.

I ran my gaze over her body again, noting the bandages and abrasions that seemed to litter her usually perfect skin. Gently taking one of her hands, I stared at it and began to carefully rub my thumb across her palm. Her hand was cooler than usual, and looked so small and vulnerable encased in mine that I felt another sob rise in my throat. Fuck. I needed to get a grip. She was alive, that was all that mattered.

'I'm here, sweetheart. Can you hear me?' I stared at her eagerly, but there was no response, not even a flicker of her eyelids, or a squeeze to my hand, and I felt disappointment flood my system. My initial rush of adrenaline and emotion began to leave my body as I realised that my wait to be properly reunited with Sasha was going to have to continue for a little longer, and I suddenly felt my legs wanting to give way below me.

Dragging a chair closer to the bed, I sank down into it, staring up at her sleeping face. 'You're going to be OK, and I'll be here when you wake up.' Resting my head onto the soft mattress I let my eyes close. I'd just rest here until she woke up.

Chapter Thirty-Four

Sasha

Beep. Beep. Beep.

The noise was continuous, but thankfully nowhere near as irritating as that wailing had been earlier. What had the wailing noise been again? I tried to recall it, and even though I couldn't place it, I felt sure that I should have known the answer . . . *ugh*. Why was my head so groggy? I felt like I had marshmallows instead of a brain. Yumm. Marshmallows. I could really eat something sweet right now. As if agreeing, my stomach growled loudly, and I realised that, actually, I was so hungry I could eat pretty much anything.

Focus. My thoughts were bouncing around like a ping-pong ball, and my head felt so weird that I couldn't think straight at all. My eyes were sluggish and stubbornly remaining closed, so instead of mustering the energy to open them I took several long, slow breaths as I tried to slow my thoughts and process what was going on.

Through the fog I managed to make out four things: I was lying down on something soft, my body hurt but I didn't know why, my brain felt drugged, and finally, there were other noises around me that seemed more familiar, one of which was oddly comforting. Given the overwhelming confusion I was currently feeling, the sensation of comfort was extremely soothing, so I focused on it as intently as I could and tried to identify what it was that was drawing my attention.

It was a soft, low sound, coming and going in regular intervals. Soft and low. Like a cat purring, except different somehow. I didn't own a cat, and my lethargic brain couldn't work out what the sound was, so I decided it was time to try and get my eyes involved to help me solve the puzzle.

My eyelids felt like they were made of lead as I tried to open them. The overwhelming temptation was to let them stay closed and fall back to sleep, but the stubborn part of me was starting to help my brain focus, and I wanted to know what the hell was going on. Blinking several times, I saw blinding lights above me, so bright that they caused my head to throb, but I persevered, opening my sticky eyes, and wincing until my vision adjusted.

My sight was still a little blurry, but good enough that I could see a ceiling above me of polystyrene tiles, with a long fluorescent tube light in the centre, the kind that my dad had in his garage when I was a kid. The bulb was humming softly and flickering, which caught my slow-moving attention for a few seconds, like a moth drawn to an oil lamp. Blinking again, I started to rotate my head in the direction of the familiar noise that I wanted to identify, but I had to pause several times to allow the throbbing in my head to settle. Fuck me, I could murder some paracetamol right now.

Breathing deeply to help overcome the pain, I rotated my head again and then felt a smile tug at my lips as I finally located the familiar sound. Marcus. My eyes were bleary, but I could make out his angular jaw and the unforgettable curve of his gorgeous mouth, so I knew it was definitely Marcus. Or more specifically, it was Marcus and the soft sounds of his snoring.

Before I could fully appreciate how glorious it felt to see my man, my foggy brain tried to work out what he had on his head. A bandana maybe? Marcus very rarely wore a hat of any kind, and if he did it would be a cap, not a bandana, but he definitely had something on. Screwing my eyes up and willing them to clear and work properly I looked again. His wild blond hair was skewed and sticking up, and around the top of his head was a swathe of white. It looked like a sweat band that people wore when they were playing tennis.

Or a bandage.

A bandage. Almost like one of those over-the-top ones you saw wrapped around someone's head in a comedy film. Yes, that's exactly what it looked like. My brain stuck on that idea, and a frown creased my brow. Why would he have a bandage on his head? Then again, why was I lying in a brightly lit room with aches and pains all over my body?

Letting out a hiss of frustration, I scowled. Jesus, I hated this fucking fluffy feeling of disorientation. It was like a hangover but ten times worse. Why couldn't I clear my head?

'Marcus?' My voice came out like a dry squeak, and apparently was not loud enough to wake him up because he continued to snore in the chair. OK, if he wasn't going to help me, I needed to try and start at the beginning and work out what was happening. I shifted my body and winced. I was in pain, quite a lot of pain, and Marcus appeared to be bandaged up, so what the hell had happened?

A car crash maybe? I sifted through my brain, trying to

recollect any fragments of memories that might help me work out what was going on, but just kept drawing fuzzy blanks. Putting my hands on either side of me, I tried to push myself upright but was immediately stopped by a searing pain in my leg. Fuck, that was painful! I prided myself on having a high pain threshold, so for me to admit that I was hurting meant I must have quite seriously injured myself.

But how?

Closing my eyes, I cast a picture of Marcus in my mind. Wild blond hair, sparkling eyes, and a smile to die for – I could remember his features perfectly, which was a good start. Expanding my vision, I pictured my flat, imagining myself walking through the rooms, and thankfully being able to recall each in quite intricate detail. Next, I branched my memories out to our friends; I knew for sure that my flat was opposite my best friend Robyn's, and that she lived with her partner, Oliver.

Robyn and Oliver. Something about them was causing my memories to falter slightly. Had I been with them today? Had we all been in an accident? Scrunching my eyes shut tighter, I focused on thoughts of Robyn and Oliver. I pictured their gorgeous home, which was like a mansion when compared to my little attic flat, and then my thoughts drifted to the local wine bar and Club Twist, both venues where we regularly met them for drinks.

Club Twist. A place for folk to explore their twisted sides – a sex club supreme, owned by one of Oliver's longest standing friends, David Halton. A place full of dark corners and naughty deliciousness, and somewhere that I felt oddly comfortable. I didn't feel comfortable as I thought about the place now, though; my stomach was knotting up with tension and a sickly feeling swept through me.

Perhaps I was onto something. Maybe the Club had something to do with my injuries? Honing my mind onto Club Twist, I pictured its grand exterior and imagined myself walking through the double-doored entrance and seeing the old theatre stage before me that was now used as a dancefloor. The long, elegant bar was situated to the side, lined with purple neon lights and leather stools and was always a hub for people to gather. The energy inside the Club was one of the things that had always appealed to me. There was always a hum of excitement in the air, not to mention the heady pulse of well-chosen dance music, always loud, but not earsplittingly so.

On that thought I suddenly had a flash of recollection. I was inside the Club, and instead of the music I was surrounded by deafeningly loud noises of terror and fear.

Panicking at the horrific images now starting to flood my brain, I felt sweat pop on my forehead and a huge, gagging gasp ripped up my throat as I wriggled in the bed, seemingly unable to control my body.

'Sash . . .?' Marcus's voice was groggy, but my writhing had obviously disturbed his sleep and through my panic I saw him sitting up and blinking away his confusion. As his face cleared, I saw shocked relief flood his features and then my man was pushing to his feet and moving even closer to me, grabbing one of my hands and clutching it to his chest as if he never wanted to let it go.

'Sasha? You're awake, thank god!' I was still so confused by what was happening, but it was so good to hear Marcus's voice that I gripped his hand back equally as tightly and smiled. Wincing, I realised that even my face hurt, but I struggled through it and put all my blurry focus onto him. His hand dwarfed mine as it always did, but then I realised that it was swollen and red with cuts.

'What the hell has happened, Marcus?'

He frowned, 'You don't remember?'

I shook my head and tried to push myself upright again but was stopped this time by Marcus as he placed a hand gently on my shoulder and held me in place. 'Stay still, gorgeous. Try not to move too much.'

Try not to move? I knew I was hurting, but why wouldn't he let me move? Getting more and more frustrated by the second, I let out a huff and repeated my question. 'Why? What's happened?'

I felt his grip on my hand tighten further, and a grimace creased his handsome face. 'We were at the Club. There . . .' He swallowed loudly and shifted on his feet as if anxious. 'There was an explosion.' He visibly paled, the colour draining from his skin before my eyes as my brain tried to process what he had just said. An explosion?

An explosion seemed way too far-fetched to be true. It couldn't be possible, I'd certainly remember if I'd been involved in an explosion, wouldn't I? My heart rate accelerated though, accompanied by the increasingly quick beeps on the machine that I was hooked up to, which just seemed to add to the thick tension now hanging in the room. Suddenly Marcus collapsed forwards onto the bed, gripping my hand and scattering desperate kisses across my face. 'Jesus, Sasha. I thought I'd lost you.'

I'd never seen him this emotional, not even when he'd talked about Celia attacking him, so I let him have a few moments to settle, and then gave his hand a squeeze.

I realised that the fuzziness in my mind was clearing by the second, presumably as my medications wore off, but frustratingly my memory was still stubbornly blank. 'I have a few vague flashes of memory. We were in the Club, and I remember a really loud noise, but that's about it. Talk me through it, Marcus.'

He finally lifted his head, and I could see that his eyes were shiny with tears, a sight that made my heart clench with worry. Whatever had happened it was obviously some serious shit. From the frown I could see that, below his bandages, he seemed reluctant to tell me, perhaps because he was worried it would upset me, or maybe because he was struggling to process it himself. Whatever the reason, I shook my head firmly, ignoring the way it made my brain swim in my skull. 'Please. I want to know.'

Sighing heavily, Marcus nodded and then carefully sat on the side of my bed, still gripping my hand tightly.

'We were out at the Club, just like normal really, and then out of nowhere there was this huge bang and before we could react the whole place started collapsing around us.' A visible shudder ran through Marcus, and it was so powerful I felt it vibrate through the bed. 'It was fucking awful, Sasha. You were right next to me one second, but then people started stamped-ing all over the place and we got dragged apart. Then the ceiling started to fall in and all I could see was dust and débris and the crowd surging towards the doors.'

My brain only had a few glimpses of what he was telling me stored as actual memories, but I still felt clammy with shock. 'Fucking hell.'

'Quite.' He nodded grimly. 'I searched for you, literally dug through the rubble with my bare hands,' he wiggled his swollen fingers with a grimace and then shrugged, 'but you were nowhere to be found. Then I . . .' He paused, letting out a dry

259

laugh. 'Well, I kinda collapsed and was forced to stop looking for you and come to hospital.'

My eyes widened as fear gripped me, and I ripped my hand from his and cupped his cheek. 'You collapsed? Are you OK?' My concern was so great I almost felt paralysed by it, and even though I knew and had accepted that I loved Marcus deeply, I was still shocked at how greatly his words had affected me. It would seem that I'd come a hell of a long way from the emotionless, independent Sasha Mortimer of a few years ago.

He rubbed gingerly at the bandage around his head. 'Yeah, I'm fine. I took a bump to the head. I've got a bit of concussion, but I'm all right.' He shrugged off his injury and looked intently back at me. 'Anyway, I didn't know it at the time, but you'd been admitted too. They'd given you a load of pain medication, so you were out of it and no one knew your name. I was here being treated and had been asking everyone I met about whether you'd been admitted. Finally, one of the doctors put two and two together and remembered my description of you and brought me down here to see if it was you.'

Marcus brushed some stray hairs back from my face and smiled down at me sweetly. 'I'm so bloody glad it was.'

This was all insane, and as a result I had so many questions bubbling around in my head. 'Is the Club gone? How are our friends? Was anyone killed?'

'I don't know the final verdict, but from what I saw when I was there I doubt that the Club is saveable.' Marcus shook his head sadly. 'I have no idea about fatalities, there were still search and rescue teams working when I left. I've gotten through to everyone we were out with. Oliver and Robyn are here at hospital too, being treated for some minor injuries, but they're fine, and David and Natalia are still in Soho with the police and investigators but they're fine too.' Marcus paused and frowned. 'Physically fine. I suspect David will be almost as destroyed as the building.'

I could believe it too, that club was his life's work; he'd put everything he had into it. I continued to cling to Marcus's hand as a heavy silence fell between us while I tried to absorb everything he'd just told me.

Suddenly Marcus stood up from the bed and walked to the cabinet on the far wall. He was frowning, seemingly deep in thought. He poured himself a cup of water, downed it in one and then strode back to my side with a purposeful look on his face. Grabbing my hand again he leant over me and stared into my eyes.

'Marry me, Sasha.' His statement was so determined it was almost a demand, but bloody hell did his words take me by surprise. A marriage proposal? That had certainly come out of nowhere! It was just as well I was already lying down, otherwise I may well have fallen over.

Seeing the shock on my face, he gave a wry chuckle. 'I know it's soon to be asking you, but I love you so much.' He squeezed my hand, and then with his other arm reached up and gently caressed my cheek. 'You were my missing piece; I feel complete now.' He shrugged, almost self-consciously. 'I nearly lost you today . . . all of this has made me realise just how much I want that connection with you. I want to be with you, Sasha, always.' He paused and licked his lips before continuing in a softer tone. 'Please say you'll marry me?'

Being me, with my aversion to commitment and emotions in general, I had expected a laugh to erupt from my throat, or

261

perhaps a burst of sarcasm, but to my surprise, I found myself parting my lips and saying just one single word.

'Yes.'

'Yes?' Marcus questioned, looking just as shocked by my acceptance as I felt, but there was no denying it, Marcus Price was my missing piece too. I'd never felt so accepted, so loved and so wanted in all my life. It had taken me a while to drop my barriers, but I was certain that he was it for me, so now that he had actually asked the question I found it incredibly easy to answer.

'Yes, Marcus. I'll marry you.'

Letting out a noise that was half laugh and half splutter, my man then leant forwards and kissed me. It was gentle, and lingering, and perfect, and I lapped up his attention until he finally pulled back with an amused chuckle. 'We might be having a shitty day today, but I think our future looks pretty damn bright.' Marcus let out another relieved laugh and bent down to kiss me again. I might be battered and bruised, but I was so happy that I couldn't help but smile against his lips.

Well, that was that then. I was now officially engaged.

Chapter Thirty-Five

David

We'd finally finished with the police, for now, anyway, and had just made it back to the quiet calm of the flat I shared with Elle and Dan. They had both taken a day off work to be here if we needed them, which was incredibly kind of them, although right now I just felt so drained that I probably just needed to eat something and then crash into bed.

My legs felt like lead, and I was so physically and mentally exhausted that I only just made it to the sofa before collapsing down onto it. Natalia wasn't far behind me, and as she lowered herself to join me, I looped an arm around her waist and tugged her so she was pulled right up close to me. I'd lost pretty much everything last night, and even though we were safe, I needed her near to ground me.

Elle was hovering in the door to the lounge looking anxious and fidgety. 'Coffee?'

Natalia stifled a yawn and then nodded. 'Yes, please.'

I wasn't sure I wanted coffee. What I *wanted* was a time machine so I could go back twenty-four hours and work out what the fuck it was that caused the explosion at my club. The accident investigators had still been on scene when we'd left and the police had warned us that it could be several days until we got a conclusive answer.

'I know it's only eleven in the morning, but do you want something stronger?' Dan offered. 'Whisky' perhaps? Or brandy?'

It was certainly tempting, and would be easy to lose myself to booze, but right now I wanted to stay sober in case there were any updates or more interviews I needed to do. 'Nah, coffee is good. Thanks, guys.'

Beside me, Natalia rubbed her hands together and then touched her face with a frown. 'Ugh. I'm covered in dust. I'm just going to wash my face, I feel gritty.' The air around the Club had been filled with dust clouds for hours after the explosion. I'd noticed it on several occasions, quite surprised by how long it had hung in the air before resettling. I could probably do with a shower myself, but right now I couldn't muster the energy to do anything other than sit here and reflect on everything that had happened.

Elle and Dan came back in with a pot of coffee and a tray of croissants. I was hungry, but the idea of eating when I was so emotionally strung out made me feel sick to my stomach and I shook my head when they offered me one. They started to eat as Natalia returned, and I frowned as I watched her. She looked on edge, and glanced over her shoulder not once, but twice as she came back down the corridor. Her shoulders relaxed marginally as she sat back down, but something was definitely up, and it seemed like more than just tiredness from the long evening.

'Everything OK, Natalia?' Elle had obviously seen it too, because she beat me to it with her question.

Natalia's eyes sprung to mine, shocked, but then she turned to Elle with a small smile and nodded. 'Of course. I'm fine. Just tired.'

Raising an eyebrow, Elle gave her an uncompromising stare. 'That smile isn't kidding anyone, Nat. I know you guys have had a horrible night, but you're jumpy as hell. What's the matter?'

Natalia's eyes widened at Elle's bluntness, and then her shoulders slumped against me as she snuggled closer and gave another anxious glance towards the windows and then the hallway.

'It's stupid, but since that police officer said the explosion might have been caused by Richard I just can't seem to relax. I mean what if he somehow tracks us down and comes here?' I heard the sound of her swallowing nervously.

I saw Dan glance towards the door and frown and then look towards Natalia and me. 'The police think it was deliberate? Like a bomb?'

I sighed and rubbed a hand over my tired eyes. 'They don't know yet, but it's one of the avenues they're looking into.'

Natalia shrugged and then attempted another one of those fake smiles, obviously trying to fool us all into thinking she was fine. 'I sound so pathetic!' Waving a hand to dismiss us, she plunged the coffee and busied herself pouring it into the mugs. 'I'm just being silly. I'll be fine, honestly.'

We all sat in silence for a few minutes while Natalia busied herself with pouring and serving the coffee, and then, once she was sat back beside me, I took her free hand in mine and turned so I could look her straight in the eyes.

'Why don't you move in with me?' The words had blurted from my mouth spontaneously, but it was a perfect solution.

Natalia was feeling edgy, and I had this flat or my massive house which was empty for most of the year. Natalia and I had spent most of our time together here at the London flat, but if we moved in together, I'd rather we had the privacy of my other house in London.

The reason I spent the majority of my time at this flat was because of its easy proximity to the Club for work, but seeing as that was now a pile of rubble and would take months to rebuild it made sense that we got away. It was a triple win; Natalia would have me with her, so would hopefully feel safer, I'd have some distance from the Club and the memories of the explosion, and to top it all off, I'd have my girl living with me twenty-four-seven which was a very tempting prospect.

Natalia blinked several times and then let out a shocked splutter of laughter. 'Umm. What?'

'If you're feeling nervous, then move in with me; we'll have each other there so you'll feel safer.' Natalia still hadn't seen the house yet; in fact, we'd been planning on going over there next weekend so she could see it. I had shown her pictures though, and she had commented on how lovely it was, and how comfortable it looked. Why not let her get comfortable by moving in?

It seemed I had stunned her with my offer, because her eyes were flicking about like crazy as she thought it over. 'I mean it's really early, we've not been together long, have we?'

Elle let out a snort of laughter and shook her head. 'You haven't, but this is hardly a standard situation, is it? There's a weirdo on the loose!' She laughed and then wiggled her eyebrows. 'Plus, let's face it, you guys are basically inseparable as it is, moving in together will just make things easier for both of you.'

Natalia had been right; things were relatively new between us, but I was old enough and wise enough to be more than certain about my relationship with her. I was in for the long haul and living together was just the next natural step. I didn't want her to feel pressurised into anything though, so I tried to keep it casual, took a sip of my coffee and shrugged. 'I have a house that needs some love and attention, and it'll be a perfect distraction for me over the next few months to keep my mind busy. We can decorate.'

My girl still seemed unsure, but I could definitely see temptation in her eyes. 'You could have the best of both worlds if it makes you feel more comfortable; live with me but leave some things at your place and come and go between the two, or move in fully and rent your place out.'

Natalia pursed her lips as she thought it through, and then plonked her coffee down so rapidly that some of the hot liquid slopped over the rim onto the table, before she grabbed my hand. 'Really? Are you sure?'

I smiled, so thankful that I had this gorgeous girl in my life. 'Of course. Regardless of what happened with Richard and the Club, moving in together would be the next step for us anyway.'

Natalia threw herself at me, pulling me into the hardest hug I had received in a very long while and then pressed a kiss against my lips. 'Oh my gosh, that would be so amazing, David. I'd love to.'

We hugged long and hard, and then Natalia pulled back and cast an embarrassed glance towards Elle and Dan, who were watching all this play out with smiles on their faces. Natalia moved away and settled herself next to me on the sofa, cradling her coffee and looking far more relaxed now.

I watched her for a few seconds, glad that we were taking this next step together, and relieved that there was some light shining through the otherwise god awful day that we'd just gone through. With my Club now in ruins I was going to have to work hard to focus on the positives in my life. Thankfully, Natalia was a big one.

My contemplation was broken by the vibration of my phone and I dug in my pocket to retrieve it, seeing an unlisted number on the screen. 'Hello?'

'Mr Halton?'

The voice on the line was deep and unfamiliar and I frowned, suspecting it was probably the police, or someone calling about the explosion. 'Speaking. Who is this please?'

'Good morning, Mr Halton, my name is Detective Poole from the Forensic Investigation Team at the Metropolitan Police.'

My Club had been blown to bits so it was hardly a 'good morning', but I didn't say that. Instead my spine stiffened and I clutched the phone tighter as I sat up and placed my coffee on the table so I could give him my full attention.

'We're able to give you some closure on the explosion at your Club. It has been confirmed that it was definitely a gas explosion.'

A huge breath rushed from my lungs as I digested his words. 'Gas? Are you sure?'

'Yes. Tests and excavations on site have conclusively proven that a pipe leading from the main had ruptured.' He paused and cleared his throat. 'Apparently the neighbour next door had been smelling gas on and off for weeks and had contacted the gas board but an engineer hadn't been sent out yet.'

'Fuck.' I ran a hand through my hair as I tried to process this information. 'I hadn't smelt gas at all.' I saw Natalia's eyebrows raise as she overheard my conversation, and it reminded me to follow up on the other possibility. 'We'd been told that it might have had something to do with a deliberate explosion, linked to a previous Club member? Richard Lincoln?'

I heard the officer hum down the line in recognition of the name. 'Before the gas leak had been confirmed we did follow that lead up, but Mr Lincoln is now residing in Sydney Australia as of two months ago. He definitely hasn't been in the United Kingdom, so there was no link to him.'

Australia? That was news to me, but would certainly help put Natalia's mind at rest.

'Things have been quite chaotic at the scene. I'm sorry it's taken us this long to get in touch.' The detective was apologising, but actually, this closure was coming a lot quicker than I'd expected.

'No, you've been really quick in following up. I appreciate it.'

'We'll have a further debrief with you shortly, to give you all the facts, but that will be in a few days' time. Have you got any other questions at the moment?'

I thought about it, and only one sprung to my mind. 'Do you have any updates on the casualties? Were there . . .' I paused, feeling a lump of fear-laced emotion wedge in my throat. 'Were there any deaths?'

The detective let out a heavy sigh down the line, which immediately made me fear the worst, but then followed it up with some surprising words. 'Currently no fatalities, no. There are four people either undergoing surgery, or in need of it, but all are expected to make a full recovery, and then an awful lot of more minor injuries. Given the nature of the explosion, I think we've been remarkably lucky.'

It felt like a weight had been lifted from my shoulders and I nodded in relief. 'It sounds like it, thank goodness. Thank you for all the help, Detective.'

'Not a problem. I advise that you get in touch with your insurance company to start the ball rolling, and don't forget to try and get some rest.'

I'd already called my insurance company, so that was sorted, and as for rest? My mind was in overdrive, so I wasn't sure I'd sleep for a while yet, even though I was exhausted. 'OK, we will. Thanks again, Detective.' I hung up the phone and placed it on the table, aware that I was being intently watched by three sets of impatient eyes, but just needing a few moments to process it all myself before speaking.

We sat silently for a minute or so, and then Dan broke first, leaning forwards in his seat. 'So, it wasn't a deliberate explosion then?'

I shook my head. 'Nope. You probably gathered as much from my conversation, but it's been confirmed as a gas explosion.'

'It's been utterly crap, but at least you have answers to your questions now,' Dan said with a supportive smile. 'Do you think your insurance will pay out?'

In this whole confusing mess, that was the one thing I was confident about. 'Yes. I've always paid top dollar to make sure I have very inclusive cover. They'll cover everything, so I'll be able to rebuild.'

'I know it must be heartbreaking for you, but think of it as a new start. Rebuild and make it bigger and better than before.' I felt Natalia give my hand a squeeze and I gave her a thankful smile. 'Exactly. We need to look at it in a positive light.' I'd developed lots of ideas for the Club over the years, and now I had the experience under my belt I knew the Club would rise again, and indeed be bigger and better than before.

Wanting to reassure my girl, I smiled at her and broke the good news. 'By the way, it definitely wasn't linked to Richard.'

She chewed on her bottom lip and frowned. 'I heard you ask about him, but I couldn't hear the answer. How have they ruled him out?'

'They followed the line of inquiry and discovered that he has moved to Australia.'

Her eyes widened in shock, and I'll be honest, I'd been quite surprised by the news too. 'Sounds like he moved out there straight after the incident with you. Must have gone for a fresh start.' Natalia literally relaxed before my eyes with relief, her shoulders softened, grip relaxed, and a little colour returned to her cheeks. 'You don't need to worry about him anymore, sweetheart.'

Realising that this new information might cause her to change her mind about moving in with me, or see it as unnecessary, I raised my eyebrows hopefully and tried to lay her with my most charming smile. 'I'd still really like you to move in with me though, if you'd like to?'

Before Natalia could answer, Elle interrupted us. 'You have to say yes, Natalia. He'll be unbearable now if you change your mind.'

Natalia chuckled and then looked me straight in the eyes before nodding. 'I'd really like that.'

I drew in a deep breath of relief, glad that I had closure, and pleased that Natalia and I would be living together soon, but still feeling completely blindsided by last night's incident. My club was gone. There one minute and rubble the next. I suppose it just highlighted how fragile life could be. I wasn't a particularly clingy person, but I found myself needing to reach out and touch Natalia, and so I took her hand and linked my fingers through hers.

As gut-wrenching as it might be to absorb, the building was gone, but at least we were safe, and that was what I planned to focus on to get me through.

Chapter Thirty-Six

Sasha

Gripping the handles of my newly bestowed crutches, I slipped my arms into the holders and then attempted a swinging step forwards. The weight of the cast on my leg unbalanced me and I swore and wobbled, and then swore again, just for good measure. Frowning down at the metal sticks I shook my head. These things were going to take some getting used to. I came to a halt at the bottom of the steps with a sigh, standing on the pavement on one leg like a hapless flamingo.

I looked up at the front door with determination. All that stood between me and the cherry red door of Marcus's building in Notting Hill were six entrance steps. Six very *large* entrance steps, which currently looked as high as flipping Mount Kilimanjaro.

'Bloody things.' I wanted to chuck the crutches aside and drag myself up, but I rolled my eyes instead and looked across at Marcus who was very visibly attempting not to laugh at my blundered attempts.

'You'll get used to them, babe,' he reassured me, finally allowing his grin to escape. Bastard. I faked a scowl, and then laughed myself. I was more uncoordinated than a puppet with its strings tangled. I'd only been given the crutches this morning at the hospital when they'd decided I was ready to be discharged, and it was the first time in my life that I'd ever used some. I'd had a few practice waddles around the ward to prove I was 'safe' to go home, but using the damn things was worse than attempting to brush my teeth left-handed.

'Here, let me help you.' Marcus looped an arm around my waist and was now trying to take my weight and hold my suitcase in his other hand. He wasn't being particularly successful at either, so I laughed and shook my head.

'How about you take my case up first and then come back and help me?'

Marcus assessed me with narrowed eyes, as if trying to decide if I was going to be stubborn and climb the stairs on my own the moment he left my side, which of course I was, so I fluttered my eyelashes persuasively and gave him my best innocent look. 'Go. I'm getting cold.'

As planned, my mention of being cold triggered his protective side and Marcus quickly disappeared up the steps and inside with my case. I grinned triumphantly and eyed the steps with determination. I wasn't going to let a simple set of stairs beat me, so I raised one crutch up and tossed it up the steps, where it landed with a clatter at the top, and then gripped the handrail with my free hand. Using a combination of sheer bloody mindedness and upper body strength, I balanced myself between the unmoving handrail and my crutch and managed to get to the top step just as Marcus reappeared at the door.

'Sasha!' he chided me with shock in his tone, so I grinned with a fake apology and then shrugged. 'I'm stuck with this cast for at least eight weeks. I've got to learn how to cope.'

Letting out a defeated sigh, Marcus nodded and handed me the crutch from the floor before pushing the door open. 'Maybe we should rent a bungalow for a couple of months,' he suggested as I hobbled into the hallway.

'Don't be so stupid, I'll be fine—' My words stopped abruptly and my little victory faded fast as I looked up at the next staircase stretching upwards away from me. Maybe a bungalow wasn't such a bad idea after all.

'For fuck's sake,' I muttered under my breath, cursing the fact that he lived on the first floor. It was better than the three flights of stairs to my top floor flat though, which was why Marcus and I had agreed that I'd live with him full time during my recuperation. Seeing as we were now engaged, we'd also decided that it would be a perfect time to have a trial run of living together, which I was actually really excited about.

'Not feeling quite so cocky now, are you, babe?' Marcus quipped with a wink, before scooping me and my crutches up into his arms and carrying me to his front door and placing me down. 'I won't carry you over the threshold,' he commented mildly. 'Not yet, anyway,' he added, before wiggling his eyebrows at me and grinning. His words, and his cheeky smile caused butterflies to erupt in my belly and I felt my cheeks heat with a blush.

We were going to get married! I still hadn't quite got my head around the idea, but I knew for sure that the butterflies in my tummy were ones of excitement, not nerves or regret.

Marcus pushed the door open and then stepped aside to allow me to go first. Currently, I could put no weight on my healing leg at all – it was full of screws and metal rods – so, grimacing, I gripped my crutch handles with all my might and started to wobble my way forwards. I traversed the hallway, making a direct beeline for the lounge and the gigantic sofas that were calling to me.

I was concentrating so hard on not falling over, with my head downturned and watching my feet, that when a huge round of applause and shrieking started, I nearly toppled backwards in shock. My fall was only stopped by Marcus, as he moved in close behind me and wrapped a supportive arm around my waist to catch me.

'Surprise! Happy homecoming!' I lifted my head in shock and to my surprise I found all of our close friends gathered in the lounge. Oliver, Robyn, David and Natalia were rushing forwards to hug me, and behind them I saw Nicholas, Rebecca, Nathan and Stella also smiling at me broadly.

The room was full of balloons and banners, half of which said 'Congratulations on your Engagement!', and half which said 'Get well soon!'. Wow! This was all so unexpected that I felt a prick of tears in my eyes as I hugged everyone in turn. Jesus. Getting injured and then engaged had obviously made me soft!

Natalia rubbed my arm and smiled at me as she and Marcus helped me towards a chair. 'We decided that after everything that has been going on lately, we needed to celebrate the good things. Congratulations on your engagement, guys!'

In total I'd been in the hospital for four weeks, only being released today when they were finally satisfied that the damaged vein in my leg was well and truly healed. In that time all of our friends had heard about our engagement and congratulated us, but it was a lovely surprise to have it done in this way. Everyone was looking at us with broad grins, and I let out a laugh at being thrust so unexpectedly into the spotlight. 'Thank you! Wow, this is such a shock!'

Oliver came across with a bottle of champagne and poured both Marcus and me a glass before turning to the room and raising a glass.

'To Marcus and Sasha. Congratulations on your engagement, and here's to a swift recovery.'

My cheeks were hurting from grinning, but everyone raised their glasses in the toast before taking a sip. Oliver directed his steely stare towards David and gave a small nod of his head before lifting his glass again. 'And here's to better times ahead for everyone.' It was obvious his words were directed at David, who had lost so much in the explosion, and my heart really did go out to him.

Marcus leant down and looked deep in my eyes, and his close contact rapidly had the connection between us fizzing to life and raising my heart rate. 'You've made my life complete. I can't wait to marry you, Sash.' He dropped a kiss on my lips that lingered for just long enough that Oliver let out a wolf whistle that caused the room to erupt in laughter and calls of 'Get a room!' until Marcus and I pulled apart, grinning.

Winking at me, he stood up and bowed to our friends, then chuckled and waved a hand towards the kitchen. 'Right, let's get this party started. Food is in the kitchen and help yourselves to drinks.'

The attention turned away from us as everyone started to mingle and chat. Natalia was still standing close by, so I reached out and touched her arm to get her attention.

'How's David doing?' It had been four weeks since the explosion at Club Twist, and although I'd seen our friends regularly when they'd visited me in hospital, I hadn't wanted to directly ask David how everything was going with the Club in case it was still all too raw for him.

Natalia smiled and looked fondly across the room to David who was swapping his glass of bubbles for a bottle of beer and chatting animatedly with Oliver. 'He's doing really well. It was such a shock, of course, and I was worried the stress was going to be too much for him, but thanks to his insurance company they've moved things through so quickly that work will be starting next week to clear the site ready for the rebuild.'

My eyebrows rose. That was quick! I was so pleased for him, though. That club had been his life's work, and I know Marcus had been concerned about David's mental state over the past few weeks, especially if the rebuild had been disallowed for any reason.

'He looks in good spirits,' I commented, and I wasn't just being polite, David really did look happy.

'We're really enjoying living together; it's going so well,' she confessed with a shy grin. 'And have you heard that Oliver, David and Oliver's friend Matius are opening up a club together in Spain?'

I vaguely recalled hearing Marcus talking about it on the phone while I'd been in hospital a few weeks ago, but I'd still been groggy on drugs, so couldn't recall many details. 'I don't know much, but yeah, I heard Marcus talking about it with Oliver. Sounds exciting.'

'It's in the early stages at the moment; they're just securing the premises in Barcelona, but honestly, I think putting attention on that has been David's saving grace. He's been able to focus on planning, rather than stress about the devastation at Club Twist.'

Natalia looked down at me with a smile. 'I'll bring you a plate of food through before the men eat it all.' She disappeared and left me to myself where I could relax and do some people watching over my nearest and dearest. I felt a warm buzz of happiness in my chest as I looked at my friends in turn. What with Richard's attack on Natalia and then the explosion, David and Natalia had been through hell in the last few months, but they were through the worst of it now, and it was clear for everyone to see just how happy they were now they'd cemented their relationship by moving in together. They were such a perfect match that I couldn't ever see anything coming between them.

Nathan, Stella, Nicholas and Rebeca might be expanding their lives by moving out of the city and having children, but as brothers went, they were still almost inseparable. After what Nicholas and Nathan had endured as children their bond was strong – anyone who survived that kind of joint abuse would be close – but I suspected they would always play significant parts in each other's lives. I smiled to myself as I looked at them both standing there in smart suits that were tailored to perfection. One thing I could say about the Jackson Brothers – they were always the smartest, best dressed men in any room they entered.

And last, but definitely not least, my eyes moved to Robyn and Oliver. They were standing by the fireplace, her tucked comfortably by his side as they spoke to Marcus. Robyn was one of the most genuinely selfless people I'd ever met, and would always be my best friend. I was thrilled that she and Oliver were married and so happy together. With the way they still went at it like rabbits in the bedroom I suspected we'd be getting the news that they were expecting miniature versions of themselves anytime soon too.

This party was such a lovely surprise, and I felt so loved as I looked around the room full of people. I'd come a very long way in the last few years; learning to trust and let people closer, and I could now say, hand over heart, that I must be one of the luckiest girls alive. Not only did I have a fiancé whom I loved deeply and trusted implicitly, but I also had a close network of friends who I knew would always be there for me, no matter what.

Sitting back, I sipped my champagne and looked around the gathered group of people with a warm smile. As groups of friends went, we certainly had a lot of hidden histories between us. Dark stories of abuse, sadness and death that could have made us rebel against the world and give up hope of ever finding security and love. But it hadn't broken our spirits, we were stronger than all the shitty things that life had thrown at us. We'd all fought back against the world and won. We might have been through some tough times, but here we were, all of us brought together in our friendships and relationships by connections so random that they could only be accounted to fate.

We were all meant to be in each other's lives, and we'd stay that way for ever. It was as simple as that.

Epilogue

Author's note

When I finished my first series — the Untwisted Series — many of you requested a 'ten years later' type of ending so you could see where the brothers Nicholas and Nathanial Jackson were in years to come.

I had been reluctant to write such a chapter, because the boys continued to feature in my second series and I didn't want to prematurely age them at that point. Now I have completed both the Untwisted Series and its sister series, the Club Twist Series, I have written a chapter that is set eighteen years later, and it follows on the next pages.

If you want to keep Nicholas, Nathan, Oliver, Marcus, David and their partners young in your mind then I recommend you stop reading now!

If, however, you are desperate to see if they are all still up to all sorts of kinky fun with their chosen partners then read on and see what the future has in store for them.

Enjoy.

Alice xx

Sasha

Eighteen years later

I was sitting at the gigantic kitchen table in Nathan and Stella's gorgeous country house and couldn't help but be slightly jealous of how complete it was. No building supplies sitting around, no rooms to paint, just a beautiful Edwardian country house complete with conservatory, acres of land and a swimming pool. It was the complete opposite of the house Marcus and I had bought three years ago when we'd decided to leave London, which was lovely, but still midway through its revamp. Style-wise it was my dream house, so I knew I just needed patience and soon ours would look just as beautiful as this.

'Sash, you couldn't pull the beef out of the oven for me, could you?' Stella asked as she juggled a pan of potatoes in one hand and a sieve in the other.

'Of course.' Opening the oven door, I was surrounded by hot plumes of roast beef-scented air and moaned deeply at how delicious it smelt.

Just then, Nathan walked in from the garden and cast a fond glance through the window towards his son William. Moving up behind Stella, he wrapped an arm around her waist and quirked an eyebrow.

'William just told me the reason he didn't make it home for lunch yesterday,' Nathan informed us with a grin. After this summer's heatwave we were all sporting rather fetching tans, and I had to say that Nathan and Marcus with their blond hair and fair skin had taken to the hot weather rather well. Both now had vividly sun-bleached hair and tanned skin, and as I glanced across at Marcus I grinned – it really suited him, and even though I was probably biased, I'd say it made him look sexier than ever.

'Why?' Stella asked as she drained the potatoes at the sink.

'He was so busy chatting up Sarah from the florist's that he "forgot the time".' Nathan made air quotes with his fingers as he quoted their son and then leant back against the counter, grinning.

'What?' Stella threw her hands up in disbelief. 'What about Molly? I thought she was his latest interest?' I chuckled at their conversation, putting the sizzling beef joint on the side to rest and then joining them at the window.

Nathan laughed and wrapped an arm around Stella. 'Molly was last week,' he informed us, almost sounding proud of how many hearts their son was probably breaking in the village while he was home for the summer from his first term at university.

Leaning to the left, I looked through the open windows into the garden and saw William tinkering with his mountain bike. He was the spitting image of a younger Nathan; with his dad's tall broad build, blond hair, and startlingly blue eyes. He definitely had the looks to be a heart breaker, that was for sure.

Stella joined me and sighed as she watched him too. 'Where has the time gone? He's so grown up now, and such a handsome young man that it makes my chest tight.' She laughed and poked Nathan in the ribs. 'And apparently, he's turning into a quite a lady's man too, from the sounds of it, which wouldn't be far from what you were like when you were younger, hmm?'

Nathan laughed and held his hands up. 'Don't blame me! It's

not my fault he's taken on my startlingly good looks and suave charm.' Sobering his expression, he moved closer to Stella and slid a reassuring arm around her shoulders. 'Seriously though, don't worry. I've spoken to him about it. He respects women, Stella. He doesn't sleep around, he just like a good flirt.'

William and Stella were really close, but the bond his son shared with Nathan was exceptionally sweet. He clearly idolised his dad, and much to my surprise, Nathan had turned into quite the doting father figure and a great example for their son to grow up learning from.

'He confided in me last week that he was still a virgin. Did you know that?' Nathan suddenly said, and I almost felt bad for the kid as we all stood just a few metres away discussing him so intently.

Stella gave Nathan a startled glance and even I raised my eyebrows, not entirely sure if Will might be telling his dad a little lie there. Every time I saw him he was always surrounded by girls.

'I don't know why you look so surprised, Stella, you know he's a good lad. He's sensible. He said he was waiting for someone special. I'd like to think he's using us as an example.' Nathan nuzzled Stella's neck and hummed contentedly which seemed to be my cue to give them a little space, so I turned for the dining table and went to join my man.

A feeling of warm contentment swept through me as I looked at Marcus and watched him as he entertained our two crazy chocolate Labradors, Teagan and Bracken. We hadn't had children, instead getting the dogs that we had both always craved. I loved them beyond belief, and soon we'd be getting a third addition to our crazy fur-baby family – a Springer spaniel puppy named Jasper who would be joining us as soon as he was weaned from his mother. Marcus and I were still so in love that it was probably sickening to outsiders, but it was just how we were; happy, loved-up, and constantly covered in dog hair. It might not be everyone's idea of a perfect life, but to Marcus and me, it was heaven.

Stella

Nathan kissed my neck and then gave a gentle suck on the skin there. Even after all these years together he still liked to mark me whenever he could, but today, he settled for nipping my skin and then soothing it with a brief kiss. Maybe it was because we had company that he stopped there – not that that would usually stop him; he was still just as naughty and cheeky as he'd always been.

'Ugh, get a room, you guys.'

Turning, I saw Nicholas and Rebecca joining us all in the kitchen. Nicholas was grinning at catching his brother in the heated embrace.

'Yeah, yeah. You can always head home if you don't like the view, brother,' Nathan joked lightly, crossing his arms across his chest.

They could too, seeing as Nicholas and Rebecca lived just down the road from us now, and had done for the last sixteen years. Technically they were our next-door neighbours, but with a strip of local conservation land separating our properties it was about an eight-minute walk door to door. Perfect really; we got to spend lots of time with them, but all still got our privacy.

Marcus and Sasha were now living in a neighbouring village too. David and Natalia were still London based, and along with Marcus and Sasha hadn't had any children. They seemed perfectly content as they were, and still lived the London lifestyle of parties and sexual exploration most weekends, so I suspected they'd be in the city for the foreseeable future.

Oliver and Robyn were the only ones of our close group who were absent today. They had broken our hearts last year by deciding to take early retirement and return to Oliver's home country of Spain. They had clearly been rutting like rabbits, because they were now the proud parents to three young children – Rosa, Emilia and Samuel – and they'd decided they wanted to bring their children up in the Spanish countryside surrounded by Oliver's huge family. I couldn't blame them really, but we were all sad at their departure. Sasha and Robyn were so close, so she had found it the hardest, but she and Marcus now flew out to visit them regularly and Oliver still kept a small house in the UK which they had promised to visit at least four times a year. It still wasn't quite the same without them in our little gatherings though.

Glancing back out into the garden, I saw Ben and Holly join William. Becky and Nicholas's twins had grown up into lovely young people too. Both with exceptional manners and looks which were a perfect mix of their parents.

Ben dropped to his haunches beside the bike to offer his opinion while Holly flopped into a sun chair beside them and began strumming on her guitar. Both had followed their dad with his love of music, Holly with the guitar and piano, and Ben with the drums. They loved spending time with Nicholas in his music room, composing pieces together, and would sometimes perform them to Nathan and me when we were visiting. It was really rather sweet. Nicholas literally couldn't be any prouder of them.

'Mummy, Dad guess what!' The loud squeal disturbed my gazing, and I turned to see a tornado of blonde hair and flailing limbs come careening into the kitchen straight towards Nathan and me.

'Pumpkin!' My heart melted as Nathan lifted Sophie aloft and spun her around. Our youngest daughter, and the most gorgeous little girl I've ever seen. Although being her mother obviously I might be slightly biased.

We hadn't been planning on having any more children. Nathan had been so utterly terrified of me going through childbirth again that we'd agreed to just stay as a family of three and spoil William rotten. But eight years ago, whilst still on the contraceptive injection, I had fallen accidentally pregnant again.

Nine months later, and with Nathan gaining several more grey hairs in the process from the stress, Sophie was born. Nathan had now had the snip to avoid any more 'accidents', because he hadn't wanted me to be fitted with a coil (too invasive), wouldn't dream of using condoms (too fiddly), and couldn't bear to go more than one or two days without sex (unbearable). Even in his late forties my man still had the sex drive of a prize stallion.

'The blueberry bushes we planted have got fruit!' Sophie exclaimed excitedly, and as Nathan popped her on the kitchen counter, I saw that her face and fingers were covered in purple stains.

'And let me guess, you had to pick a few to check if they were ripe?' I asked with a smile as I watched Jean enter the kitchen too – Nathan's mum, and Sophie's beloved grandma.

'I did. Gran told me they'd almost fall off when they're ready, and that they'd be really sweet, and they are! Look how many we collected, Mummy!' Sophie still called me 'Mummy', and I loved it, but she'd shortened Nathan's 'Daddy' to 'Dad' a few months ago, and I suspected it wouldn't be long until I got the same treatment. She was seven going on seventeen with her intelligence and wit, and growing up so fast, but I couldn't be prouder of her.

Jean popped a tub on the counter that was indeed full of blueberries and then rinsed her fingers under the tap. 'Looks like there'll be another crop in a day or so,' she said, giving Sophie's hair an affectionate ruffle.

Nathan and Nicholas had taken it very slow rebuilding their relations with their mum, but after all the years that had passed, and several joint therapy sessions along the way, Jean was now a very welcome member of our family.

'Maybe we can have blueberry crumble tomorrow, if you two haven't eaten all of them,' Nathan murmured, giving his mum a fond smile and then looking at our daughter's sticky fingers with a frown before turning to the kitchen sink to grab a cloth.

My lips pulled into a smile as I looked across at Nicholas and Rebecca and saw them also giving Nathan an amused look as he began to thoroughly clean Sophie's hands and cheeks.

He was still a clean freak, but he was my clean freak. The stress of attempting to keep two children clean over the last eighteen years had probably added to his grey hairs too; although they only graced his temples, the rest of his hair was still as blond as ever.

'We'll set the table,' Nicholas commented with a grin as he

rolled his eyes at Nathan's over the top cleansing routine. 'Are Kenny and Tom still joining us?'

Glancing at the clock, I nodded. 'Yes, but Kenny texted earlier to say they're running late. Set a place for David and Natalia too, they should be here any moment now.'

'Kenny and Tom running late? Aren't they always?' Rebecca replied with a grin which instantly caused me to nod. Tom was Kenny's husband and as punctual as could be, but Kenny was still late for everything. Literally. He'd even been late for his own wedding, which had nearly caused poor Tom to pass out from nerves. They were still going strong though, and as much a part of our family now as the rest of the gang was.

Scooping up the cutlery, Becky rolled her eyes with a chuckle as she and Nicholas carried it out to the patio followed by Marcus and Sasha who gathered up the condiments and took them out to the table.

Adding a blob of handwash to the cloth, Nathan was about to initiate round two of his cleaning when Sophie leapt from the counter with a giggle and galloped back into the garden.

Frowning at his daughter's escape, Nathan turned back to me and I couldn't stop the bubble of laughter that rose up my throat.

A thrilled giggle filled the air, breaking our gaze, and I turned to see William in the garden, hoisting Sophie into the air with a grin.

'All right, trouble?' he teased, giving her a tickle and then lifting her to sit on his shoulders. He was so good with his little sister, and she absolutely adored her brother.

To be honest, it was like Sophie had three older siblings looking out for her, because William, Ben, Holly and Sophie spent so much time together that they had an exceptionally close bond. It had been hard on all of them when William had gone off to university last September, not to mention difficult for Nathan and me to adapt too, but luckily our boy was quite homey. As well as enjoying his new-found freedom he was still regularly making time to come home on some weekends and in the holidays.

Looking back at Nathan, I saw he still looked disgruntled, but obviously also sensing his discomfort, Jean leant across and took the cloth from him. 'I'll take it outside and clean her fingers off before we eat,' she said with a smile.

'Thanks, Mum,' Nathan mumbled, watching her as she left the kitchen and then turning his stare back on me.

Cupping his jaw, I ran my thumb over his slight stubble soothingly. 'See? Gran to the rescue. You can calm down your clean freakery.'

Raising an eyebrow at my cheek, he gave me a wicked, narrow-eyed look that instantly heated my blood. 'Just because we have company don't think I won't redden your arse, Mrs Jackson,' he warned me in a heated whisper by my ear. He would as well. Not in front of our guests, or the children, of course, but Nathan and I still regularly used our soundproof 'bedroom' when everyone else was fast asleep.

I guess once a Dom, always a Dom, not that I was complaining. I loved it now just as much as I had when we'd first met.

Looking back at Nathan, I grinned and brushed a few stray blond hairs back from his brow. He was still startlingly handsome, just with the touch of grey in his hair, and some laughter lines at the corners of his eyes that I'd like to think I was responsible for.

Sighing contentedly, I took a second to appreciate how

fortunate we all were. Yep, I was a lucky lady. My children were incredible, I was surrounded by family and friends whom we loved dearly, and I had certainly found my someone special. I was never ever going to let him go, either. Smiling up at him, I found him still watching me with a dark grin so I leant onto my tiptoes and gave his neck a brief nip.

'Bring it on, Mr Jackson, bring it on.'

The End . . . again!

Author's note continued . . .

The characters in these books have played a huge part in my life over the last seven years, and I truly hope you have enjoyed this final instalment of the Club Twist Series and found the happy endings you were hoping for with all my beloved characters.

As always, I love to hear from readers, so feel free to get in touch and tell me your thoughts!

E-mail: aliceraineauthor@gmail.com
Twitter: @AliceRaine1
Facebook: www.facebook.com/alice.raineauthor
Website: www.aliceraineauthor.com

Thank you all for reading.
Alice x

Newport Community
Learning & Libraries

Acknowledgements

Crashing to a Halt is the final book in my Club Twist series, so I want to take a brief moment to extend a special to all of you, my amazing readers. Without your positivity, feedback and support I would never have made it this far. Thanks must go out to my fabulous editor Kate Byrne, for putting up with my tardiness and reigning in my rambling manuscripts! Not to forget all the brilliant staff at Headline and Hachette that work tirelessly behind the scenes to bring my books to life.

Finally, a huge thanks to my partner for backing me every step of the way, and my family for their support of my writing, not that they will ever be allowed to read this, or any of my other books!

Alice x

Welcome to Club Twist,
where the owners are just as
sinful as the patrons . . .

Available now from

ACCENT

Don't miss the Untwisted series!

An all-consuming affair with famous pianist Nicholas Jackson
engulfs Rebecca in a whirlwind of passion and dominance.
But is she ultimately destined for heartbreak?

A dizzying, all-consuming affair . . .

Available now from

ACCENT

Try the Revealed series!

When schoolteacher Allie Shaw took an impromptu cleaning job to cover for a friend, she never expected to wind up snowed in with a devilishly handsome sex god.

A tale of dark secrets and the forbidden world of desires ...

Available now from

ACCENT

Addictive thrillers. **Gripping** suspense.
Irresistible love stories. **Escapist** treats.

For **guaranteed brilliant reads**

Discover **Headline Accent**

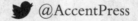 @AccentPress

24/09/21

Newport Library and
Information Service
John Frost Square
Newport
South Wales NP20 1PA

ACCENT